VESSEL: BONDED EARTH
BOOK ONE

VESSEL: BONDED EARTH BOOK ONE

SAMANTHA JO

To Patrick, for giving support that is borderline delusional. And to my children, Lila, Lenora, Hadley, and Everett, for giving my life more color than I ever could have hoped for. I love you all.

Contents

Dedication	iv
One	23
Two	31
Three	39
Four	43
Five	53
Six	61
Seven	73
Eight	83
Nine	91

Ten	113
Eleven	121
Twelve	127
Thirteen	131
Fourteen	135
Fifteen	141
Sixteen	151
Seventeen	165
Eighteen	167
Nineteen	175
Twenty	187
Twenty-One	195
Twenty-Two	209
Twenty-Three	213

Twenty-Four	219
Twenty-Five	225
Twenty-Six	231
Twenty-Seven	235
Twenty-Eight	243
Twenty-Nine	255
Thirty	259
Thirty-One	265
Thirty-Two	275
Thirty-Three	279
Thirty-Four	285
Thirty-Five	289
Thirty-Six	293
Thirty-Seven	301

About The Author 307

RECLAMATION

- ⊙ Fort Hope
- ⊙ Fort Iceridge
- ⊙ Fort Seven
- ⊙ Fort Beacon
- ⊙ Fort Willamshire
- ⊙ Fort Marshwood
- ⊙ Fort Vulhaven
- ⊙ Fort Breakwater

NORETHERLAND

Upper Plains

Fertile Plains

Grandview Academy

Bierden ⊙

The New Colonies
Circa 600 PM

RIDGEMOUNT

BLACK ROCK

NORTHERN DRIFT

WHITEHALL

THE WELL

OLD ROAN

SOUTHERN DRIFT

GROVE

PART ONE

May 21, 608 PM (post meteorum)

Amelia

In the delicate space between awake and asleep, Amelia Tobins swayed back and forth, which was odd in a vague way she could not grasp in her current drowsy state. But her head ached, and her tongue felt fuzzy, and she just wanted to go back to sleep. She was slipping seamlessly back into the dream of riding a giant maple leaf down the side of a butter mountain, when her body went momentarily airborne, before bumping the hard surface from which she had risen, and dropping to an even rougher level of what she was now completely certain was not her bed.

Amelia forced her heavy eyes open, searching her surroundings. Wooden boards, horse noises...horse smells, boots... on someone's feet. Someone else was there.

"Well, that'll wake you up," said an unfamiliar voice.

Amelia panicked, attempting to sit up but her hands were bound together, as well as her feet. Fear surged through her, hot and steady, and she jolted upright. She was in a carriage, and the voice had come from the passenger sitting on the back bench. She must have rolled from the front bench. But why was she there in the first place?

"Welcome back," they said, clearly less concerned about the situation than Amelia was.

They leaned forward, and she could see their face in the dim light of the carriage. They seemed young but rough, with sunken in, dark eyes, dry lips, and a shaved head. Their slim neck was tattooed along the left side with unrecognizable markings.

"Hey, relax," they said, looking down at her. "Slow your breathing or you'll hyperventilate. I really don't want to deal with that tonight."

Amelia could not think of a single reason to relax. In fact, every part of her wanted to scream and run, but terror had her locked in place.

"I'm serious. Relax, you're fine." They sat back, looking out the window of the carriage. "We've just been on a really long ride so far. At least you got to sleep for most of it."

They looked at her again, then pantomimed breathing in an exaggerated way, as if she had simply not heard them. Amelia closed her eyes and focused on breathing in and out, and the tension left her limbs.

"You gotta piss?" they asked when she opened her eyes.

"What? Uh, no. I'm okay, I guess."

"They always gotta piss at the worst times."

The absurdity of the conversation cracked the hold of her fear, and her thoughts resumed a more normal pace.

"Who are you?" she quavered. "Where am I?" She clamped her eyes shut against the throbbing that was growing worse by the moment.

"I am Rhine," they answered. "This is a carriage."

"And... what's happening?" Amelia asked.

The stranger eyed her for a long time before letting out a long breath.

"Look kiddo, nothing I can tell you is going to make this any easier," Rhine said, in a tone touched with sadness, or regret. Maybe both. "And nothing *you* can do is going to change your circumstances. It's probably best if you just try to go back to sleep and save your energy. You'll need it later."

"It's really uncomfortable on the floor," Amelia whined, rolling her shoulders.

"I'll bet it is," was their only response.

"Why am I on the floor?"

"Well, that bump you felt was the carriage hitting a rut," they answered, matter of fact, "and the feeling of falling to the floor was, in fact, you falling to the floor."

"Can I... can I get up?"

"Are you going to try to fight me and jump from the carriage?"

"Are you afraid of a twelve-year-old girl?" Amelia shot back, with what her mother would call 'more sass than she had earned.' Rhine raised their bushy eyebrows, and Amelia shrank back, covering her face.

If only she could keep her mouth shut. Peeking through her fingers, there was amusement in the upturned corner of Rhine's mouth.

After a moment, they gestured with their free hand for her to get up. Their other hand held a large, wide-bladed knife that looked like the one her father used to clear brush. Her stomach flipped as she instantly realized this knife was probably not used to cut branches. Suddenly, her father's voice was there, in her ear, reminding her that the only way to solve problems was with a calm mind and clear thoughts. Of course, he had been talking about a nanny goat trying to push out a kid hooves-first, not whatever mess she was in now.

"Get up, if you want," Rhine conceded, "but don't be stupid."

"Can you cut these off?" Amelia asked, holding out her bound wrists.

"Not a chance."

"Be easier to get up, if you did."

"Probably."

Amelia let out a sigh and set to the task of first finding her way to her hands and knees, then pushing her way up squatting. The carriage was too small for her to stand upright, but she made her way to the bench, nonetheless.

"Well, would you look at that?" they responded dryly, not actually looking at her.

"Why did you say I would need my energy later?" she asked. "Where are we going?"

The only sound was the slick *whsk whsk whsk* of a whetstone sliding across the edge of Rhine's blade. No answers, then. What could she piece together herself? She had been taken from home, no doubt. Kidnapped. She had been kidnapped. The realization of that was such an odd sensation that it did not feel real, not for many moments. But with each bump of the carriage and every swish of the whetstone across the blade staring at her, the more solid the notion became.

Rhine had taken her from her home, most likely with the help of other people. At the very least, there was a driver helping with her kidnapping. Why would someone take *her*, of all people? And where were they going?

She slid to the side of the carriage and peered out the small window that made up the top half of the door. When she squinted, she could just make out the shadowed shapes of jagged peaks in the distance, which was mildly helpful. They had not made it out of the Green Ridge Mountain Range. Maybe she was not so far from home. She leaned further, trying to see if there were other carriages in her caravan, but with the low light of the new moon, she could see next to nothing.

"Hey," Rhine snapped. "There's nothing out there for you except coyotes and cold."

Amelia lowered her eyes. "There's nothing in here for me except you and that knife."

"That's right," Rhine said, "and frankly, I liked you a whole lot better when you were asleep. So, you'll be quiet for the rest of the ride, or I'll put you back to sleep, understood?" To further accentuate the threat, they released their mana and allowed it to shine through their pupils, casting them in an eerie glow, like a wild cat at night.

Calm mind, clear thoughts. Calm mind, clear thoughts.

"Okay," Amelia conceded.

In the stretching silence that followed, her renewed fear chewed away at her stomach, making her nauseous. No one had ever prepared her for something like this. How could they have? Did anyone know she was gone? Was anyone coming to help?

Amelia tried to remember the last time a Seeker had visited the village closest to the hollow where her family lived. It had been a few months, so one must be due soon. Not that it mattered much, unless someone outside the hollow found out about her disappearance. There was no way that her parents would ask for help from The Second Order. Even if a Seeker could be pressed upon to look for her, that help would come far too late.

The entirety of her family lived in Tobins Hollow. Who else could her parents ask for help? Would they send her brothers out looking for her? She shivered, realizing that she was still in her sleep clothes. Goose flesh pebbled her exposed arms, and she pulled her legs up to her chest, leaning into the corner of the bench, feeling very small and very alone.

Calm mind, clear thoughts. If no one was coming to help, she would have to help herself. She just needed a plan.

Amelia needed to figure out why she had been taken in the first place, and perhaps where she was being taken.

It was common folklore in the mountains that sometimes children were taken from families who could not afford to feed and care for them and given to families who could. But those tales were mostly meant to keep teenagers from eating their weight in food each day. True or not, that explanation didn't really fit. She was helpful at home, always taking care of her younger brother and sisters, and seeing to the animals. She was a decent cook and had a knack for finding wild game when her family needed it. No, they would not have sent her away.

She looked around for clues in the carriage. It was pretty basic, two benches, a small lamp, and a door on either side. The cushion on the bench was worn down, and smelled like too many dirty, sweaty bodies had pressed their filth into it. And if she was not mistaken, there was a blood stain not half a foot from where she sat. The removable cloth top was thread-bare in places, letting night air whistle inside. Doors with pliable, mana-made glass windows rattled as they rambled along the rough valley path and had probably needed to be replaced many journeys ago. Maybe she could elbow...Rhine noticed her studying the door and cleared their throat conspicuously, so Amelia resumed her study of the rest of the carriage, trying to pretend as though she was not. There were no other weapons, and if there was luggage, it was most likely stashed inside the benches. Aside from the general air of misery and misuse, the carriage yielded no clues.

Then there was Rhine. Their clothing was plain but clean. There were no patches or writing on the thick, hunter green sweater that they wore. Their boots looked well-used, but maintained, with high ankles and a sturdy heel. All of which told her...nothing. They might work in the mountains, or on a farm, or in one of the many places Amelia had never visited before. The only distinguishing feature to their appearance was that tattoo. Amelia leaned her head to the side, trying to study it more closely.

"Can I help you?" they asked, sounding annoyed, but at least there was no threat to their tone.

"What does your tattoo mean?"

"That I spend most of my time with violent idiots," they answered, "and I never have enough to eat."

"So, you are part of a group? What kind of group?"

Rhine sighed. "What did I say about keeping quiet?"

Amelia averted her gaze. "Sorry," she said, "but I'm scared, and I just want to know what is happening." It sounded childish, but desperation spurred her on. "Are you going to hurt me?"

Rhine studied her for a moment, squinting.

"Yes and no," they finally said.

"Yes, and no?" she asked. "How can it be both?"

"*I* am taking you to *him*," Rhine clarified, hitching their thumb toward the back of the carriage, indicating the road behind them. "There is a good chance he will hurt you. He seems like the type."

The words were blunt, but Amelia heard the guilt in their voice.

"Not that I expect your forgiveness or anything, kid," they added wryly, "I know what I am and how I got here. Life's unfair and all that."

Amelia flexed her fingers and bent her wrists, trying to keep the blood flowing to her hands. Rhine watched her fidget but made no move to help. She let out a sigh.

"And there is really nothing I can do?" Amelia asked, a thick ache settling in her throat. "You won't help me?"

"Right," Rhine whispered.

"Well, can you at least tell me who he is?" Tears welled in her eyes, against her wishes. "Why is he so awful?"

Rhine's brows pinched, the guilt in their words spreading to their face for a faint heartbeat, before they smoothed away all emotion, their cool mask sliding back into place. They started working the whetstone across their knife once more and answered simply, "You'll find out soon enough."

***

Amelia had never realized what a gift it was to be able to stay inside a cozy cabin on a cold spring night. But as she stood shivering in the shadow of the ancient mountain before her, she planned to hug her old, beaten-up, cast-iron stove the moment she returned home.

She shivered from the terror of her situation as much as from the cold of the night. It had coursed through her, settling into her muscles, leaving her feeling ragged and worn. At least the jittery movements of her half-frozen body kept her awake.

She and Rhine had been joined by the carriage driver as they left the road and made their way, on foot, to the mountains. Nearly an hour of hiking later, they stood in a narrow clearing alongside a stream issuing from the mountain. Neither had spoken the entire trip, and Amelia had been too focused on her feet to spare energy for anything else, save the occasional, irrational thought of running away. Ultimately, Rhine was right. There was nothing out here but coyotes and cold. And bears. They had forgotten to mention the bears.

Another shiver racked her body and Amelia was almost tired enough to lay down on the damp ground, but then she heard the rustling of underbrush being trampled. A moment later, a man emerged from the pine trees and stepped into the small clearing, slapping the red cloth that hung from the lowest limb of a hemlock tree. They had been following the small banners all the way from the trail, but Amelia only just now pieced together the reasoning. This was a smugglers path.

The man looked older than her brothers, but younger than her father. His clothes were nice, if a bit fancy for hiking, and his brown hair looked freshly cut and styled. He was muscular and tall, and when he looked at her, his face twisted like he had smelled something particularly unpleasant. The only thing she could smell was the earthy tang of soil where it met the stream, and pinesap. She had never met him before, she was certain. But as he moved closer, a figure appeared from behind him that she did recognize.

"Mattias?" she asked, squinting to be sure it really was her older brother picking his way out of the trees. Before he could answer, Rhine spoke up.

"You're late. We'll be lucky if we can get this done before sunrise," they accused, pointing a finger at the other man.

"I'm paying for a service," the newcomer spat, "not for complaints. Let's get this done."

Amelia could only stare at her brother, pleading for answers with her eyes. He had yet to meet them, busy studying the small boulders at his feet. It struck her as odd that he was fully dressed, in his normal work clothes, and not in his pajamas. Amelia shivered in her night gown.

"We'll have to hike in closer than this," Rhine instructed. "Probably half a mile or so. The leak isn't as strong along this tributary as it used to be."

The muscles along the man's jaw jumped as he clenched and unclenched his teeth. He looked like he wanted to argue, until Rhine spoke up again.

"If you want this to work, I need to be as close to The Well as I can be. Mana leaks tend to disperse in these streams and run off into the dirt. If we try to consecrate her here, she won't be able to take as much. Is *that* what you paid for? A half-cooked Vessel? Or do you suppose you could walk a little further?"

Their voice was heavy with sarcasm, and even though they were much smaller, they did not seem intimidated by the man. Amelia thought they should be.

"Fine," the man spat.

"After you," Rhine said, taking Amelia by the arm. It was an effort to get her stiff legs moving again. Her brother fell in step with her, and she took his hand in hers, squeezing to confirm the comfort that came from his solidity. They walked, surrounded by Rhine, the mysterious man, and the two carriage drivers. There was no chance she would escape, now. At least her brother was there. Maybe he knew more. Maybe he could protect her. Amelia broke the silence, the small burst of hope in her chest refusing to be contained.

"Matti, what's going on?" she whispered. "Do you know why they've taken us?"

He winced.

"Not us, Millie," Mattias answered. "You. Just you."

A painful longing for home struck her chest at the sound of his voice. They should not be here; they should be home. Just Matti and Millie, playing in the trees, far from a world where grown-ups stole you from your bed at night. Best friends whose biggest worry was whether mama would be mad they were out late.

Then his words registered.

"Wait, what do you mean just me?" she asked. "You're here, too."

He took a long time answering. "First of all, Millie, I'm real sorry. I am. I'm so sorry. But I had to. We're all stuck there in that hollow, and you have a gift you should be using, and I wish it was me, but it's not...this will...you can..."

"Matti, get your foot out of your mouth," she said, "I don't understand what you are trying to say."

Mattias blew out a long breath and squeezed her hand. "Millie, you are special," he started, "Not just, y'know, for our family. You are *special* special. You're a Vessel. Or you will be. You can be. It will give you a good life. You'll never be hungry, and you'll have nice clothes and you'll get to travel. You'll have a nice house and..."

"Oh, stop that, Mattias," she said, cutting him off. "I can't just be a Vessel; you can't just make someone that way. They have to be born that way. And I wasn't." Her attendance at Basic had been spotty at best, but everyone knew that a person was either born a Vessel or they were not. She had not been. She stared at him, waiting for him to agree, or to laugh it off as a joke, or break into a run through the woods, but he just looked back at her, his dark brown eyes sorrowful.

"Yes, Millie, you were," he said. "Mama and pap know. They've always known. Why do you think they always keep you home? You never get to go into town. They're hiding you from the Seekers. They don't want you to leave, so they hide you."

"I don't believe you," she spat out, anger making her cheeks hot. Why was Mattias playing games at a time like this?

"C'mon, Mill, you know mama and pap," he said, holding his hand to his chest in mock dismay. "They would never let one of their children be taken to serve as an *unnatural abomination*. They would never let that happen." He stepped over a rotting log and instinctively reached back to help her, but Amelia pulled away. She was not going to play along with whatever game he was up to.

She studied the ground as she walked, trying to make sense of what Mattias had said. He had to be lying. Because if that was the truth, and she really was a Vessel, she would never be able to return home again. She would never braid her little sister's hair, never sneak treats to her favorite dog, and never play in the stream with Matti again. She would be shunned. To her family, it will be as if she never existed.

Most people in town accepted that Vessels were a natural, normal, and even important part of society, but superstition and old-world religion had a way of twisting the minds of the folks who dwelt in the dark, sheltered nooks of mountain hollows. Folks like her parents.

"How did they know?" she shot out. "I was never even tested."

"Millie, everyone knows," he answered. "You think it's normal that you always know how to find schooling fish? You think everyone can tell when they goat is sick just by sittin' close to it? How you gonna tell me you never noticed that our garden makes twice as much food as anyone else in the hollow? You are special, and you haven't even taken your minna, or whatever they call it."

"None of that proves anything," she whispered, but she knew he was right. She had noticed that she was different, and she had definitely heard folks talking about her when they thought she could not hear. But she never understood what any of it meant until now. She was not just different; she was an abomination.

The trail had begun to climb, and Amelia had nothing left to give the journey. She was dreadfully tired and ready to collapse, but everyone else continued to move, so she mustered one last, small burst of energy, and started uphill. She gave a side-long glance to her brother, who had gone silent again.

"How did you know? Did they tell you?" she asked.

He nodded. "They said we all had to protect you," he said. "That you couldn't go with the Seekers when they came to town looking for recruits. But mama and pap were wrong." His voice wavered when he spoke ill of their parents. "He's a Brother of the First Order," he said, pointing at the man walking with Rhine, "and he says it's more dangerous for you to stay at home, untrained."

"And how did he know I'm a... a Vessel?" she asked, watching the man move with an unnatural grace in the moonless night.

"Well, honestly, that part I don't know," Mattias answered, biting his lower lip like he always did while trying to solve a puzzle. "He just said that he knew people who kept an eye out for untrained Vessels, and they had told him 'bout you. He came at me and Jonas a few weeks back when we went into town for the new horse bits pap ordered." He looked at her again. "Jonas said we shouldn't do it," he said, his voice quiet. "But I knew you would be okay. You're tough, and smart, Millie. You'll be fine."

How could she ever be fine with this? She was a twelve-year-old girl whose whole world was a few acres of wilderness, and the family she loved more than anything. She was too small, too quiet for the life of a Vessel. Already, she could feel her sacred mountain hollow slipping away from her.

But then, something else began to nag at her over-tired brain. She saw it, but did not want to see it.

No, there was no way that they would...

"Mattias, what do you mean by 'do it?'" she asked slowly. "And what exactly are you doing here? Did you just come to see me off?"

The group had apparently come to their destination, as Rhine and the Brother from the First Order stopped in another, larger clearing beside the stream. It was wider now, and the current dragged by them at a steady clip. She nearly had to shout to be heard over the low rumble.

"Mattias, what do you mean?" she asked, facing her brother. "What did you *do*?"

Right on cue, the man crossed the distance and dropped a heavy looking pouch in Mattias' palm, all the while staring at her. His face contorted into a cruel smile, and Amelia flinched as the truth hit her like a slap across the face.

Rhine released a low whistle between their teeth. "Damn, that was cold," they said, then turned their back on the group.

"You...you sold me?" she shouted, her voice shrill against the heavy rush of the stream. He did not answer. "You sold me to him, Mattias?" There was no other sound for several heartbeats. She looked at the bag in his hand. "That's all he gave you Matti? You sold your own sister for a bag of coins, you big dummy?"

"I'm sorry," he finally whispered, looking far more injured than Amelia thought he had the right to.

"You're sorry?!" she screamed. "That's all you have to say to me, Mattias?"

She expected someone to break up their argument. But the cruel man just watched Amelia and Mattias with amusement in his eyes, while Rhine and the carriage drivers pretended to not hear.

"Well?" she demanded.

"I wish it was me, Millie," he said, fighting back his own tears as he reached out to her for a moment, before letting his empty hand drop back to his side. "I really do. I wish I was the one with the gift, but I'm not. You are."

"Yeah?" she said around the ache in her throat, "but I don't care about gifts. I don't want to be special. I want to go home."

He shook his head and grimaced at the pouch, as if realizing how dirty it was. "Please Millie, do this for us. Do this for yourself."

Rhine turned and looked at her, expectant. What were they waiting for?

"What happens if I say no?" she asked to no one in particular. "Do I get to go home?"

"No, you don't," the man answered. "We stay here until you change your mind, because you absolutely have to do this." She would probably have to learn his actual name if she was leaving the mountain with him.

"But I don't want to do this," she said, turning to face him. "Does that matter?"

He rolled his eyes. "No," he answered. "Besides, your brother is right. Your life will improve once you become a Vessel. Coin, travel, esteem, power. It's a hell of a lot better than anything that incestuous hollow could offer you."

His words stung, but he was probably right. The two times she had seen a Vessel while in town, they had looked well-fed and clean. They had nice clothing, and they spoke of their travels to anyone who wanted to listen. Besides, what was the alternative? She could not return home, now that the truth was out. Seekers would come for her after all, but this time they would take her to The Well themselves. Then, she would be sent somewhere else for training. Even if she wanted to choose that path, the hateful glare of her captor told her she probably would not leave this mountain until she agreed.

Amelia let out a heavy breath and gingerly rubbed her wrists where they were sore from the bindings Rhine had finally removed at the start of the hike.

"Fine, I will do this," she said, resigned. Then she turned to her brother and pinned him with her eyes. "But I hope you know I will never forgive you. You hear me? Never. And when everyone asks where I went, you better have the nerve to tell them what you did to me." Her voice broke as his betrayal struck home in her heart. "And I sure hope that those stupid coins are worth it. I hope it's enough to make you feel better when you miss me. It won't be enough to make me feel better when I miss you."

The words landed like a blow, and he shrank back from her. Amelia wanted to say more, but she had begun crying and her thoughts blurred.

"Well," the man purred, "now that's done." He turned to Rhine, thrusting his hands toward the stream. Through her tears, she could see that a large, old sycamore tree had fallen, fording the water into an oblong pool that was calmer than the rushing current.

"Right, you get into the water," Rhine said, pointing their chin at Amelia, "as deep as you can go. Once I start pulling the mana toward the pool, you'll only have a few minutes to gather as much of it as you can. It's not like at the actual Well. You won't have access to all of it. Just whatever has leaked into this stream, and whatever I can pull together for you."

"We're doing it here?" she wondered. "How?"

"See that pass up ahead?" Rhine asked her, gesturing further up the mountain. Amelia nodded. "The meteor hit just over that pass, on the eastern side of the mountain. It leaks, and the Seekers can't seem to get it to stop. We take it. Gather it, anyway. Then you have to take it."

Amelia frowned. "How do I take it?"

"Once you are in the water, close your eyes," Rhine explained, and Amelia was surprised by their patience. "Imagine the power flowing into you and becoming a part of you. The mana will do the rest."

It sounded easy enough.

"How will I know if it's working?" she asked.

"Oh, trust me, you'll know," Rhine responded, chuckling.

"Will it hurt?"

"Enough questions," the man interjected.

Rhine let out an annoyed sighed and turned to him. "Once she starts pulling mana, you'll need to be in there with her. Do you have a stone ready?"

He pulled a stone the size of his hand out from under his shirt, where it was already attached to a golden chain.

"Good, be ready to open right as she is almost full or we'll miss the window and your bonding won't be successful," Rhine advised him.

"Yes, I know," he said with a scoff, "I've bonded Vessels before, I'll have no problem bonding this one."

"Bonding?" she asked, but no one seemed to hear her.

"Are you sure you wanna do this?" Rhine asked him in a low voice. "She's just a kid, and you'll be stuck with her no matter what. If she's rejected by all of the Orders, or she washes out…No one wants to be bonded to a stray."

"I'm certain," was his curt response.

They turned to Amelia. She took one last look at her brother, all but forgotten as he leaned against a tree, silently crying.

"Tell everyone I love them. And goodbye," she said, the salt of her own tears burning her cheeks. Mattias nodded once, then turned away.

Amelia stepped into the water, gasping against the shock of frigid water that swallowed her legs instantly. It was late spring in the Colonies, but mountain streams cared little for calendars. The smell of half-rotted fish invaded her nose, and she knew that if she looked, it would not be difficult to find the source. She kept walking, though, and made it up to her chest before the crushing cold made her stop.

"What now?" she asked through chattering teeth.

"Be quiet and focus," Rhine answered as they plunged their arms in up to their elbows.

Nothing happened, at first. But then, she saw it. A thin stream of iridescent liquid flowing toward her in the pool. It was unlike anything she had ever seen before, creamy and shimmering, somehow reflecting a wide array of colors despite the low light of the night. No, not reflecting; *it is the source of the color and light.*

The small thread pushing through the pool grew as other wisps of mana converged with it, first becoming a rope, then growing to the girth of a small log, all the while flowing and moving toward her in the water.

"Take it," Rhine grunted, sweat pooling on their forehead.

Following Rhine's advice, Amelia closed her eyes and imagined the beautiful force moving closer and filling her. It did not seem to work. Then...she felt a tentative pushing at the space beneath her rib cage. She opened her eyes and saw that it was there, touching her belly, and spiraling her whole body under the water.

May I? It asked without words.

You may, she somehow answered in the same unspoken language.

In a flash, it filled her, heat and excitement rushing through her bloodstream, across her chest, down her arms, burning through her finger tips. At the same time, it pushed down, cramping her leg muscles and digging her feet into the rocky stream bed. The mana invaded her mind, forcing out all thought and crushing her vision to a single speck of white light before bursting into a cloud of dancing colors. Turquoise, first dark, then fading to light, swirling so fast she feared she might pass out. She squeezed her eyes shut, but the colors were *in* her eyes, in her mind. Singing unlike any human voice she had ever heard built to a crescendo and vibrated her entire body. It was too all intense, like a separate beast trying to find a way to share her skin and bone and muscle. Any second now, she would surely burst from the power coursing through her. She made to shout, but then Rhine and the man were there, in the water with her. He pressed the stone into her right hand with his. Rhine clasped Amelia and the Brother's joined hands between their own, trapping the stone in the center.

The sensation of warmth bloomed on her face, and she pulled open her eyes. Rhine's hands and forearms were radiating heat and light, and their face was now slick with sweat. They spoke no words, but focused intently on the cluster of hands in front of them. The heat spread, down Amelia's right arm, across her chest, and into her belly. Her eyes went blurry staring at the celestial glow, but she welcomed the warmth. As this newer, somehow stranger force moved through her, the mana she had pulled from the stream settled, moved out of her limbs. Amelia could never figure out how she knew, but it was a ball of energy, living beneath her belly button.

How very lovely.

"Almost done," Rhine whispered through gritted teeth. But the fury of sensation had abused Amelia's small body, she could not hold on any longer. As she finally gave into the pull of unconsciousness, her last thoughts were of a mountain hollow when the sun breaks over the jagged horizon at dawn.

One

April 10, 622

Calen

As far as death shrouds went, Calen thought hers was quite beautiful. The fitted bodice of the creamy chiffon gown was embroidered with delicate golden vines and leaves, the likeness of flowers made up by tiny, iridescent pearls. Below her waist, it flowed away from her body and encased her in a stream of soft fabric. The sleeves matched the style and hung loose from her shoulders, cascading down past her hands to conceal her twin obsidian rings and the inelegant fingers that hardly deserved them. As with other ritual days, she wore her hair down, and it insisted on laying in wild waves that contrasted with the delicate nature of her dress. Its saving grace was the beautiful crown of fresh violets the villagers had crafted for her. Woven through the waves and across her forehead, just above her dark eyebrows, it made her feel a little less plain.

She was not actually dead, nor would she be soon. But the events of the day would lurch her closer to the point at which she would wish she were. Not exactly the typical thoughts of a Third Order Vessel on ritual day, but she was powerless to stop them. At least she was in the mountains for the next month, rather than far from the only place she would ever consider home. Maybe she should try to convince Stokely to request ritual work that kept them in the mountains year-round.

"Ha!" she chuckled. Convince Stokely of anything? Good one.

As if sensing her thoughts, he appeared in the doorway of their shared suite. "Are you almost ready?" he asked. "Their insufferable elder is circling, and I cannot have one more conversation with that man."

"Yep," she answered, smoothing her hands over her gown.

"Are you wearing shoes today?" he asked, disgusted.

"Yep," she lied.

"Good. We're walking today. Apparently, this dirt path village is too small to even need carriages."

"Cobblestone," she responded.

"What?"

"Their roads are cobblestone," she clarified, "not dirt."

He shot her a look that said he could not care less.

Stokely was not wrong about the size of the village, she had to concede. Within a few moments, they had left the Graymount Inn and were halfway to the blessing site. The village was really quite lovely, despite what Stokely had said. His disdain meant little to her now, as she had learned how easy it was to earn over the eight years they had worked together. Along the main street as well as the neighborhoods, single-story houses of earthen bricks and river rock were bordered with busy gardens and small enclosures for rabbits and chickens. They were built in efficient, tidy rows stretching away from the thoroughfare in a way that made it easy to find one's way around. Today, the houses looked particularly charming, with their ceremonial wreaths hung on each door.

They passed the last house on the main road before entering a town square that enclosed a pretty river rock fountain. It appeared to have been freshly scrubbed, and the steady flow of water crashing against bare stone was loud, but not unpleasant. It made a nice backdrop to the low hum of the villager's voices as they milled around the square, some headed toward the blessing site, some on their way to a large, low building on the eastern side of the square that Calen guessed was the

Community Center. Its large front doors stood open, and a boisterous woman stood in the entry, waving a wooden spoon at folks of all ages as they carried dishes of rich-smelling food, candlesticks, and crocks inside. She made eye contact with Calen and waved. Calen nodded, and meant to smile, but instead felt her face contort in confusion at the strange sensation coming from her belly, where her mana rested like a sulking child. She flashed a forced smile at the woman and looked around for Stokely. If he had gotten lost in this small crowd and was using their Stone to pull at her...But no, he was standing just behind her. She followed to where she was being tugged, and the origination of her discomfort materialized in the form of a young woman, probably about fourteen years old. She was tall for her age, and thin, with pale brown hair, walking to the blessing site, arm in arm with another girl her age.

The crowd had parted and grown quiet at the urgency with which Calen moved. The young girl was so engrossed in her conversation that when she croaked a laugh, its only competition for attention was the fountain, happily splashing away behind them. The girl followed her friend's gaze and turned, coming face-to-face with Calen. Her eyes went wide before she cast them down, and Calen realized that she probably looked frightening, worked up as she was. She smoothed her expression, and when the girl looked up again, Calen grinned.

"Move out of the way," her friend instructed.

"Oh, yes," said the girl. "Sorry, Mistress Revered."

"Well, that's not necessary," Calen said, infusing warmth into her voice. "What is your name?"

The girl stared, her head tilted to the side. "Oh, Avonelle Bishop," she eventually offered. "My name is Avonelle Bishop, but most folks call me Nelle." Her voice had the soft, rounded quality of a girl raised in the mountains. Over the years, Calen had learned how to push out her words with greater distinction, but her accent found a way to slide across her tongue anytime she returned.

"Well, Avonelle Bishop. It is a pleasure to meet you, and there is no need to apologize to me. I am but a humble guest at your gathering and

I would be honored if you would show me the way," she finished with a gentle nod.

Stokely scoffed, and Calen watched Nelle's eyes shift to him. The girl looked him up and down, taking in his gaudy, golden robes, and the corners of her small mouthed turned down. Her hand came up to her stomach and her pale dress crumpled as she clutched at it.

"Well, of course, Mistress Revered," she answered, as she dragged her eyes back to Calen.

"Please, my name is Calendula."

Nelle's eyebrows shot up as she silently mouthed the name. A laugh bubbled up from Calen's throat.

"Meaning no offense, Mistress," Nelle said, "that is just a... unique name."

"That it is," Calen agreed with a tilt of her head. "And if we are lucky, I may get the chance to tell you of its origin. For now, you may call me Calen. The *gentleman* behind me is Brother Stokely."

"It is a pleasure to meet you, Revered Calendula, Calen," Nelle said. "It is also a pleasure to meet you, Brother Stokely." He ignored the girl and cleaned his impeccable nails, which were never dirty, she knew. But he loved to distract himself by admiring his own perfection rather than interact with people he felt were beneath him, which was almost everyone. She suppressed a sigh and offered a hand to help carry Nelle's burdens. The girl's eyes locked on Calen's ring and her mouth fell open. It was an odd distinction Calen did not necessarily relish, but the rings were sacred to her, and she hated to be without them.

Calen wiggled the fingers on her outstretched hand and nodded at the basket. The girl straightened and handed it to her, then went back to squinting at the large obsidian stone. Calen leaned in and whispered conspiratorially, "You do know the way to the field?"

"Oh, yes!" Nelle said, nodding in the direction of the wide-open expanse behind the Community Center. "It's just this way."

Calen walked alongside Nelle, who seemed to be having trouble deciding what to do with herself.

"I haven't been back to this side of the mountain range in years,"

Calen said. "Your village reminds me of where I lived as a child. Well, we didn't actually live in the village, but in the mountains just beyond. I always wondered what it would be like to have one of these lovely stone houses," she added, waving her hand at the small homes along the road.

"That's where you lived before you went to The Well with the Seeker that found you?" Nelle inquired.

"Mmmm. Not exactly," Calen said, instinctively looking back at Stokely. "But close enough."

"Where do you live now?"

"We live in a small city in the Fertile Plains Colony," Calen answered, "just a few days travel from here. I actually have a cabin now, but I mostly stay to myself."

"Do you live with him?" Nelle asked, the acid in her voice surprising.

"Not exactly. But close enough."

The girl shuddered, and a curiosity tickled Calen's mind.

"How did you become a ritual worker?" Nelle asked. "Did you get to pick?"

"No, we don't decide for ourselves," Calen said. "Our distribution of mana, the way it settles in our body, is what decides for us after we've been consecrated at The Well. I have what is called a 'sacral distribution' of mana, so that is what decided my fate."

"Sacral distribution?" Nelle asked, her eyebrows pinching down.

"Yes, it means that I hold my power right here," Calen explained, making small circular motions in front of her lower abdomen, "and I can move it and release it as necessary. Once it has been released from me, it will pass its energy onto the next willing recipient. In this case, your seeds will receive it, and it will help them germinate and grow."

"But what happens then?" Nelle asked, her face growing animated. "Where does it go after the soil and seeds? And does it feel weird? Does it hurt? Can you pass it on to a person?"

Calen grinned.

"Sorry," Nelle apologized. "I just have so many questions, and our little library here doesn't have a whole lot of books about your Order.

I got to meet a Seeker, once, and they were real nice, but they didn't help much."

"Asking questions is a fantastic way to learn about the world, Nelle," Calen offered. "Is it alright if I call you Nelle?" The girl nodded. "To the best of our knowledge, mana eventually returns to The Well. That is how we have failed to exhaust its reserves, despite pulling from it for six-hundred twenty-two years. It does feel weird, but it does not hurt," she paused there, considering her slight omission of the truth, "and I can pass it on to another person, but only if I'm healing them. I am not much of a healer, however. Even then, it would temporarily exist within you, but only enough to perform whatever act was necessary to make your body whole, then it would leave. The only way mana can pass from one *person* to another, and stay there, is if they are both Vessels. One must pull from, or push into, the other. It's difficult, painful and... generally frowned upon."

Nelle was nodding, and Calen imagined her filing away the information somewhere in her mind.

"Is there a reason you are so curious about the Third Order?" Calen asked. "Are you hoping to join?"

"Oh, no," Nelle answered, smiling. "I don't think I have it." She pointed at Calen's abdomen, then at her own. Calen was not so sure. They had made it nearly to the field, and she could still feel a slight pull toward the girl. Nelle being a Vessel would not exactly explain the strange occurrence, but it might help make sense of it.

They passed through a thicket of trees and arrived at the blessing site. Men and women were spreading blankets on the grassy patch between the trees and the farm fields. A child nearly collided with Nelle as they ran from a friend, playing a game of tag. The girl giggled, then turned to Calen, beaming with pride. She swept her hands out to take in their surroundings.

"This is Zimmern Farm," she stated. "Up ahead is Darrow's, they grow real nice tomatoes and peppers. My favorite is strawberries, they come from Emond's, which is down that way." She nodded in the opposite direction of Darrow's farm.

To the north, south, and east, open fields ran in furrowed mounds of soil, straight and stretching as far as Calen could see. The villagers had undoubtedly been working the ground for weeks, gently tilling and seeding in preparation for her arrival.

They have done their job, now you do yours, she told herself.

"I love the smell turned soil," Nelle confided, inhaling deeply, "don't you?"

"Mmhmm," Calen answered, not wanting to open her mouth. The sour taste of bile filled the back of her throat.

"Mistress Calen, are you okay?" Nelle asked.

Calen glanced at the girl but did not answer. What could she say? That blessing rituals, her main duty as a Vessel, were a horrendous affair? That she could not think straight over the sound of her heart pounding in her ears? How could she explain the coiled energy in her legs that yelled for her to run? She closed her eyes and focused on the feel of her feet on the cool ground. It was soft, and tender blades of grass tickled her soles. She pulled breath into her lungs, the spring air smelling of impending rain.

"Calen," Stokely said, suddenly close enough to whisper in her ear, "you have a job to do. I will force you to your knees in front of all these people, if I must."

His hand slid up her spine and he wrapped his hand around her shoulder, pressing his thumb into the sensitive space between her vertebrae. Pain spiked as he squeezed, and she grunted, biting her tongue to keep from yelling. Blessed Vessel, why did he need to wear so much cologne?

Turning toward Nelle, she handed the girl her basket. Eyes that were entirely too keen for someone of such a young age studied the interaction between her and Stokely. Nelle had not missed a thing.

"Mistress Calen?" she asked.

"It was lovely to meet you, Nelle," she managed, not meeting the girl's eye. "Have a wonderful blessing day."

Forcing her legs to move, Calen stepped toward the field and was surprised Stokely did not follow. She glanced over her shoulder and found him studying Nelle, playing with the consecration stone that hung from his neck. Nelle stared back, hunched, but holding his gaze.

"Stokely," she called back. An inkling of concern began to unfurl in her belly.

The girl is ordinary. Nothing to see there, Stokely. Move along.

Stokely lifted his chin and swept away from the girl, his golden robes less than resplendent in the clouded afternoon gloom. The ambiguous fear abated, and she breathed a sigh of relief, her shoulders sagging.

Picking up the hem of her gown, Calen stepped into the field and focused on the task ahead.

Ready to make a miracle? She asked the stagnant coil of energy living within her. As usual, it did not answer. Just once, she wished it would.

Two

April 10, 622

Calen

"Settle in, now. Settle in," Elder Karimo attempted to quiet the crowd. His gnarled brown hands were raised above his head, slowly flapping up and down as if the noise was a physical entity he could beat into submission. "Settle in, folks."

"We are joined today by Brother Stokely of the First Order and Revered Calendula of the Third Order. They honor us with their presence on this blessing day, to give freely of themselves so that we may live in abundance and security." He paused to allow the crowd a moment of praise and appreciation. "These lovely Vessels have traveled a long distance to join us today and shall be staying with us until the week's end. May the blessing take root and may we all take the appropriate measures to show our immense gratitude over the coming days." Then, his weather-worn face cracked in a wry grin. "And may tonight's celebration be rowdy enough to be heard on the western side of these mountains!"

Calen rolled her eyes. It was not that she did not enjoy a party, but ritual work robbed her of any desire to celebrate afterward. Most other ritual workers could perform a seed blessing, party the rest of the day, and enjoy a partner (or two) for the night. But Calen would consider it a victory if she remained upright for the rest of the day. It was, at the very least, unfair.

Calen wiggled her toes in the damp, cool soil and listened as the crowd started to grow impatient behind her. The rambling elder would need to shorten up his speech or he would soon lose them entirely. The man had to have seen close to fifty seed blessings at this point in time (not to mention a multitude of lesser ritual works) and Calen found it annoying that he still insisted on making such a meal out of it. Everyone in the Colonies depended upon the food grown in fields just like these for survival, there was no need to play up the importance of the day.

He flapped his hands again, and when the crowd quieted, he finished by intoning the traditional closing.

"Blessed are the Vessels." The crowd murmured their assent. Now, it was her turn.

Many of the ritual workers made an absolute performance of their blessings, talking and chanting and dancing. Some even exposed their naked breasts to the Earth in a display of their own sensual abundance. As if that could confer a greater gift to the soil. It was all as ridiculous and useless as the grand speeches made by statesmen on their behalf. Calen did not have the dramatic flair or the desire to indulge all that nonsense. She would rather just get this over with.

She turned to the crowd, passing her eyes over as many of them as she could. Every time she performed ritual work, the same question bubbled up.

Do they know?

Did the people of this quaint little village understand what they were asking of her? What they were taking *from* her? It was difficult for her to fathom that people would celebrate ritual workers slowly pouring themselves out until they were empty, but humans once performed sacrifices to their perceived gods, so it was possible. Though, it was more probable that most citizens of the Colonies lived their entire lives oblivious to what had been given to ensure their "security and abundance." They didn't understand what seed blessings required.

The ritual didn't require song or dance. Or breasts. It *required* the force that lived within her, mana. It *required* her to rip herself apart and leave pieces behind. A sadness settled in her chest, realizing that there would be less of her left after she finished her work this afternoon.

Regardless of her dislike of dramatics, Calen was expected to give a speech. Holding her hands toward the townspeople, balanced between the sky and the earth, she spoke.

"The Well has bestowed upon me this incredible gift to share with you. I will bless the soil and awaken the seeds that lie there now, but I do not give you abundance and security. I give you the *opportunity* for abundance and security. I will use my hands to bless you, but you will use your hands to tend the crops and harvest these lands."

Calen glanced to the side, wondering if Stokely would notice that she had gone off script, again. He quieted the sickle-shaped elder with whom he was speaking as his eyes slid to Calen standing in the field. She smirked to herself.

"Know that I am in awe of your dedication and hard work that feeds our great colonies," she continued. "This is an act of partnership. I thank you."

She truly did believe that the people surrounding her were deserving of appreciation for their hard work and dedication, regardless of how difficult her role in the process would be. They would still toil away through sweltering summer days to feed the Colonies, but that wasn't the only reason she commended them. Stokely believed himself (and most other Vessels) to be exceptional, and when she praised commoners as equals, it made him so angry that his left eye twitched. It was one of the few joys left to her in this world.

"Blessed are the Vessels," she said in closing, and lowered her hands to her sides, turning back to the nearly black soil of the mountain valley.

Taking a few steadying breaths, she knelt in her delicate, feather-light gown, her knees registering the discomfort of the cold almost immediately. Her feet were far more accustomed to the elements, as she often walked barefoot. The feel of crisp, half-frozen grass snapping beneath her had always reminded her of living in the mountains as a girl, sneaking out at dawn to catch the first blinding rays of sun as they crested the horizon. If she were a commoner, she would be well on her way to catching an illness, but holding the essence of the universe within her *did* have some perks, and never getting sick was certainly one of them.

Calen leaned forward and dug her hands into the ground, feeling the tiny grains of earth slipping beneath her short fingernails as an energetic earthworm wriggled restlessly beneath her palm. She had read once that these miraculous little creatures were covered with taste buds on the outsides of their bodies, and she was suddenly remorseful that she had washed them clean of her lunch before leaving the inn this afternoon.

"Sorry little guy, you'll have to settle for the taste of soap," she whispered. The smell of hyacinth floated on the breeze, heady and floral, and she could see them sitting in an old jar on her windowsill back home, awaiting her return. Calen clung to that morsel of beauty, knowing how much she would need it in the moments to come.

A small group of women had begun to sing and sway. Even though Calen had no desire to do so herself, she was always grateful for the cover their noise would provide. It didn't matter that she tried to keep quiet during her ritual work; the power she was about to unleash was wild and unruly. Just like all other primal acts of nature, wielding her mana was a loud and messy affair.

One last deep breath, and she prompted a miracle. Calen *opened*. In her mind's eye, she envisioned the tight ball of power that lay mostly dormant, just below and behind her navel. She embraced the power, imagining her hands gently stroking the sides of it as it awakened. It swelled slightly and came unfurled, and she was washed in the sensation of lightness, a gentle buzz of intoxication that always accompanied opening.

Her mana swirled softly at first, then began sending out small tendrils questing around her abdomen. It was a coil of energy, circling and shifting and changing from light to deep turquoise and back again. Being open to her power felt like nervous butterflies, but more pleasant and somehow more natural. A hauntingly sweet song accompanied the energy, for her ears alone, she knew, and Calen was always touched by the intimacy of it. The more time she allowed herself to stay like this, open to her mana, the more awake and alive it became.

When she was at Grandview, she had been taught that mana had poured into her at the moment of consecration, and she would act as its Vessel. It was her power to be wielded as befit her duties. But she never quite believed that. It was more like an extension of herself, a limb that humanity hadn't known it was missing until six hundred twenty-two years ago. Her mana moved and acted of its own accord, as if sentient and alive, until she directed it. Her shoulders sagged as she gathered the courage to do exactly that.

With the same inherent ability to awaken the power and open herself, Calen envisioned herself grabbing ahold of one of the sweet, beautiful tendrils, and with every ounce of fleeting nerve she had, she *ripped* it away from itself. Her mana immediately reacted, flashing red and angry, recoiling into itself, and screaming inside her mind so loudly that she visibly flinched. It took an incredible effort to keep her hands on the ground and not reach to shield her ears, even though she knew it would be useless against the sound. As always, it was within her, and she could not escape their shared misery.

As quickly as she could, she silenced her mana. She imagined cupping her hands around the inflamed power, and in an action similar to clenching down with a muscle deep inside herself, she closed off again. The power rested once more, dormant, and quiet, waves of sadness rolling from it. Just as she believed it was likely sentient, she also believed it could feel. And right now, it felt betrayed.

I'm so sorry, she thought. She hoped it understood.

Separate from the poor, sorrowful ball resting in her pelvis once more, was the piece of power she had stolen away. She would have to work quickly before it reattached, which could happen in mere moments. Calen began heaving, working the energy up from her belly because, despite what she had said during her speech, the blessing did not come from her hands.

In an act beyond her own comprehension, the mana was suddenly lodged somewhere above her stomach. As it continued to move, she panicked at the momentary inability to breathe, her guttural sounds of choking providing a hacking drumbeat for the singing crowd of onlookers. But then, it slid from the back of her throat and across her tongue. Calen leaned forward and pushed her lips into the soil, imitating a kiss. One last heave and the cool, tangy energy left her body and sank into the Earth.

As always, the blessing happened all around her, but she was wrapped in a blur of bodily pain and soul-crushing despair. The power that had sunken into the ground would send a wave of color and energy pulsing across the fields at incredible speed. Visible to the naked eye, everyone in attendance would react with awe. Her mana would light up the soil with shades of turquoise, but Calen never got to see the beauty of it. Ritual work took an exacting toll, and she was lost to the world in the moments after she gave her mana to the Earth.

She had allowed her hickory-hued hair to sheet around her face, hiding the torrents now staining her cheeks. This was a private heartbreak that she did not wish to share with the townsfolk gathered. Blessing their soil was her duty, and it was not meant to come with a helping of guilt. Whether or not they knew what they had asked of her, she did not intend to give them her pain.

The tears streaming down her hot cheeks splashed into the crumbled black and were immediately absorbed. The Earth had caught enough of her tears to recognize them as family and welcome them home. Every part of her ached. She worried she was going to vomit again, but this time it would be plain old stomach contents leaving her body, instead of the power of the universe. Breathing in the clean mountain air, Calen calmed herself and discreetly wiped her face dry. Sitting back to rest on her knees, the pressing sensation of being watched tickled the back of her neck.

Calen could sense someone standing close by, in the field with her. Turning to look over her shoulder, in stark contrast to the jubilant people behind her, was the girl with keen eyes and intelligent questions. Nelle. Her body was rigid, and she gripped her blush pink dress in white-knuckled fists. The look on her open face was one of abject horror. There was no joy in her eyes. No awe at the miracle that had been performed.

Calen had the distinct feeling that the girl had seen *everything* that had happened. For all the fine fabric cocooning her now, she felt stripped bare. Perhaps the rest of her village did not notice what a seed blessing truly was, but Nelle did. Somehow, she knew.

Three

April 10, 622

Stokely

Stokely stood by the window of the Graymount Community Center, watching as the citizens piled into the large space. The rain had held off until after the seed blessing, then had let loose in a deluge that sent them scattering to the closest trees and buildings for cover. He had the sense to head back to the center before that had happened and was spared the indignity of spending the rest of the evening half-soaked and smelling like a wet dog. The men and women drifting past him would not be so fortunate.

If he were in a generous mood, he might have given a bit of credit to Calen for saving him. But she was deserving of exactly no praise right now.

Calen. She was growing more worthless by the day, and on this particular day she did so by leaps and bounds. Hot irritation surged in his muscles at the thought of her scampering across the wet dirt, demanding that he escort her back to the inn as soon as the seed blessing concluded, and he squeezed his hands behind his back as he fought the urge to hit something. The sycophant elder at his elbow had overheard and insisted that they take their meal at the Community Center, as all the best cooks in the village would be working those kitchens. He had effectively prevented Stokely from having to spend the remainder of the afternoon listening to Calen's incessant weeping, which she was most definitely doing in the women's room.

How could such a powerful Vessel be such a pathetic person?

Three partners in, and he was losing hope that he would find the right one. The two partners he had trained before Calen had been far quicker to understand his requirement for submission and compliance. Zolya had been a lovely woman, and he had even grown fond of her in their years working together. If only he hadn't accidentally pulled too much power from her, he wouldn't have burned her out prematurely. Jamilla had been far weaker in her ability to hold mana, but easier to break. However, she had also been far too clever for her own good. Death at the bottom of a ravine was the least she deserved after the accusations she had leveled at him.

Then, there was Calen. He had waited so long for her to be ready for their partnership, invested so much of his time, energy, and coin. Stokely had built a foundation of hope on which he and Calen could have built something incredible. He had the ruthlessness necessary to understand exactly how their power should be used, and the vision to create a future worthy of their stature. She had an astounding capacity for holding mana, and a way of working with it that was both intuitive and explosive. He was so close to sharing everything with her. She could be the one woman with whom he could disclose all he had learned while training at Black Rock, locked away in the secret cellar with the most important tomes written in human existence and the librarian capable of understanding them. But she continued to insist that her power was different from everyone else's, and that working with it was painful and difficult.

He released a sigh and suppressed the twinge of regret he felt every time he considered what he would have to soon do. He could not afford the weakness of remorse, not even for Calen. A hundred years from now, she would be a distant memory, and he would be the living representation of the next leap in human evolution.

Still, Stokely would have to find another way to bond to an apprentice once he had used her up. There was no way the new Head of the First Order, Marcus, would grant him another partnership. His predecessor, Fineas, had been much more malleable. When Stokely needed a new ritual worker, he would simply drip honey into the man's ear and whiskey down his throat, and all previous missteps would be forgiven. He had a feeling that Marcus was not the type of man to be convinced so easily. Stokely had heard rumors of his plans to elevate the standards by which new First Order members were judged, and "strict" didn't even begin to describe them. Marcus had even allegedly allowed a Seeker to help sort out some of the stickier complaints made about Order members at Black Rock. No, he was not the man to help Stokely find a new partner once Calen was out of the way.

Stokely raised his chin and grinned. He was not a man to be denied, and if he needed a new partner, he would find a way to get one.

The villagers continued to pour in at a casual pace, their deep-seated manners winning out over their need to find shelter. A dozen-or-so of them had come back early and were busily cooking some kind of stew in the kitchen adjacent to the main hall. The promising aroma of rich meat mingled with earthy vegetables, and his stomach rumbled. Perhaps he could find the voluptuous woman carrying the crock of apple mead to keep him occupied while he waited for the meal to be prepared. Mountain trolls like these often mixed their meal with dancing and talking, so it could be a while. His stomach burbled again, and he thought of his favorite restaurant back home, where they understood how to properly honor a man of his stature. If he had his way, he would never work in the mountains again.

The space beneath his ribs began to warm, and he realized that his Stone was activated. The sensation was not strong, but it was definitely there. He scanned the room for Calen but found that she was still absent. Then, he spotted the girl from earlier, the one who had interrupted the seed blessing by walking straight into the field. It was not his imagination that his Stone had reacted toward her earlier. It was doing so now. The gentle pull of the Stone tugged, and he began to move toward her, almost unconsciously, as she weaved through the sodden crowd.

He watched her shuffle silently across the room, hands still holding her dress in tight fists, shock and sadness etched into the down-turned edges of her delicate mouth, tension in her shoulders. A woman who appeared to be her mother pressed a kiss into the top of her head before passing under the hanging pine bough and into the kitchen with an armful of food. The girl settled into a booth in the corner, finally releasing the death grip on her dress. Her eyes darted around the room, as if just now noticing that there were other humans present. She made eye contact with him for one tense moment, then her eyes shot wide and swung to the table in front of her. In a fruitless attempt to avoid his attention, she shriveled into the corner of the booth.

He wanted to approach her, but a much stronger pull came from the direction in which Calen had fled earlier. He ground his teeth, knowing he would have to keep a tight leash on her tonight. Something had her completely off-kilter, and she was likely to act irresponsibly if left to her own devices.

"I'll be back for you, little mouse," he mused to the girl in the corner. Large, hazel eyes set in a thin, not entirely unpretty face, with a small mouth, and pale, limp hair made the nickname true. Perhaps he would not need Marcus to help him find another partner, after all.

Four

April 10, 622

Calen

Calen closed the pale green umbrella she had borrowed from the front desk at the Inn and propped it against the wall, careful not to drip rain on her fresh dress. She had returned to her room to clean up and change from her dirt-smeared gown after spying herself in the women's washroom mirror. She had looked feral, with clumps of soil stuck to her tear-stained cheeks under a mane of hair that had grown even more wild in the humid, pre-storm air. It was pinned back now, but she still donned the crown of violets, wilted as they were. There were dark circles under her puffy eyes, but she had never learned to properly apply makeup, so there was nothing for it. If she had, perhaps she could brighten her lips to a color closer to a living human's, rather than the wan shade of a dead trout.

Stokely appeared at the end of the hall, a dark shape in the warmly lit doorway. She shuffled across the distance and made to edge around him, but he caught her by the elbow.

"Calen," he growled.

She looked up at him through dark lashes. "I'm starving, can we please just get in there?"

He studied her face, his discerning eyes darting from one feature to another, and his lips pinched. "You look awful."

"Thanks," she said, "that's what I was trying for."

His eyes went hard. "Are you at least done crying? This isn't exactly the time or place."

If he had shown any softness, she might have allowed herself a moment of vulnerability. She might have told him how her joints ached, and her head throbbed. She might have even asked to be held. But every time he spoke, his words were a knife held to flesh, ready to expose bone.

"I'm fine. Can we please just get in there?"

He released her arm and turned his back on her. If only she had a knife of her own, she could end this slow-moving disaster once and for all. But no. This was her fate, her duty. She would follow in his wake, and cling to the small mercies this life offered. One of which turned out to be the main hall of the Community Center.

The high ceilings were strung with pine boughs in a criss-cross pattern, tied together with yellow ribbon where they met. The wood-paneled walls were adorned with sconces holding spice-scented beeswax candles that had been lit for the occasion, and candelabra were sprinkled about on every table, giving the enormous room a warm, intimate feel. Pitchers of chilled water were set between oblong wooden bowls filled with dinner rolls and crocks of butter, inviting folks to help themselves before the real meal began. The floor had been buffed to a high shine to entice dancers to enjoy themselves. Calen could not help but smile.

They settled themselves in the small booth situated to allow them a view of the festivities. Through the cacophony of festive voices, she heard one cut through the rest.

"Revered Calen, Brother Stokely, we've done made quite a feast for you!"

The boisterous woman from earlier was making her way to their booth. She flourished two pristine ceramic bowls and laid them atop the woven placemats before her and Stokely. A jolly-looking, ruddy-faced man was on her heels, carrying pots of stew that made her mouth water instantly. The woman took them from his hands, as well as a bowl of bread, a small pot of butter, and cooked cinnamon apples from the short parade of helpers following him. She arranged each just so, then leaned forward to begin heaping spoonfuls of the rich stew into their bowls. Stokely stopped her with a sharp look, and her hand paused, hovering halfway to its destination, brown sauce dripping onto the white tablecloth.

"Apologies, sir," she said, her smile turning nervous, "it's common manners here to serve our guests. If you don't mind."

"Actually," he said, "I do mind. Quite a bit. It would appear that you have little control over the portions that you serve and eat." He scanned her body with unkind eyes and the woman pulled back. Calen winced. "Revered Calen and I would prefer to serve ourselves, so that we may remain healthy and nimble enough to continue our work without our hearts giving out prematurely. Set down the spoon and walk away, if you don't mind."

The woman glared at Stokely and straightened her spine.

"I see that you folks don't share the same sense of decency as we do here," the woman said, "so I suppose it would be best if we just left you to yourselves. I'll have my niece bring you some water, and wine, if that's not too offensive to your *nimble sensibilities?*"

Perhaps she did not need Calen's sympathy.

Stokely narrowed his eyes. "Actually, I think we would prefer the apple mead."

"Just so, Brother Stokely," the woman said, all the warmth in her voice gone. "Revered Calen, enjoy your meal." Then, she turned on her heel, lifted her skirt, and made for the kitchen.

"There was no need to be that rude, Stoke," Calen said.

"There was no need for her to be that big, Calen."

Calen lifted her spoon and squeezed the smooth handle, imagining what it would be like to shove it into his eye. She dipped it into the food, instead. It was incredible. Hot, but not scalding. Flavor that was so intense it exploded on her tongue. Salty beef, soft potatoes and sweet carrots, small peas that popped when she bit down, thyme and rosemary in perfect proportions, and the bite of black pepper at the end. If she could cook like this, Calen would probably have the village woman's bearing, and wear her figure as a badge of honor. Calen reached for the bread, and *blessed Vessel* it was still warm.

"Easy, Calen," Stokely warned.

How long would it take to smother a human with a piece of bread? Too long, she decided. That would be a waste of a good piece of bread, anyhow. She would have to settle for a dirty look.

"You'll thank me when you are still thin enough to wear your gowns at the end of the season," was his clipped response to the heat burning in her eyes.

They finished their meals, and Stokely stood to find more mead. Perhaps if he had not been so rude, the villagers might have been more willing to bring refills. She looked across the dance floor, to the kitchens where the woman had disappeared. Calen had really been looking forward to finding out what other dishes the villagers had prepared.

Beyond the dancers moving with the steady rhythm of the hand drum being played, a lone figure stood, motionless save the rise and fall of her shallow breathing. Nelle. She looked as frightened as before, and perhaps a little angry. They locked eyes, and the girl made her way across the busy divide. She appeared to be on a mission that brought her to Calen's booth.

"I need to talk to you," Nelle blurted out. Calen watched her open her mouth and close it. She did it a second time, then pinched her lips shut and crossed her arms. Concerned, she waited for the girl to say more.

Nelle cleared her throat. "Excuse me, Mistress Calendula. May I speak with you?"

The apprehension she had felt earlier crept back into her chest. Glancing over the girl's shoulder, Calen could see Stokely watching the two of them, his hawk-like eyes demanding to know more. Why could he not find business beyond her for just one evening?

"Actually," Calen said, "I think it would be good if you went back to your booth, Nelle. Or better yet, you should go and dance with that handsome, albeit sweaty, young man. Please." She pointed her chin at the young man waving for Nelle to join him in a dance.

"But, Mistress Calendula, I really must speak with—"

"No, you really must not," she pushed out, a weak desperation sneaking into her words. "Please, do not draw attention to yourself. Just go join your friends and try to enjoy your evening."

"I saw what you did!" Nelle yelled. Calen watched surprise register on the girl's face. "Apologies, Mistress. It's just that, well..." she trailed off, her eyes darting back and forth. "I just want to understand what happened. I don't know what I saw, but it wasn't right. It wasn't right, Mistress Calen, and I want to know why."

With a forced air of boredom, she rose to her feet and nodded toward the hallway. "Let's find somewhere quiet to talk." Nelle followed, and when they were safely out of sight, Calen rested her hands on the girl's shoulders.

"Nelle, please try to calm down. We can speak here, but it would be best if we kept quiet."

Nelle looked at her with that same mix of anger and confusion. "Why?" she asked. "It's a secret, isn't it? That's why my mama had no idea what I was talking about when I told her what I saw. How it felt. Why did it feel like that?"

Calen could see the tears gathering in her eyes, and the tip of her nose was red from where she was continuously wiping it with a napkin. She lifted her hands to her head and began massaging her temples.

"Hurts so bad," she whispered.

"What hurts, Nelle?"

"My head. The screaming. It still hurts. When does it stop?"

There was no way she meant...

"What screaming, Nelle? No one is screaming."

"N-no, not a person," she winced and rubbed her head again. "Your... was that your mana? And you ripped it, and it changed, and then...screaming."

No. Not possible.

Calen rubbed at the dark stones on each of her middle fingers, a nervous habit that accompanied the rings. Of all the reasons Nelle could be different, Calen had not considered this. Somehow, the girl could see her mana.

"Come with me," she said, and started for the women's washroom.

Calen checked for feet under each of the stall doors. Once she was certain they were alone, she locked the door and turned back to Nelle.

"Nelle, I don't know how much time we have to speak. Stokely will notice I'm gone and come to find me. I will answer as many of your questions as I can but I can't promise the answers will make sense to you right now. And if you want answers, I have conditions."

She counted them off on her fingers, surprised at how steady they were.

"One: You will answer my questions first. That may help us both to make sense of all of this. Two: When we are done speaking, you will wait until I leave this washroom, give me ten minutes to get my partner out of the hall, then you will leave and go straight home. In fact, you will have one of your friends walk you there, if your parents are still busy. Yes?"

She waited for Nelle to confirm with a quick nod, then continued.

"Three: You will avoid Stokely," she said, punctuating each word. "We are set to stay here for two days more, and you need to stay away from him. If you and I both know something strange has happened, then he certainly will have realized it as well. You will avoid him at all costs. Do not defer to him as you would other Vessels. If he comes looking for you, hide. If he finds you, run. This is the most important condition and I need to know that you understand what I am telling you."

Nelle's slim body shuddered. "He's...not right." Just as before, the girl's hand went to her stomach.

"Do you get stomach aches often?" Calen asked on a hunch.

"No more than most kids. But he makes my stomach hurt. Don't worry, I'll stay away from him."

Realization washed over Calen. Nelle held mana, and she had a Seeker's intuitive distribution. That was how she could feel the imbalance in Stokely's character, and why it made her stomach hurt. But how could she hold mana? And how was she pulling Calen with it?

Calen crossed her hands in front of her and intentionally softened her features.

"Okay, Nelle. I need you to be absolutely honest with me. You won't be in any trouble, and neither will your parents."

Nelle gave her a confused look.

"When did you go to the Well?" she asked the girl.

"Wh-what? I've never been to the Well," Nelle answered.

"Never?"

"Never."

"Not even when you were younger, maybe?"

"No. I've never left the Southern Drift. I've only ever left Graymount to visit family a couple times."

Well, that made less than no sense.

"When was the last time a Seeker came to your village looking for potential Vessels?" Calen asked.

"Two years ago," Nelle answered. "There was two of 'em, and they brought candy from every Colony they had been to."

If Nelle held mana, the Seekers would have been able to sense it with a simple touch and infusion of their mana into the girl.

"Were you tested?" Calen asked.

"No," Nelles said, her eyebrows pinching together. "I didn't, because I had the worst case of poison ivy in my life. I think they felt bad about getting too close, since I was covered in hives head-to-toe. Couldn't even wear clothes. They said I could always try next time."

"How old were you?"

"Twelve."

"Two years is too long between visits," she said, mostly to herself. Not that there was anything to do about it. Seekers were from The Second Order, and just like the First and Third, they kept to themselves and answered to no one but the Head of their Order.

"Well, they don't come out here much. We don't have a lot of trouble, so they mostly come around when there's testing to do. They took two that year, Leto and Elanor."

So, it was possible that the Seekers had missed her, but that would not explain how she had been consecrated in the first place. Surely, she would have to know about it, had it happened. Maybe there was a different explanation altogether.

"Nelle, can you explain what you felt out in that field?"

The girl's eyes went wide, then she launched into a hushed recounting of what she had seen. And felt. And heard. There was no doubt that she had witnessed the innermost workings of Calen's power.

"Was that *thing* I saw your mana?" Nelle asked.

"Yes, Nelle, it was." She let out a measured breath. "I don't know how else to say this, but what you are telling me is impossible. No one can see mana except for the person who holds it, unless and until they release it. When it is still inside of a Vessel, it is private. It is only visible to us. When we use our mana, for a blessing or a healing, or during a fight or a balancing, it is visible to the naked eye. I don't understand how you could have seen my mana."

"It was like a swirling ball or cloud," Nelle whispered, as if she had not heard Calen. Her eyes were glassy and unfocused. "I don't know. It somehow made sense to me. It was like everything in life was connected to you through it. It was like everything in life was connected to *me* through it. Then, it —"

Nelle took a shuddering breath and looked into Calen's eyes, fear and pain radiating from her wide, searching face.

"Why did it hurt like that?" she asked. "Why is it like that? Did you do something wrong?"

"No, I didn't do anything wrong," Calen answered. "At least, not that I know of. Yes, it always feels that way. It didn't used to. But for the past few years, my mana has gone a bit wild. Difficult."

"Is that why you left the seed blessing right away?"

"Yes. I didn't want to vomit on the field. Tends to make people upset."

Calen let out a huff as she sat on the small stool beside the sinks, resting her head in her hands. It was an embarrassing exposé of her loneliness that she wanted to confide her shortcomings to a young stranger while on the floor of a public washroom in a village far from home, but it was inevitable. The girl already knew too much, and Calen had no one else to tell. Stokely had successfully isolated her over their shared years, and in the place where her former friendships had lived, he had salted the Earth with his vitriol and condescension. The absence she felt the most acutely belonged to the one person who swore they would never leave her side. That promise, that vow, had for years been a lifeline. Now, it was a frayed connection to a person who had been swallowed up by her own self-importance.

"It's not like that for everyone else, is it?" Nelle asked.

Calen shook her head, a precarious violet tumbling free and falling to the floor beside her.

"But maybe there is a reason that it feels that way for you? Maybe...maybe there is something wrong?"

"Are you accusing me of mishandling my mana?" Calen shot back, instantly regretting the harshness in her tone.

"Sorry, I shouldn't have said that," Nelle said. Her cheeks flushed, and she looked away, fiddling with the cold-water knob.

"No, it's okay," Calen said. "It has just been a long day, and this situation is making me anxious. I think we need to find a way to figure this out."

Calen closed and fought against the dizziness swimming in her head. The smell of fruit pie of some type had seeped into the washroom, and she realized that she was still hungry, as well as exhausted.

"I am staying in your village for two days more," she said, looking up, "if I can get away from Stokely—"

As if summoned by her thoughts of him, the man's voice accompanied three loud bangs against the washroom door. Calen jumped up, her heart pounding. She glanced at Nelle and held a finger to her lips, then turned toward the door.

"Yes?" Calen asked, false casualness in her voice.

"Calen? What are you doing in there?" Stokely asked, his words slurred around the edges. "It's time to go. That mead went straight to my head, and I need to get away from these people."

Without looking away from Nelle, she answered.

"Okay, Stokely. You can head back to the inn; I'll be there as soon as I'm done in here."

She heard his normally precise feet clumsily shuffling away from the door and back toward the celebration. She closed and opened her fists in rapid succession, trying to move the hot, jittery feeling from them, and turned away from Nelle.

"Mistress Calen," the girl said from behind her, "can I ask you a question?"

"Sure," she said, her voice like a cord strung between two moving objects.

"Brother Stokely hurts you, doesn't he?"

Her head fell forward in a surrendered nod.

"And...and no one helps you?"

"It's complicated."

"I don't understand," Nelle said, stepping toward her, "With what you have inside of you...with how powerful you are, why do you let him?"

Calen whispered back over her shoulder, "Because, dear Nelle. There are forces in this world more powerful than what I have inside of me."

Nelle moved closer still.

"No, Mistress Calen, I don't think that there are."

Tears welled in the corner of Calen's eyes, but she held them in as she squared herself to the door. Some lessons were better left for adulthood.

"Remember, ten minutes," she said.

Then she twisted the lock, turned the doorknob, and swept out of the restroom.

Five

April 10, 622

Calen

Calen watched a drop of rain meander down her nose and splash on her hand hovering above the brass doorknob. She and Stokely had been given the best room at the Inn, complete with its own soaking bathtub and breathtaking view of the mountains through floor-to-ceiling windows on the wall opposite the bed. The bed itself was large and comfortable, and there was a wood-burning oven in the corner that kept the room cozy. It was truly a spectacular space. If only she didn't have to share it with a monster.

Despite the rain-soaked run across the town center, the warmth from the fire blazing in the open foyer behind permeated her tired body. The aromatic wood smoke reminded her of the small, tidy cabin that was waiting for her at the end of their two-month trek across three Colonies to perform seed blessings this spring. Several weeks into the tour, she was determined to make it to the last city. Calen could survive this season.

She laid her palm on the worn knob and rested her forehead against the ancient wood of the door, savoring one last moment of peace before facing the brutality that awaited her on the other side. Stokely's preternatural hearing must have detected her movements, though, and a moment later the door flung open. She shot a foot out to catch herself and would have face-planted on the wide-planked oak floor had he not been standing just across the doorjamb. Instead, she smashed into his firm chest, immediately righting herself to edge around him. He let out an irritated huff and closed the door.

"You're soaking wet," he commented.

"Yes, well. You may have noticed that it is raining." She held an outstretched hand toward the wall of windows.

She was not welcomed to their room by sultry wood-smoke musk. No, their shared space smelled like sandalwood and spice, a predator's den properly marked. Her back to him, she could feel his scowl as she searched for the fluffy, cotton towel with which she had bathed earlier in the day.

"Are you going to get an attitude tonight, Callie?" he asked.

She gave a scowl of her own. She hated that stupid nickname, and he knew it. Which was why he used it as though he was talking to a small, idiotic child, or an unimpressive pet dog. Calen found the towel, gave it a sniff, and started to dry her hair, turning to face him. Stokely glared from his most intimidating pose, arms crossed over his broad chest, legs in a wide, space-claiming stance. His sodden clothes had already been discarded and he wore only his underclothes and their Consecration Stone on a chain around his neck. He must have used his mana to burn the alcohol from his system, stone-cold sober as he now was.

"There's no attitude, Stoke" she said. "I'll be dry in a minute."

"Good. I'm really not in the mood for a fight tonight."

Liar. He was always in the mood for a fight. It was, perhaps, his favorite thing to do in all of the world.

"Get undressed and get into bed. And so help me, if you get my pillow wet, you will sleep on the floor," he said, as though to an unimpressively *wet*, pet dog.

Calen watched him saunter toward the bed, fidgeting in place. She haphazardly folded the towel and set it on the dresser, lowering her hands to her belly.

"Listen, Stokely. Today was...intense. I'm—" she paused.

Just say it.

"I don't want to do this tonight," she said in a rush, closing her eyes against his reaction.

He turned smoothly, his condescending gaze sweeping the room before landing on her as he sauntered back toward her.

"Excuse me?" he asked, cupping his ear as if he had not heard her properly.

The wood oven was so warm, and she knew the perfect softness that the mattress would give when it cradled her once more. She really wanted nothing *more* than to undress and get into bed, but no amount of comfort could lull her into voluntarily laying with him tonight. Although, 'voluntarily' was a subjective term to Stokely. He routinely *took* what was not volunteered. She could already hear the speech building in his voice.

"It is our duty, your duty, Calen. Just because you are a terrible ritual worker, you are not excused from your responsibilities, and embracing your fecund nature is well within your job description."

Many Vessels of her Order felt that their ritual work fed their sexual energy, and vice versa, but those women were different. They chose who to share their sensual abundance with, whether it be their bonded partner, or someone else entirely. And to her knowledge, basic decency and shared consent were every bit as important as the need to "embrace their fecund nature." Stokely had never once fulfilled those intimate, human needs before demanding from her what he wanted. While many women would envy her position (literally), that was only because they did not know Brother Stokely the way that she did.

He stopped with less than a foot between them, forcing her head back to maintain eye contact.

"Mind repeating that, Callie?" he said, disbelief dripping from his voice. "Because it sounds to me like you are trying to neglect your duties for the second time today."

"I'm not being neglectful, Stoke," she pled, "I'm just tired and today's blessing was really difficult. I just want to go to bed, please."

"Do you think this is what *I* want to do?" His eyes roved up and down her body in a way that made her fidget nervously, a sneer pulling at his upper lip. "No," he said in a way that was quiet without being gentle. "But we have a responsibility. I do this because I have to. Now, undress and get into bed. I won't say it a third time."

She let her arms fall to her sides, her eyes pleading for understanding.

"Now," he let out in a low growl.

He started to turn again, but was stopped by the single syllable that left her lips.

"No."

It was barely a whisper, but it hit him like an avalanche.

"No?"

It was far more dangerous coming from him.

Stokely's narrowed eyes were hot coals. His posture shifted almost imperceptibly, and she recognized the loaded moment that usually signaled he was about to unleash his unnatural speed and brutality on a sparring partner. Only this time, there was no well-trained, equally powerful opponent. There was only her, with her small, weak frame, and unwieldy, unhelpful mana to accept the consequences of this refusal. There would be no witnesses to his barbarity, save the rain drops streaking the windows.

The strike came so quickly that at first, Calen did not know what had happened. One moment, she was standing firmly on her own two feet. In the next, she was sprawled on the hardwood floor, tasting metal. Thankfully, she had caught herself with both hands, but within seconds, the pain flooded into her jaw with the clarity that he had hit her. Her suspicions were confirmed when she shot a look over her shoulder and saw him opening and closing a fist glowing blue with his mana.

Calen remembered two seconds too late exactly what came next. His large, bare foot connected with the exposed ribs along her side, kicking out with so much force that she left the floor and crashed down on her back with a painful grunt.

Stokely walked leisurely to her, placing one foot on either side of her hips, looming over her with all the concern of a man making a cup of tea. He was completely exposed to her, the action meant to highlight just how powerless he believed her to be. As if she couldn't possibly pose a threat. As if he could show his soft underside and she would not strike.

"You know, I change my mind," he let out with a contented sigh. "Turns out I am in the mood for a little bit of a fight tonight. But I feel better. So now, you're going to fucking listen. Undress. Bed. Now."

He walked away from her for the second time.

Under the haze of ritual-induced exhaustion, Calen was a seething mass of agony as she lolled on the floor. Her vision spun and she sucked in a breath, instantly regretting the sharp pain in her chest that was probably cracked ribs. When she tried to close her mouth, a sickening ache blossomed in a jaw that didn't work right, and her lip was going numb where it had split. Her mind wanted to retreat, wanted her to stop feeling, stop seeing, stop knowing, but that was a luxury she could not afford. If she did, she might not return.

Calen fought through the raging storm of sadness and memory and pain, desperately trying to regain control of herself. Pushing weakly to her side while gingerly cradling her broken midsection, she tried to crawl away to somewhere, anywhere safe, but there was nowhere to go.

Then, from somewhere in the mess of her mind, came a voice that was as healing as a salve. Sharp and strong and undeniably *her*. All the chaos of the moment smoothed away, the sharp edge of pain abated, and she heard it as clearly as if the woman was sitting in front of her.

Cal, get up, Rosalind's voice whipped in her mind.

"Rosie?" she whispered to herself.

Stoke must have hit her harder than she thought if she was hallucinating. Calen had not spoken to Rosie in at least a year.

Cal, please, the not-Rosalind Rosalind voice begged. *Run.*

"Run?" she asked the empty airspace in front of her.

Leaning on shaky arms, she glanced at Stokely but he did not so much as look back in her direction.

Calen, don't let him do this. Her voice was growing quiet, as if she were being pulled away. *You're stronger than this.*

A memory.

There are forces in this world more powerful than what I have inside of me.

No, Mistress Calen, I don't think that there are.

Holding onto the lip of the dresser, Calen pulled herself to standing, biting down on a whimper. She waited until the room held still, then she bolted for the door.

Stokely's speed won out, again, and he crossed the room just as she was reaching for the doorknob. He smacked her hand away with such force that she cried out in shock and pain. Then he took her by the waist and *threw her* toward the bed. She came down with a thud that only slightly muffled the sound of her shoulder popping, her limp body sliding the last few feet before bumping into the foot of the four-poster bed she had spent so much time admiring.

Calen had not been trained as a warrior at Black Rock. She did not know how to wield her power in a way that could protect her from Stokely, but she had to try. She closed her eyes and tried to focus on the mana resting in her core.

Please. If you can hear me. Help.

It began to stir, but before she could open fully, he was there, standing over her.

"Calen..." he crooned, his voice low and menacing. "I thought we were past this. Don't get me wrong, I do actually love when you put up a bit of a fight. But refusing me? Running away?"

He tsked as he lowered himself into her personal space, straddling her belly as he rolled his shoulders. He twisted his head to the right and left, loud cracks issuing from his neck. Just a man warming up before a bout of exercise.

"That simply cannot be allowed."

A whip of lightning flashed outside, and Calen saw the crazed look in his eye. She shook her head, and tried one last time to get away. His thighs tightened on her frame.

"Please," she begged.

Stokely stroked a disgustingly gentle finger down her cheek, tracing the tears that could no longer be held in. When it reached the soft underside of her chin, he tipped her head back and wrapped his fingers delicately around her throat. Manicured and beautiful. Cruel and lethal. He squeezed.

The last thing Calen heard before she lost consciousness was her own ragged voice, choking on her words.

"No. Please, no."

Six

April 10, 622

Rosalind

Rosalind was drowning. Spinning in the churning ether between dreaming and awakening, she was incapable of discerning up from down. With a jolt, she broke through the surface of sleep and sat bolt upright in her bed, sucking in a noisy breath of warm night air. Her skin was coated in a light sheen of sweat and her heart galloped beneath her ribs as she tried to catch her breath and orient herself to the room. Frederick was there in an instant, practically leaping from the twin bed he slept in, positioned against the wall opposite hers. His chestnut brown hair was a tousled mess and there were creases on his left cheek. He had definitely been getting better sleep than her.

"Freddie, put that thing away," she said, as her vision caught the firelight playing on the blade of his dagger. He may have been fast asleep, but years of practice as her bodyguard had instilled instincts so strong they kicked in before he was fully awake.

"Are you okay?" he asked as his eyes flitted around the room, searching for the danger.

"Ummm…"

She shook her head and blinked to clear the sleep from her eyes.

"Yeah" she let out in a sleep-hoarse voice. "Yes, I think I'm okay, Freddie. Just a really bad dream."

He sheathed the dagger at his thigh, the holster incongruous with the complete lack of clothing save his fitted undershorts. They had never been attacked in the night before, but Frederick had asserted that as her influence in the Colonies grew, so too did the target on her back.

"Do you want to talk about it?" he asked, with his usual slow, lumbering way of speaking.

"Not much to—"

Rosalind cleared her throat and reached for the glass of water on the bedside stand, taking a few hearty sips before trying again.

"Not much to talk about, it was just a bad dream."

Freddie watched her, waiting for her to say more.

"It was Cal, I was dreaming of Cal. Only..." her voice broke again, this time from the raw emotion that seemed to hover close to the surface of nightmares. "It was awful, Freddie. She was being attacked. *He* was hurting her," she finished.

A rare flash of anger lit behind Frederick's warm, brown eyes at the mention of *him*. She knew that her partner took it as a personal affront that men like Brother Stokely were allowed to remain within the good graces of society. They were from the same Order, had been through the same candidate process, had made the same vows to protect and honor their partners and the institutions of the New Colonies. Yet Brother Stokely had taken that responsibility and twisted it into something awful and ugly. It was a black eye on their organization that he was allowed to behave the way that he did. The man did make a considerable effort to conceal the true nature of his relationship with his partners, but it was the worst kept secret in the Order that he was abusive and cruel.

He shook his head and the heat receded from his face.

"How bad was it?" he asked softly.

"Bad. But it was just a dream. Nightmare. It was just a nightmare. Please, tell me it was just a nightmare?"

"Only you know the difference, Rosie. Was this just a nightmare, or was this time...more?"

"Blessed Vessel, I don't know. You know how it is. Sometimes I dream of her because I miss her. Other times, it's like I'm watching her life play out."

She pushed her palms into her cheeks, the weight of exhaustion pulling her back toward sleep.

"But if it wasn't just a dream," she continued, "she's in trouble. He was...he did..."

She could not bring herself to say it aloud and risk giving the horror oxygen.

"Well, what do you want to do about it?" Frederick implored.

"What do you mean, what do I want to do about it?" she asked. "It's not like I can leave. Gwendolyn started talked to herself at dinner tonight. You know as well as I do, that means she's only a day or two off from a full-on relapse. I won't be able to leave her side for at least a few weeks."

Her throat burned with helplessness.

Rosalind's great many skills had gained her favor with the Archfamily over the course of her eight-year career in the capital. However, it was her particular skill with manipulating the mana of others that had elevated her to the status of personal advisor to Gwendolyn, the Archmother, when she began suffering.

Five years ago, Gwendolyn's power had begun acting erratically, shifting through her body in ways that were unnatural, influencing the actions of her brain in ways that shouldn't have been possible. Her fits were becoming more frequent. During these times, Rosalind was required to stay by her side until her mana settled and the Archmother felt well again. She knew this was likely the last night she would spend in her own rooms at the Homestead before she was called to lend her abilities once more.

"Yes, I know," he answered, "but the last time you had vivid nightmares, you slept through them for four nights before you sought her out. I don't need to remind you how sick Calen was by the time you finally went to her."

"No, you do not."

"And that was when she was in the capital. Do you even know where she is now? How long will it take to get to her?"

He leaned in and raised his eyebrows.

She let out a small huff of sad laughter.

"Not sick, last time. Poisoned."

"Poisoned. By *him*," he added.

"By him," she confirmed. "But I can't leave this time."

A sharp silence descended as each searched for a solution. Rosalind looked at her partner, shirtless on this abnormally warm spring evening. Freddie had a warrior's physique from years of sparring, but a far softer soul, his adult life spent in the relative safety and comfort of the capital. He preferred the solitude of the woods over the bustling noise of the Archfamily Homestead, and often took trips into the wilderness to hunt morels and wild berries, or to just be. The knowledge and skills he'd earned over the collective years spent in solitude would make him uniquely qualified to set out on his own, even into the mountains...

"Don't even think about it," he answered, his thousand-yard stare into the fire unblinking.

"I was just thinking..." she started.

"I know what you were just thinking," he said, swinging his gaze to her. "And I am not leaving your side, particularly if Gwendolyn is going to need you. You are going to need me."

He was not wrong. But she was not ready to give up.

"I'll be fine here, Freddie," she said. "Calen's just in the Southern Drift. You could be there and back in a fortnight."

Stokely had gone to extreme lengths to ensure that the women no longer had regular contact, but Rosalind had never stopped tracking Calen's movements. She always knew where to find her best friend.

"It's only a few days ride southwest. You'll be able to find them in no time, make sure she's okay, then come back home."

"And if she's *not* okay?" he parried, "Ros, what if the Order has to get involved? You know I'll be called away to testify. They could hold me at Black Rock for months for that process. I won't leave you for that long. Absolutely not."

People tended to believe that Freddie's main purpose in life was to serve as her resident doormat. If that had been the truth, she would have chewed him up and spit him out their first year working together. Instead, they were chosen brother and sister. Equals, despite how things looked from the outside. And if he said 'no,' she respected it. Most of the time.

"I can't just leave her out there with him, Freddie," she pled.

"That's true," he conceded, "but you also can't solve the problem tonight. You need sleep, Ros. I need sleep." His wide yawn prompted her own, and he crossed back over to his own bed.

Her mana hummed within her core, still perturbed by the nightmare. She stretched and rolled her shoulders, trying to relax her body.

"You're right," she said, "I will get up at first light and make some call requests. Maybe it was just a dream and I'll find her healthy and well."

His skeptical look mirrored her own, she knew.

"Good night, again."

Rosalind gathered up her long, cinnamon hair and twirled it into a bun on top of her head as she laid down on her blessedly cool sheets.

"Freddie, did I abandon her?"

For a moment, the only sound was the blood pumping in her ears.

"Go to sleep, Ros," he answered, the placid words muffled by his pillow.

"I have to know she is okay," she added, as she closed her eyes and tried to find sleep again.

It never came.

***

After hours of fitful rest punctuated by heart-pounding fear, Rosalind had risen before first light, dressed, and made her way to the local calling station. It was beginning to occur to her that she might have been better off walking the extra half mile to the next closest station, if only to avoid the call operator sitting in front of her, oblivious to how deeply he was testing her patience this morning. The boy was clearly new at this job, evidenced by the fact that he had been put on early bird duty, and that he struggled to find the right frequency to make her call.

Making a two-way call to the Southern Drift should have been fairly simple for the young man, considering how close the Colony was to the capital, but he had searched through the frequencies once already and was having a difficult time making the connection. The current state of her dress was probably exacerbating matters. In the confusion of dressing in the dark, she had accidentally thrown on one of Freddie's front-lacing tunics that was entirely too large, and the neckline hung precariously low on her chest. The boy, who was clearly old enough to notice, was trying desperately not to notice.

The call office of the Southern Drift would have a schedule of the comings and goings of all persons of interest, as well as any pertinent information travelers wanted to leave for family or friends who might inquire after them. All traveling Vessels were required to check in with the nearest call office when they arrived in a new Colony or large city.

These same schedules were submitted in the main records hall on the Archfamily Homestead. Paper records were considered to be among the most important public possessions within the Colonies and every citizen had access to them. Every year, as soon as Stokely submitted his itinerary for the year (and thereby, Calen's schedule), Rosalind tracked it down and committed it to memory.

This year was no different. Rosalind knew that they were expected to be in a small mountain town in central Southern Drift Colony for a seed blessing. Barring some dramatic schedule change, they should still be there. She figured this would be the first place to call. Or...try to call, anyway.

"Mistress, I'm so sorry. Just, let me check one more time," he spoke, in a lilting way that marked him as a northerner. He fidgeted with the call device.

Rosalind had spent considerable time at the libraries of Black Rock while traveling with Freddie early in their careers. She had quickly become obsessed with learning about pre-meteoric history, particularly technological advances. Most of it had been wiped out or rendered obsolete with the arrival of the global meteor strikes and the strange celestial matter (or energy, depending upon whom you asked) they had brought with them. The librarians thought her obsession to be quaint, but they suffered her endless streams of questioning with gently clasped hands and placid smiles.

It was not as though she would ever have the chance to experience the ancient devices that had apparently permeated human existence. Scholars and scientists alike agreed that life pre-meteor was barbaric and difficult, and no one was in a hurry to send society back to those dark days. None of that stopped Rosalind's unyielding need to know, to want to experience. Especially now, as she watched the operator work in vain to make her call. *Malor*, she mouthed the name printed on his wrinkled, pale blue shirt. Oh, how much simpler life would be if she just had a personal calling device of her own. At this point, homing pigeons would be preferable…or smoke signals. She sighed and looked to the ceiling for reprieve.

"Ah ha!"

The boy's eyes lit up as he un-hunched himself behind his desk and his eyes landed on Rosalind's. Then, he melted like honey in a tea pot, blissful admiration crossing a smooth face that was just a few years into needing a razor. At twenty-seven, Rosalind was well aware of the affect her beauty had on people. Her flirtatious, upturned, deep green eyes were what captured attention (aided, of course, by a tasteful application of makeup), while her smooth, slender, freckle-specked nose drew that attention down to her rosebud mouth (tinted the color a shade lighter than her hair) in a confident but coy smirk she had spent many nights practicing in her mirror. When she needed to go in for the kill, she would flash a broad, unabashed smile that put twin dimples on full display.

Not that she would need that now. The poor kid had finally let his eyes travel to the view afforded by Freddie's shirt, and the look on his face said he might have forgotten his own name.

"Ahem," she said, delicately but deliberately.

He started, sitting up straight again. In an instant, he seemed to not only remember his own name, but where he was, and that he had a job to do. For her. He blushed.

"Em, sorry. I found the frequency," he stuttered out. "What inquiry would you like to make?"

To that, Rosalind extended her hand across the desk, palm open and awaiting the receiver. She had no intention of letting him make the *actual* call for her.

"Oh, em. That's not really allowed," he said, shrugging his commiseration.

Rosalind's only response was to lean further over the desk, pushing her hand (and cleavage) closer to him. His arms went slack for a moment, then he handed the caller over to her, knowing he had lost the silent argument.

She placed the earpiece firmly to her ear, avoiding the three golden rings pierced into the lobe that indicated her Order, and adjusted the volume dial until she clearly heard the voice on the other end of the line.

"Southern Drift, central station, how may I help you?" asked the sleepy voice on the other end. The woman had probably been working all night like the boy sitting in front of her, but she had the bland disposition of someone who had worked this lonely shift for years. Rosalind figured it probably was not a glamorous job, but it did offer purchasing coins for people whose trade was not a part of the basic barter system that set the prices for all goods and services in the Colonies.

"Yes," she chimed in her most professional tone, "I would like to inquire into the individual schedules of Revered Calendula of the Third Order and Brother Stokely of the First Order."

Rosalind heard the woman working on the other end of the line, identifying their unique schedule log.

"Who requests this information?" she asked flatly.

"Revered Rosalind of the Third Order."

Rosalind had considered giving a false name to prevent Brother Stokely from learning of her inquiry, but she knew that she would not be granted their personal, up-to-date schedules without the security clearance of an Order member. Schedules may have been public property, but allowing the public to know every step a Revered took, as well as any calls made, was a security hazard.

Using her own name to gain access to private information was a measured risk. Stokely was possessive and violent, and if he had an inkling that Ros was looking for Calen, he would likely take it out on her.

"Code word, please?"

Ros looked across the table at the operator watching her and pantomimed for him to cover his ears. He obliged.

"North Star," she whispered, cupping her hand around the receiver.

"And what information do you request, specifically?" the faceless voice droned.

"Schedule of movements for the past six days, call logs- incoming and outgoing-, and ummm…" she paused, trying to figure out how to word her next request, "if either Vessel has requested the aid of a healer?"

Without preamble, the woman launched into their itinerary.

"Revered Calendula and Brother Stokely arrived via the northern border way station of the Southern Drift on April 6, 622, PM. Both traveled to Everspring Peak on April 8, 622 PM. Both passed through central way station, Southern Drift on April 9, 622 PM. Both traveled to Graymount, Southern Drift on April 9, 622. No further travel within Southern Drift logged at this time."

So far, so good, they were exactly where Rosalind had expected them to be, and they hadn't made any unusual stops along the way. April 9th was two days past, so they had probably arrived that day, stayed the night in Graymount, and performed the seed blessing last night. Nothing out of the ordinary.

"Call log, incoming and outgoing," the woman had spoken.

"One call from Everspring Peak, Southern Drift, April 8 at 1517 hours to Sun Grove. Duration: twenty minutes."

She took a breath.

"One call from Graymount, Southern Drift, April 11 at 0300 hours to Hopa City. Duration: two minutes. End of call log."

Wait, what?

"Excuse me, ma'am," Rosalind asked, "But did you just say that there was a two-minute call in the middle of the night to Hopa City? Last night?"

"Yes, Mistress," she answered, "That is what the call log shows."

"Was there a message attached or a name given for the recipient?"

"No, Mistress."

"Can you tell me which call center was contacted in Hopa?"

"Yes, Mistress. It was the western way station call center."

That would put it on the edge of the city. It was only there because the various people who lived scattered outside of Hopa City had made a big deal about having to travel so far to make calls. A call center had been put in, despite the fact that the area fell short in all criteria required for one. It was such an odd affair that Rosalind had even heard about it in the capital.

"Hmm, okay. And the other information I requested?" she asked, cautiously optimistic.

"Cannot be provided to anyone beneath the rank of Head of Order. Is there anything else, Mistress?"

"No, ma'am, thank you for your help."

The operator did not even respond, but instead played the tone that was universally known as a polite request to hang up the caller and open the frequency. She handed the receiver back to Malor, thanked him for his help, and left the office even more irritated than she had been upon arrival.

Something, well, *everything* about that call last night felt odd. Who treks out to a call station in the middle of the night? To make a call to Hopa City, no less? Hopa was just a few miles from Graymount, and it would have been just as easy to take a quick ride over and meet with the intended recipient in person. No one would waste call privileges making a short-distance call.

Unless...unless it was an emergency. Had Calen called someone in Hopa City for help? The thought of Calen being hurt and alone...it made Rosalind's chest ache. But the idea that someone *else* would be sitting at her bedside, nursing her wounds, made her want to weep with frustration and jealousy.

She strode down the main thoroughfare, anger and fear simmering in her veins. Her mana had begun to churn on its own, no longer a quiet, calm presence within her. Its apprehension was feeding into hers, making her uncomfortably nauseous. She would have to close off until she could figure out what to do.

Shop keepers and restaurateurs were opening their doors for the day, and the smell of warm, fresh biscuits, smoky bacon and hot tea permeated the warm morning breeze. Her stomach grumbled an appropriate response to its current state of emptiness, and the nausea of a moment ago passed.

Rosalind rounded the corner and, in the distance, could see the Archfamily Homestead sprawling across the northern end of the city. It was built into the scenery with the intention of highlighting the natural splendor of the area. Single-storied and made of bricks all shades of red clay, wisteria vines climbed up and around each of the large, accommodating windows that faced the southern sun. In a few short weeks, those vines would wake from their winter slumber and begin crawling across the parts of the building it had not yet graced with its pale purple clusters of flowers. While they were gorgeous and heavenly-scented, they would have to be pulled back from the roof panels that provided power to the buildings but required sunlight to work.

There were 'wings' of the Homestead that stretched to the east, north, and west, used to house the Archfamily and the staff required to maintain the constant buzz of activity. It was, in its truest sense, a homestead. To the northeast, rolling, fertile fields of crops of all sorts meandered into the distance, their food used to nourish the members of the Archfamily as well as common citizens of the capital. To the northwest was a series of barns and paddocks that held all manner of livestock for similar purposes to the crop fields. And to the south, slightly downhill to capture rainwater runoff from the Homestead proper, was a wonderfully symmetrical orchard of dwarf fruit and nut trees and berry patches, all edged in by a generous border of native wildflowers and medicinal herbs.

Running her hand along the slender, sleeping grapevines, Rosalind reminded herself that she needed to take a bottle of vintage to—

Then, the idea hit her.

She may not be able to leave the capital, and Freddie may not be willing to leave, but that did not mean she was completely helpless. Rosalind knew exactly who she would ask for help. Her stomach growled loudly again, uncaring how pressing her mission was.

"Right, right. Breakfast," she mumbled to herself and made for the Homestead kitchen.

Seven

April 11, 622

Nox

Nox surfaced from a pleasantly deep sleep at a deliciously slow pace, the soft rays of morning sunlight filtering through the thick curtains at his windows to dance across his face. Then came the warm scent of vanilla and musk shampoo that was a perennial favorite among women in the capital, and a tickle from the hair that emanated the sweet aroma. The final pull came from the gentle wiggling of the supple body he had spent the night wrapped around. Well, *half* of the night.

She let out a quiet mewling noise as she stretched her arms and legs under the blanket, then turned to face him, a sleepy smile playing across her smooth, round face.

"Good morning, handsome," she greeted.

"Good morning, beautiful," he responded, and stroked his callused thumb across her cheek.

It was an oddly intimate exchange to share with someone he had only met the night before, but until he found someone to permanently fill the position of 'partner to share intimate gestures with,' he would settle for his current situation.

Nox had not planned on sleeping with the woman, at first. At first, she came across as being one of the many women who were merely attracted to him for the mana distribution that marked him as a Brother of the First Order and endowed him with a certain physical adeptness. He felt far too predatory taking advantage of that reputation, and he was really only interested in spending time with women who were actually attracted to him.

Memories still fresh from the night brought a satisfied smile to his face, and he continued the journey of his hand through her hair and down her bare back. Perhaps she would be interested in spending time together again this evening.

"Would you like to have some—"

His offer to fetch breakfast for the two of them was cut short by an urgent knocking, and a woman's even more urgent voice, from the other side of the door.

"Nox are you home?" she called.

Cassiopea sat up, pulling the thick quilt to her chin, panic in her almond eyes.

"Are you expecting someone?" she asked tersely.

"Um, no." He held his hands out to her, trying to keep her from bolting. "But I know who that is. Just give me a moment to—"

He was once again interrupted as the woman on *that* side of the door became the woman on *this* side of the door, holding a bundle of what smelled to be cinnamon rolls. The hinges squeaked in the tense moment that followed.

The biggest downside to converting his actual, intended bedroom into his own personal library was that the only other room large enough to contain his enormous bed was the intended living room. The Homestead staff tasked with helping him move in twelve years ago had done so with hesitation and many shared looks of disbelief. But the lighting in the 'bedroom' was better for reading and having a bed in his living room had certain undeniable perks, so it had all made sense at the time.

Now, however? Now he was regretting the decision deeply, as he could feel the woman behind him bristling.

"Are you still in bed? I expected you to—" Rosalind started to ask but cut herself short. Her view was blocked by his towering frame, but when he leaned to the side, her eyes locked on the beautiful brunette in the bed, currently trying melt Rosalind with her incendiary gaze.

"*Oh*, I see," she said. Then she wiggled her fingers in a flirtatious wave for Cassiopea and *winked*.

No one could ever accuse Rosalind of being subtle. Or chaste.

"Rosalind," he said in a flat tone, but she just shrugged.

"I actually do have a reason for being here," she said. "My whole plan wasn't to barge in and ruin what I'm sure was going to be an eventful morning for you. I need to talk to you, Nox. Could I please have a moment of your time?"

Nox was fluent in the many voices of Rosalind, and if she was using manners, then matters must be serious. He turned to Cassiopea, who was now blushing and looking as confused as she was curious and pulled her attention back to him by brushing a light kiss across her knuckles.

"Cassi, would you mind giving us a minute? I need to speak with my *friend*, Revered Rosalind of the Third."

The use of Rosalind's honorific seemed to quell the woman's concerns and she let out a small huff of relief and smiled.

"If you would like to, you're welcome to enjoy a bath and I'll make some coffee to go with the cinnamon rolls that Mistress Rosalind so graciously brought for us," he added, looking innocently back at Rosalind, who rolled her eyes and handed him the bundle.

"Sure, but don't take too long. I'll be waiting...Nox?" she said, with a slight hesitation that told him maybe Cassiopea had forgotten his name. Ouch.

Rosalind had turned away to give them a moment of privacy as the woman crawled out of his bed and made her way to the bathroom. Nox adjusted himself into a seated position at the head of his carved, decadent bed, and folded his hands over his lap, turning to Rosalind.

"Would you like me to step outside so you can dress?" she asked him.

Her eyes played across the large, intricate tattoos that spanned from his shoulder blades and down each arm, and he could swear he saw a hunger there.

Nox remembered reading once about how chimpanzees behaved

when they faced a stressful event. They had sex with whatever willing partner was close by. Funny enough, that was also how Rosalind responded. How stressful must her news be that she was looking at him that way?

Their eight years of close proximity had started as a professional partnership but had grown into a friendship over their mutual love for the Archson, Augustus. They were both wise enough to avoid allowing their relationship to move beyond that and worked to remain on faithfully platonic terms. Besides, he knew that someone else had her heart, whether or not they could actually be together.

He snapped his fingers loudly, breaking her trance. "Snap out of it, Red. What do you need?"

She blinked and shook her head.

"You're not going to dress?"

"No need," he answered. "The tub fits two and I plan on joining her shortly."

She winced, and something about the look said she was going to ruin his morning.

"Well, actually," she started, "I need your help."

Damn.

Rosalind never asked for help, because Rosalind never *needed* help. He, on the other hand, had accumulated a small pile of IOUs over the years. It was not so much that Nox was in the habit of getting himself into tight situations. It was that the few times he had needed aid, Rosalind had the appropriate connections to pull the requisite strings. And, of course, there were the coveted first-edition books that she always seemed to get her hands on, despite the fact that she rarely had time to read them. Naturally, they ended up in Nox's library, and he found himself a little deeper indebted to her.

He let out a sigh. So much for finding out all the different ways his tub could 'fit two.'

"What do you need my help with, Ros?" he asked.

"Well, Nox. As you may have noticed, the Archmother is at the beginning of another episode," she said, shooting a glance at the bathroom door and the woman quietly humming to herself. "Therefore, I will be unable to leave and complete the task that needs to be completed."

He nodded in understanding. Everyone in the service of the Archfamily knew of the 'episodes' the Archmother experienced periodically. As Rosalind's friend, he knew what would be required of her over the next few days or weeks, depending upon how long this one lasted.

"So, you need me to complete this task on your behalf?" he surmised.

She settled herself at the foot of his bed and busied herself with flattening her skirt. "Yes. I trust you and believe in your abilities more than any other, Nox."

Manners and flattery? He was about to be knocked on his ass by her request, and he knew it.

"And just what is this mysterious task, Ros?" he asked.

"Someone who is…very dear to me…is in trouble," she said. "I believe she's been hurt, and she needs assistance. I would like you to find her, protect her, and return her here. To me."

The need in her eyes from a moment ago was a matchstick to the flame that danced there now. He knew of whom she spoke but asked the question anyhow.

"Who is it you want me to rescue, Rosalind?"

"Cal," she said, her voice wobbly with contained anxiety. "*My* Cal. Nox, she's hurting, and she needs help."

He let out a long sigh and ran his fingers through his hair, scratching at the base of his neck. Knocked on his ass, indeed.

"You have been saying that for years," he replied, his voice sharp with a much darker emotion.

"This time is different. This time it's really awful, Nox."

"And Freddie?"

"Refuses to leave my side for long enough to see it done."

So, Nox was the next up on her list. A small part of him was flattered that she would ask for his help. A small, deranged part of himself, because what she was asking of him involved in a convoluted relationship between a violent man and his bonded partner. Not that he would not enjoy the opportunity to force Brother Stokely into a fair fight, but this was a matter to be taken up by the Head of the First Order, not a mere member of it.

"Rosalind, please do not ask this of me."

"What else am I supposed to do?"

"Contact Brother Marcus, the new Head of the First," he said, trying to keep the sting from his answer. "He's a good man. He'll send someone from Black Rock to investigate. That's the only way you will get resolution."

"I don't have that kind of time!" she yelled. "Calen doesn't have that kind of time! Besides, if anyone from Black Rock cared, they would have fixed this mess long ago!"

"Ros, I can't," he pled. "I'm not in a position of power."

"I don't need someone in a position of power, Nox," she said, and the venom in her voice raised the hairs on his arms. "I need someone strong enough to make him pay for what he's done to her."

His eyebrows shot up. "I know you're not asking me to..."

"And why not?" she said. "If he can do whatever he wants, why can't you?"

"Because I'm not a monster," he responded. "And the First Order doesn't dish out vigilante justice."

"Ha!" she barked, and stood up from his bed, pacing. "No, you just sit back and let this happen."

"And what about you?" he retorted. "If she means so much to you, Rosalind, why haven't you stepped in."

She stopped pacing then and turned to him, guilt in the wide expanse of her tear-heavy, jade green eyes.

"I'm sorry," he said, "that came out more harshly than I intended."

"No, you're right," she whispered. "I think that's why I'm feeling so desperate. I tried for years to help her, and he did everything he could to push me out of her life. The truth is, after a while, I let him. I promised her I would be there, then I just let him push me away, and...I have to make this right, Nox. Please. I will never ask anything of you again."

The intensity of her plea was an odd contrast to the relaxed sounds of

Cassiopea lazily splashing in the tub, humming loudly enough that they could hear her.

He pulled the quilt around himself and moved to the edge of the bed, taking her hands in his own.

"Even if I wanted to help, Ros, I think you are forgetting that I have duties of my own to fulfill. Augustus and I leave next week for our vernal tour. Meeting his people, touring the Coastal Colonies, shaking hands, eating regional delicacies…any of that ring a bell?"

"Actually," she added, optimism returning to her voice, "I thought that this could provide an excellent opportunity for him to travel *and* for you to help Calen. You could talk to him and explain the situation, see if he would alter his plans. Slightly." She held up her thumb and forefinger to show him just how slightly the plan would need to change.

"Is Calen in one of the Coastal Colonies?" he inquired.

"Well, no," she conceded.

"Is she anywhere east of here? On the way to or from the Coastal Colonies?"

"Also…no."

"Rosalind?"

"She is in the central part of the Southern Drift Colony," she blurted out and winced. Her usual composure was all but absent, and that struck Nox more than anything.

"So let me see if I've got this all straight," he started, "You want me to convince Augustus, the most regimented young man I've ever met, to abandon the plan he's been crafting for the last five months, and head in the *opposite* direction from his favorite place on the continent on a mission to help a woman who is wrapped up in a semi-illegal situation with a dangerous man of unknown strength and motivation?"

"Well, when you put it like that…" she said, looking crestfallen once more.

"Please tell me," he asked, looking at the ceiling, "that you at least have evidence of her being hurt? How did you even find out that something happened?"

She avoided his glare and answered. "From a dream."

He looked at the top of her bowed head, incredulous.

"From a dream?"

"Yes," she clarified, "but sometimes my dreams are more like...visions...of people whose mana I've touched. I don't really know how it works, but it does."

Nox closed his eyes and sighed. What was she roping him into?

"Besides, you said it yourself! This has been happening for the duration of their partnership. Even if he didn't nearly kill her this time, he will eventually! We have to help, it's the right thing to do."

His leg twitched irritably. He was not meant to chase down Vessels and decide their fates. He was meant to stay put, protect the Archson, and allow the right people to handle these situations.

"He almost killed her?" he asked.

"Yes."

If she were anyone else, he would have no problem dismissing her. There was no way he would risk himself or Augustus on a mission to help someone based on what was seen *in a dream*. But she was not anyone else. She was Rosalind. She was smart and strong and sensible. If she truly believed that Cal needed help, then he could believe it on her behalf.

"I will do this, Ros," he conceded, "only because it's you doing the asking. I personally don't think this is a great idea, but if this is what you need from me, I can try. It's going to be a hell of a lot more difficult to convince Augustus."

She smiled at him, her shoulders sagging.

"Does that mean you'll help? You'll talk to Augustus?" she implored.

"It means that I will support you while *you* talk to him," he answered firmly.

"Oh, I think I can convince our little prince to do the right thing," she said, suddenly playful.

"Don't let Corian hear you using that title so loosely, you know how Seekers are about artificial titles of subjugation," Nox said, half joking.

"Oh please, he is far too busy with real matters of balance to worry about my terms of affection."

"You are far too confident in your own abilities, Ros," he said, already making his way out of the bed. "But I guess we'll see what Augustus says...right after I take my bath."

"Mind if I watch?" she joked.

"You are absolutely shameless, Red. Now get out."

***

Despite their back-and-forth jesting, neither Rosalind nor Nox enjoyed Cassiopea's company that morning. Both were people of action, and once Nox had agreed to help talk with the Archson, they had a single-minded focus to see it done. Within twenty minutes of Rosalind first entering his rooms, Nox had scarfed down a cinnamon roll (leaving the second one, along with the promised cup of coffee, to the woman still lounging in his tub), cleaned up, and dressed.

The two of them strode the short distance from Nox's rooms to the doors that led into Augustus' small apartment. Nox reminded himself that he would need to pick up more writing supplies before they left, whichever direction they ultimately headed. At sixteen, Augustus would be able to sign minor documents on the Archfamily's behalf, though he wouldn't be capable of making major changes or additions until he was named Archfather.

There was never a clear line of succession in the Archfamily, as it was customarily decided by a quorum of the most successful and sensitive Seekers. Nox held no doubt that Augustus would succeed the current Archfather, Dante, when the time came. He had unimpeachable morals, a keen intellect, a healthy physical constitution, and a strong enough mana distribution to have been an excellent candidate for training at Black Rock with the First Order. Add to that the fact that his love for his people was only matched by their love for him, and there was no denying his right to the title. His younger brothers and sisters were likely to serve important roles in the capital, but Augustus was most likely to be named the next Archfather.

The two stopped at the large, wooden door and Rosalind lifted her hand to knock. He caught her gently by the wrist, and she looked up at him with a raised eyebrow.

"Ros, you know I trust you," he said, "and so does Augustus. But Aug doesn't know about Brother Stokely. He's still young enough to believe that being a member of the First Order requires an unblemished soul. He won't understand that a sworn Brother would intentionally hurt his partner. You know how he will react if you tell him the whole truth. Have you thought about how to get around that without lying to him?"

"Not exactly," she admitted. "But this has to succeed, Nox. I don't know what else to do and..." she trailed off, looking at the door. He released her wrist, and she crossed her arms.

He was not accustomed to seeing vulnerability in Rosalind, and he did not think she was used to showing it.

"She is everything to me, Nox, *everything*," she whispered. "We have to find her, and we have to protect her."

"Alright then, let's go."

Eight

April 11, 622

Rosalind

"Who is it?" asked the tenor-voiced young man from inside the apartment.

"It's me, sweet prince," she answered, "And I've brought your knife-wielding baboon with me."

Nox looked at her as if wounded, but she knew it was fake.

"Come in," was the sing-song response from the other side of the door.

She watched as Nox held his hand over the door and released a small amount of royal blue mana from his palm. It stroked the doorknob, winding around and into the small keyhole that had been fitted with a piece of rock similar to a Consecration Stone, which only responded to the mana signature of direct members of the Archfamily and Nox. It was incredibly secure and allowed the young man the privacy and dignity of solitude when he needed it. Not even Rosalind could let herself in once the lock had been set.

The door clicked and slid open a few inches, but Rosalind was too distracted to storm in, as she normally would. She nudged it open and shuffled inside, the speech she had prepared rolling itself into a jumbled mess within her mind.

She immediately spotted the Archson hunched over his desk,

oscillating between reading small-print lines from the book in his right hand, and copying notes into the journal pinned under his left. He was the type of person who could become so engrossed in his work that a real baboon could have walked in, and he would have kept on writing.

Rosalind and Nox lowered themselves into the well-worn leather chairs on the opposite side of his desk and waited for him to finish. If they interrupted him now, he wouldn't be able to focus on their conversation, too distracted by whatever inquiry was currently driving his furious scribbling.

The sun had just begun its climb across the large, partitioned window behind Augustus when he finally looked up, closing his journal and book, and tucking the pencil behind his ear for safekeeping. His smile was warm and genuine, and she was made a mental note that she would soon need to talk to him about how to handle attention from young women, if no one else had. Where Nox had been excellent at teaching hand-to-hand combat and weaponry, as well as philosophy and literature, Ros had tutored him in the ways of people. While he had always been a quick study, he was still naïve. She had hoped he would maintain some of his innocence as he matured, but it was growing more difficult to protect the young man, given his position. He was about to get a lesson in making decisions that were a solid shade of gray.

"A visit from both of you, and at the same time," he intoned. "I'm guessing I'm either very lucky, or very unlucky." His mature demeanor was spoiled, slightly, when his stomach grumbled loudly enough for them all to hear. "And I'm guessing I should probably eat."

"You sit," Nox said, rising from his chair. "I'll grab some food. Besides, it's Rosalind who needs to speak with you. I'm merely here to lend my support," he added, smiling down at her as he made his way into the kitchenette.

Thanks for that, pal.

She waited with Augustus in a companionable silence until Nox returned with the tray of food, anyway. Augustus might be mature for his age, but he was also sixteen, and would be far more amenable to her plan once his stomach stopped attempting to digest itself.

"Nox, don't let me forget, I finished reading your copy of *Lies & Fables*," Augustus said, ripping a muffin in half and shoveling it into his mouth. "You were right, the author's commentary was far more insightful than what was left in the originally edited version."

"If you're done with it," Nox put in, handing Augustus a peeled orange, "you really need to read the academic paper that was published a few years after the author's version, discussing the importance of the editorial redactions while also providing evidence that the redacted material was historically accurate..."

Rosalind cut him off with a sharp look. The two men shared mutual love for pointy weapons and rare books, and if they were allowed to run away with a tangent about either topic, Rosalind was likely to spend her next birthday sitting in this room. There wasn't time for that. Nox took the hint.

"You know what, we can talk about that later," he said, pressing the coffee, and pouring a mug for each of them. The chair released a low groan as he sat back, crossing an ankle over his knee and bringing the steaming mug up to his face. A dark eyebrow quirked up, prompting her to begin.

She was far too practiced at this to need a deep breath to steady herself, but the desire to do so bubbled up in her chest.

Rosalind made firm eye contact with Augustus, and to the young man's credit, he didn't flinch. She began by explaining the situation in which her friend, Revered Calen, found herself. She had been hurt and needed help. Rosalind told him as though she had seen it with her own eyes, sparing him the more private details of the encounter.

"As you know, Augustus, your dear mother is not well. She is in the beginning stages of another episode."

Here, he did look away, studying his hands crossed on the desk. Rosalind knew Augustus loved his mother dearly, and it was difficult for him to see her suffering the way she did when she slipped into the abyss of her own mind.

"I cannot leave her," she lulled. "It is my duty to be here. But also, I care for her, as you do, and I want to see her well. And so, you see why I am conflicted. I cannot be in two places at once."

He glanced up again, and it only took a moment for the pieces to click into place.

"So, you will need someone to go to your friend, in your stead?" he surmised. Then, he shifted his keen gaze to Nox. "And my dear 'knife-wielding baboon' is the person you have in mind?"

"Yes, Augustus," she answered.

"You know that we are set to leave for our annual tour next week? We are going to the Coastal Colonies."

"Yes."

"But you need us to go somewhere that *isn't* the Coastal Colonies?"

She knew he was not playing at being dense, he was fishing for more details.

"As you well know," she said, trying to infuse enthusiasm into her proposal, "as Archson, you are not required to visit any specific set of Colonies each year, so long as you are visiting *some* of them. I thought that, perhaps, if you were to adjust your schedule to accommodate a tour of the Southern Drift Colony, and then travel further south into Sun Grove, you could still have a fantastic spring on the road and meet more of your people."

He sat back in his chair, his mouth agape.

"In Sun Grove, they preserve the fruit from last year's harvest in sugar and serve it as a treat at their blessing day rituals. Not to mention, the spring bloom in the mountains is forecast to be absolutely phenomenal this year—"

He stopped her gently by raising his hand, a move she would be loath to tolerate from anyone else.

She watched him study his hands, but this time his brows were knit together in a show of concentration. Then he took a deep breath and released it slowly, shifting his discerning brown eyes back to her.

"Where, exactly, is your friend?" he asked. "Calen?"

"Yes, Calen. Well, today, she is still in Graymount, in the central part of the Southern Drift Colony. But she is scheduled to travel east, toward

Old Roan, over the next few days. She will be there for a fortnight, as they hold their large, multi-day blessing ritual and celebration. Perhaps, you would be able to meet her there?" That was *not* desperation making Rosalind's voice rise to a high, tight timbre as she asked.

"Rosalind, I notice you keep saying 'her' instead of 'them.' But she is a traveling ritual worker, so you are intentionally leaving her bonded partner out of the conversation," he commented, a gentleness now reaching his voice. She knew that move. She had taught him that move. He had found a problem with the plan and was angling toward refusing her request. "Which tells me that you don't think he will be a part of getting her to safety, and furthermore, that he is not actively keeping her safe now. That is his sacred duty, no?"

She nodded.

"So, you believe he is neglecting his duty to protect his partner, best case scenario. Worst case scenario…Ros, do you believe he is complicit in this attack? Is that what you are saying?"

Rosalind would have to walk the knife's edge with what she said next. She had built up years of good will with both men, the older and the younger, and she knew they trusted her word. Augustus, however, was a firm believer in the system to which he belonged, and it would take a great leap of faith for him to follow where she was about to lead.

"What I am saying, dear Augustus," she started, leaning forward in her chair, "is that I would not come to you, I would not ask such a thing, if this weren't an absolute need borne of a desperate concern. I understand the position that I am putting *both* of you in with this proposition. I am asking Nox to help me because he is strong, competent, and exceedingly trustworthy. His tracking skills are unmatched, and if anyone can find and protect Calen, it is him." She turned to look at her friend as she said this, the rounded softness of his eyes revealing an appreciation for her praise. "And I am asking you to attend with him, because I also know you to be capable and intelligent, and Nox may need your help. Furthermore, if the situation is as dire as I believe it to be, she will need someone in a position of influence to help rectify the situation." He looked sidelong at her, as she knew he would. He was young and idealistic enough to believe that his position was merely one of servitude and not one of power.

Rosalind intentionally avoided an outright accusation of Brother Stokely. She knew as well as he did, that Augustus would be duty-bound to refuse aid. Not even a Seeker could be called in to sort the matter, regardless of the fact that a good Seeker could lay one hand on Calen and know definitively that Brother Stokely had been mistreating her. If she openly accused him, the matter would have to be submitted to the Head of the First Order. They followed very strict rules when investigating potential misdeeds. The matter would have to be fully vetted, witnesses would be called, academic members of the Order would provide testimony on precedent, and the whole circus would take months to reach a resolution. Calen might not have months to wait.

So, Rosalind tip-toed into the Land of Gray Decisions, hoping that Augustus would follow her.

"I need you to trust me that this is the right thing to do," she finished. She was definitely not wringing her sweaty hands under the desk.

Augustus and Nox eyed one another, a silent dialogue playing out between them. Augustus leaned forward, placing his forearms on the desk, and lightly drummed his fingers on the surface. Rosalind reached across the desk, but instead of demanding something from this young man, she placed her small, honey-colored hands atop his milk chocolate-toned ones. His gaze found hers.

"Augustus, please," she whispered, tears gathering along her lower eyelids. No demands, no maneuvering; just complete vulnerability, and an aching hope so potent it was clogging her throat.

His face softened, and compassion shown through his eyes. With one slight nod, he assuaged the agony in her chest, and she sagged in relief. She looked at Nox, who nodded as well.

"We will help you, Rosalind," he said quietly. "This is…this is a lot to ask, and we will need time to plan. I know you need to return to my mother, so please have two of her aids come and bring pencils and paper. If we need to ask questions of you, I will send them as runners."

She was nodding, squeezing his hands too tightly, she knew. But they had said yes, and she could finally breathe past the weight that had been sitting on her chest since last night.

Was it really only last night that I dreamed of her?

"I cannot promise we will succeed," Augustus said, "but I can promise that we will give every effort to ensure that we do." Then, he turned toward Nox. "Now, where shall we begin?"

Rosalind had never been so happy to be dismissed.

"Nox, Augustus, thank you. You have no idea..." she trailed off. She would not cry.

They both nodded, and she made her way to the door. In a testament to their already-firm dedication, both were standing over a map of the Colonies that Augustus had produced from his desk. Augustus began writing on a blank sheet of paper and Nox was using a small tool to measure the distances on the map and report numbers in between bites of the dried fruit still on the desk. Rosalind knew it would be best to leave them to their work. She quietly left the room and let the door click shut behind her. She pulled in her first full breath of the morning, and headed back toward the western wing, and the Archmother waiting there for her. This was going to work.

She smiled to herself.

Hold on just a little longer, Cal. Help is on the way.

Nine

April 11, 622

Calen

Calen woke before dawn. Or rather, was awakened by the overwhelming ache in her wrists that radiated down her arms and wrapped around the joints in her shoulders. She tried rolling them to coax away the pain but found herself unable to move her upper body. A small spike of panic coursed through her core, and she hastily tried to blink away the crust from tears that had long since dried on her lashes. She could make out the sash hanging lazily between two of the four posts of the bed, and remembered where she was. Rolling onto her left side, she peered up to where her forearms were bound and tied to the bed.

"Fuck," she muttered. Her jaw was swollen, and her lips were caked in blood, so the word came out as more a puff of useless air than a curse word carrying any weight. Stokely hadn't left her like this in years, he must have really lost his head last night.

She tried propping herself up on her elbow, but the movement was difficult with two arms that did not want to work, and a body so weak that it couldn't support its own weight.

"Ow."

In her half-seated position, she narrowed her eyes, willing them to adjust to the low light of the room, and scanned the corners to see if he was watching her now. No Stokely in sight. He must have taken off once he was done with...whatever he had done to her last night. She could not remember much past their initial confrontation, when she had refused him, then tried to run away. She searched herself for any feelings of remorse or regret, if only for the pain it had caused, but she found none. Leaving was the right thing to do, of that she had no doubt. He had worn away at the part in her soul that allowed her to endure years of abuse. Now, all that was left in its place was a rock-solid core as cold and jagged as the rings she wore.

Her lapse of memory would not last. It was a temporary reprieve from the horror she had faced. A little trick her brain played on her to give her just enough time to recover before allowing the traumatic incident to flood back into her consciousness. Then, at least, she would be able to reconcile each injury she had sustained with the assault that had caused them, like the world's most gruesome game of Match. *Ah yes, that bloody lip belongs to that time he bit me...And this bruised thigh goes with that sucker punch.* Had she really endured eight years of his terrorizing? Eight years of violence and degradation? Eight years of him attempting to beat her into submission and eight years of her somehow finding just enough will to not succumb.

She desperately wanted, no *needed*, to get these ropes off of her arms so she could survey the rest of the damage. She could tell, even from her limited movement, that her body was in bad shape.

Carefully, she used her hips and feet to shimmy into a more comfortable sitting position against the headboard. Being upright made her head throb in time with the beats of her heart, and between her broken mouth and reduced field of vision, she knew he had hit her in the face more than once.

Loss of control, indeed.

Calen tried working her hands loose. They were pale and cramped from a lack of blood flow, but already she could feel the stinging pins and needles that told her they were filling up by the second. Her wrists were touching, but it was actually her forearms that had been tied together. Being the practiced sadist that he was, Stokely knew how to hide injuries when he wanted to, and he absolutely wanted to hide these.

On the occasions that he did tie her up, he used a frayed rope, and tied high enough on her arms that the bruises and grotesque abrasions would be covered by her usual gowns and shirts during the day but exposed by her short-sleeved sleepshirt at night. It gave him a secondary thrill to not only see how badly he had hurt her, but to run his fingers along the wounds when she was least expecting it. No matter how hard she tried to deny him the gratification, she flinched and cried out every single time.

Beyond the injuries that she did remember being given (head, face, ribs), she could see bruises on her upper thighs that were silhouetted by half-moon indentations where his trim fingernails must have broken the flesh. Between her thighs...between her thighs was a sticky mess of half-dried blood and *something else* that she would rather not consider. Calen tipped her head to the side and retched. The bastard had made her bleed and left her a mess on purpose. Nausea rolled through her and she began panting against the hot saliva rising in the back of her mouth, her emotions threatening to spill over. The sudden heaving of her chest was punctuated by a staccato of jolting pain that felt like being stabbed by tiny shards of glass in the space between her ribs and her belly button.

Using her elbows to edge away the stained sheet that was still partially covering her naked body, Calen exposed the strangest looking mark she had ever seen. Just above her navel, there was a cluster of lightning bolt-shaped streaks all angling away from a central point. Wincing against the soreness there, she twisted her abdomen, and she could see that directly in the middle of the angry-looking purple-red lines, was a perfectly unblemished patch of skin. The shape seemed familiar, but she couldn't immediately place it...a teardrop, with a small bulb at the bottom end...

"Our stone?" she whispered, apprehension climbing her throat. "How...what did you do, you bastard?" The simple truth was that he had been wielding mana for longer than she had been alive. He knew so much more of her power than she did. This mark could mean anything.

A spike of light, a sharp noise.

You know what he did.

Calen had felt the message more so than she had heard it, and though she instinctively knew it had come from inside her, it wasn't the voice of her own internal dialogue.

Her mana *shifted*.

You know.

Had it just...communicated with her? No. Impossible. Stokely had hit her hard, and she was hallucinating again. Her disbelief was short-lived as a bright light flashed behind her eyes and she squeezed them tight against the shock. For the span of a split second, an image, *a memory*, filled her vision. It was her, from the night before. Pinned between her and Stokely, just above her naval...was their Consecration Stone. It was glowing and *snarling* as power rushed through it, out of her and into him. As quickly as the vision had appeared, it was gone. Calen did not have long to process the image, for in the next moment, the door to her room banged open.

Fear and anxiety surged in her chest as she became hyper-aware that she sat tied to the bed, completely naked and entirely exposed to the intruder. If it was Stokely returning, she was out of time to escape her bonds. Who knew what kind of mood the morning would find him entertaining, and Calen could not face any more abuse. She pulled her legs up under herself, trying to huddle against the headboard and hide behind whatever futile shelter was provided by the over-stuffed pillows.

It was not Stokely who entered, but a tall figure dressed in a cloak with a hood pulled up over their head. The disguise was a bit ridiculous, but at least it was not Stokely. Her emotions shifted in quick succession from relief to shame at her filthy, naked state, to anger as the woman lowered her hood to reveal a shaved head. Calen knew exactly who this woman was and the reason for her early morning visit.

The woman turned to close the door far more delicately than she had opened it. In that watery, predawn light, Calen could make out the serpentine tattoo snaking from behind the woman's left ear, down her neck, and disappearing beneath the cowl of her woolen cloak that marked her as a member of the extremist group True Eternal. Calen knew that while the group had long ago stopped committing acts of violence on a grand scale, their members were perfectly content to commit them on a smaller one. A human-sized one.

The tall, gaunt woman turned and looked over her shoulder, her cold, hazel eyes passing over the ball Calen had made of herself.

"Do you remember me?" she asked in a low, severe voice.

"Yes," Calen answered through a jaw too misaligned to be able to close.

"Good. Then I won't have to remind you what will happen if you fight me or try to use your mana in my presence?" she asked, raising an almost-nonexistent eyebrow at Calen.

She sighed. "No, you won't."

It had been years since Stokely had been this rough with her. Shortly after she left Grandview and they had begun their formal work together, Stokely had tried his absolute hardest to break her spirit. She always fought back. He would spout on about the need for her full submission as a tool for their successful partnership, but she never bought in. She drew boundaries, he crossed them. She refused his perverse demands, he issued punishment. When the punishment got too out of hand, he had called on *this* traitorous bitch to clean up his mess afterward. Calen had hoped that at some point over the past few years she had met a horribly painful death. But alas, here she was, a vulture in human form.

The woman moved quickly to the bedside and sat down the small leather duffle she had concealed under her cloak.

"Lie down," she commanded.

Calen considered disobeying the order, looking the woman directly in the eye and refusing to move. But the woman grabbed her by the face and squeezed, and any resistance Calen held was blasted away by the pain exploding beneath the vise-like grip. Calen gasped raggedly and let out a pathetic whimper.

"Lie down," she said, this time through teeth clenched so hard that it made the muscles in her wiry face jump out.

"Untie my hands," Calen asked.

The woman looked at her for a moment, considering.

"Do not test me," she warned. Then, she unsheathed a dagger strapped to her forearm, and sliced through the ropes with a ferocity presumably meant to demonstrate what would happen to Calen if she did.

Calen untangled her arms, sucking in a breath as she dislodged the rough fibers of the rope from her skin. As carefully as she could, she unfolded herself and laid down on the bed, eyes watching the wall opposite the woman now hovering over her. She knew this stranger was not at liberty to attack her unwarranted, and Calen simply did not want to face the indignation of watching what would happen next.

"Damn. He really did a number on you this time," she mumbled.

Calen could hear the admiration in the woman's voice, and it took everything she had not to use her last bit of strength to lash out at this foul beast. Stokely and this vulture were a perfect match.

The stranger's cold, rough hands were on her in an instant, pressing down on her lower abdomen. She felt a warm tingle as the woman's mana entered through her skin. Just another uninvited intrusion into her body.

"You aren't ovulating right now, so I don't think he impregnated you. But, just in case…"

Removing her hands from Calen, she rifled through her worn leather bag, emerging with two small, oval-shaped clumps of dried herbs set in pig lard.

"Open your mouth."

Calen opened her mouth as wide as it could comfortably go.

"Swallow."

She did that, too.

Calen wasn't foolish enough to ever allow herself to become pregnant with Stokely's child after one of their "bonding" sessions, but the herbs she normally took were far more friendly to her system than the ones she had just had shoved down her throat. Her monthly would come within a few hours and would be as bloody and painful as the ordeal that had put her here. Insult to injury. At least there would be no chance of accidentally carrying the cursed spawn of a monster.

Again, without preamble or permission, the stranger put her hands on Calen, this time starting at her feet. She could feel the light gray mana from the other woman probing her body, checking for major injuries: broken bones, internal bleeding, major brain damage. Stokely wanted her broken, not dead. Her pace of movement slowed as her hands hovered over the mess between Calen's thighs. Calen looked at her then, and could swear she saw something…jealousy? Anger? But the moment passed, and her hands were moving again. They stopped entirely as they hovered over the strange markings on Calen's abdomen. This time, a malicious grin spread across the woman's pale face.

She knew what this was. She knew what Stokely was doing.

Concentrating on her hands again, the woman scanned up to Calen's face, pushing her palms into either side with a gentleness that was completely at odds with the rest of the encounter. The woman was only being tame because it was necessary to ensure she did not accidentally scramble Calen's mind while she cleared any injuries there. The sensation of the queasy, gray mana probing her brain was like all of her senses being triggered at the same time. Random bits of knowledge and memory pushed into her awareness, and her body wiggled involuntarily in response to the stimulus. This was, by far, the worst part of the encounter.

Then, the woman shifted her fingertips until they were pressing in where Calen's jaw met her skull. The woman flexed, manipulating her mana into a rope that twisted, and Calen's jaw snapped back into place with a crack that was accentuated by the miserable moan that left her throat. Lastly, the woman smoothed her hands over Calen's face, flushing away the blood and fluid that filled her swollen, bruised flesh. Her work done, the stranger stood suddenly, causing the bed to bounce back, and for Calen to roll onto her side.

"I'm leaving that nasty one on your lip to remind you that you should keep your mouth shut and do what you're told," she scolded as she crossed around the bed and toward the door. The woman stopped at the sink, pushing the bag up under her cloak and over her shoulder once more, before turning on the tap and furiously scrubbing her hands with steaming hot water and soap.

Good, you should feel dirty after what you've done, Calen thought.

Everything about the partnership between this hateful woman and Stokely was wrong. Sure, they shared an almost reverent penchant for violence, but they were supposed to be on opposite sides of a centuries-old feud.

True Eternal was the demented brainchild of former Vessels who had been consecrated at the Well, but then had chosen to reject the Rule of Four that governed the citizens of the New Colonies. They espoused a doctrine that was simply too severe for most people to stomach, so they existed on the fringes of a society that had long since rejected them.

Calen had once spent a great deal of time trying to figure out why they were working together. In fact, the last time Stokely had employed the stranger's 'housekeeping' skills, Calen had asked him about his connection to the woman and True Eternal. His response had been a tight-lipped refusal to answer, followed by poisoning her morning tea with just enough hemlock to bring her to death's door, one agonizing step at a time. If it hadn't been for Rosalind's deft intervention, she would have crossed that threshold.

The woman was adjusting her hood in the mirror, readying to sneak out again. Stokely had never wanted to answer, but maybe…

"Why do you help him?" Calen blurted out through a newly restored but still-sore mouth. The woman rounded on her slowly.

"You are educated enough to know the doctrine of True Eternal," she answered, as if that was explanation enough.

"I know that four hundred years ago, your group was almost strong enough to topple the New Colonies. I know that no matter what they tried, they just kept failing. And I know that you people are still licking your wounds, hoping that one day all of humanity will suddenly accept your archaic and perverse beliefs. I also know that will never happen." She fixed the woman with a challenging glare.

"And I know that mountain trash like you will never be wise enough to understand the inner workings of the universe, no matter how much mana you hold."

The insult meant nothing to Calen. She had been called far worse.

"Still. *Brother Stokely*," she emphasized his title, "is not a member of True Eternal. In fact, he stands directly in opposition to your doctrine. Why help him?"

The other woman seemed to consider for a minute.

"Let's just say, he's a member in spirit. He understands that women like you will always have a difficult time understanding the natural order of things. You do not know your place. You refuse to learn your place. So, it is his job to *teach* you your place. It is the only way to achieve balance and find a truly eternal peace," she finished, a self-satisfied smile crossing her awful face.

She should not have been surprised by that answer, but she was. Surprised, and angry. Calen could feel rage building, burning in her throat. She sat herself up, no longer ashamed of her nudity.

"Wait, you actually think I deserve this?" she spat out, gesturing to the semi-repaired wreckage of her body. "I've heard that you people believe in some pretty horrific shit, but you think what he did was *righteous?*"

"You practically asked for it," the woman retorted, eyes narrowing.

"Fuck. You." The words were liquid heat flowing from Calen's lips.

The stranger stood a little straighter, the look on her face saying that Calen had just proven her point. She made her way to the door, opening it and stepping through before turning back just long enough to add, "You definitely deserve what's coming next." Then, she was gone.

Calen let out a feral growl, throwing what was left of the ruined rope at the closed door.

She felt like an exposed nerve, the woman's 'healing' doing little to touch the agony of her body. Alone in the quiet room again, the gravity of the situation threatened to grind her into dust.

You definitely deserve what's coming next.

What did the woman know, and what the hell did that mean? Calen had always been aware that Stokely's first two partners had met untimely ends (one in a home for burnouts and the other at the bottom of a ravine). Was this her warning that her time was almost up? Would she even see it coming?

The panic rose again, and her breathing went erratic. The old, familiar ache in her throat told her that she would soon fall apart. She would waste a day releasing all the hurt and anger that she had grown far too adept at keeping boxed up in the back of her mind. Angry at her own pathetic desire to wallow in misery, she clenched her fists over her eyes and screamed. She was sick of weeping. Sick of hiding. Sick of trying to pretend that all her petty little acts of opposition added up to anything at all.

Her mana flashed in response, pushing against its boundaries, as if equally desperate to escape this nightmare. There was an urge, there, living inside her, to open and unleash her power on anything she could destroy. It would not matter that she was a ritual worker, destined to feed the Earth and make things beautiful.

Three years ago, she had watched a Vessel burn out on a blessing site, and the woman's final act was neither nourishing, nor beautiful. It was violent and chaotic. *That* had scared Stokely, watching the woman descend into madness, only to be carried away by her partner. His face had turned white, and his shaking hands had clutched at their stone, mumbling about ending up in an Opus Home, and how he would rather die in an outhouse. She could do that, scare Stokely. She had enough power left in her to blast a crater as big as the ones caused by the meteors six hundred years ago, and part of her wanted that obliteration.

But more than that, she wanted to feel her rage. She would hold it like a coal ember, and let it burn in her chest, so that she would never again feel this broken and powerless. He did not deserve her destruction. He deserved to be starved of the power he craved like air.

"Never again," she growled, a visceral reaction.

"Never again." A prayer to anyone listening.

"Never again." A vow to herself.

She leaned forward, balling her fists in the bloodied sheets, and her panting changed into something more animalistic.

No more weeping. No more lonely tears. The last shreds of her self-pity were gone, nothing more than ashes in the swirling inferno of her heart. When they floated away, only white-hot fury would remain.

"You will never do this to me again," she spoke into the universe.

Eight years of abuse and neglect had to come to an end, and it had to be now. No one was going to rescue her, and she knew it. If Calen wanted to survive, she was going to have to save herself. She rose to start the bath and wash his filth off of her skin, a plan already taking shape.

PART TWO

June 13, 614

Amelia

Amelia sat in the comfortable, broken-in chair of Revered Jessamin's office, completely uncomfortable. She shifted back and forth on thighs still sore from where she had actually been strapped just thirty minutes earlier. Strapped, at age seventeen. Humiliation and pain rolled into one tidy strip of leather.

At least she didn't have a bloody nose to go along with her stinging thighs, like Kiely did. She glanced tentatively at her friend, who sat stewing in the chair next to her. Kiely looked as though she wanted to punch something (someone) again. She looked over at the desk of the most important woman in the Third Order, trying to find a handkerchief to staunch the bleeding. Sheafs of paper were pinned beneath a large tome, the Book of Names, if Amelia had to guess. They fluttered in a wind that came in through the open windows, lifting the lacy curtains and peeling floral wallpaper. She spotted a small wooden box with what looked like first aid supplies, but it was behind the desk, on a shelf of books that were so ancient, there was no discernable writing on the spines. Best to leave it where it was.

"Kiely," she whispered. Her friend glanced at her and her features instantly softened. "Are you okay? You're dripping again," she said, pointing at the offending nostril.

Kiely reached up and swiped at the droplets that had escaped. "That stupid bitch probably broke my nose," she spat out, her acid not directed at Amelia, but Amelia felt it all the same. She was the underlying source of the fight that caused the (probably) broken and bloodied nose. Over their years studying at Grandview, they had worked out their own dysfunctional pattern of behavior when someone (usually Doreen) made a snide comment to Amelia. It went something like:

Doreen: insult, insult, insult, you don't deserve to be here, blah blah.

Amelia: more clever insult, you are just jealous because you are terrible at wielding mana, and I'm not.

Doreen: shut up, filthy blah blah.

Kiely: punch, punch, punch.

"I told you that you didn't have to do that," Amelia said, guilt warming her cheeks. Kiely stilled and planted an intense green gaze on her.

"Listen to me, Millie," she said, her voice matching her eyes, "things aren't going to get any easier when we leave in a few weeks. You can't let people—"

Whatever advice she sought to bestow was interrupted by the office door creaking open and none other than the Head of Order, Revered Jessamin, sweeping in. Everyone knew that Jessamin was easily the most talented and powerful Third Order Vessel that had lived in the last century, but that fact had never corrupted her demeanor. She had always been infinitely fair-minded and empathetic toward the teachers and pupils of Grandview Academy of Ritual Work. Amelia hoped that those two qualities would be in plentiful supply today, or else this afternoon was about to get a whole lot worse.

Her mentor edged her way around her large, well-organized desk and settled into her seat, placing her mug of tea before her. She leaned over it to breathe in the steam of whatever herbal blend she had concocted and studied Amelia and Kiely with kind, bird-like blue eyes.

"Girls," she said, tipping her head toward them. Amelia sagged, knowing by the sound of her voice that the worst of the ordeal had already passed.

"Revered Jessamin," she and Kiely murmured in unison.

"Since this is probably the tenth time you've found your way to my office due to fighting with other students, I will skip my typical lecture," she said. "You could probably recite it back to me at this point and I do not wish to waste my voice. And since Revered Tula informed me that she has strapped you for your behavior, we will also consider your punishment fulfilled." The downturn of her lips at the mention of strapping displayed just how disappointing she found corporal punishment.

"Thank you, Revered," Amelia said, at the same time Kiely asked, "What about Doreen?"

"What about Doreen?" Revered Jessamin asked, bringing the steaming mug to her thin lips.

"Well, for starters," Kiely said, with perhaps a bit more heat than Amelia thought wise in her current circumstance, "she has no loyalty to her Order or to the future members with whom she will serve. She is cruel, immature, and unprepared for the important work with which she will be charged. She routinely misuses her mana and deserves a far greater punishment than a simple strapping."

"Let's not forget the broken wrist and black eye you so generously gifted her," Revered Jessamin said over the lip of her mug.

"Well, yeah, she definitely deserved those," Kiely said. "You know the things that she says about Amelia, the little tricks she loves to pull on her. It's not right." Kiely looked at her then, and she felt another pang of guilt for the sympathy in her eyes.

"I'm fine," Amelia responded. "Really, it doesn't bother me anymore." It was a lie, but she would tell it if it kept Kiely out of trouble.

"It's not fine, Revered Jessamin," Kiely continued. "You know how deeply I respect you; we all respect you. And I would never pretend that it is my place to tell you how to conduct Third Order business, but I think that you should seriously consider denying her request for graduation this term," she finished, lifting her chin and crossing her arms. Her round face and bright green eyes were far too beautiful to ever be considered severe, but at eighteen, she was already a force of nature, and Amelia was certain that she knew it.

Kiely had deferred her own graduation for a full year so that she could stay at Grandview with Amelia. It wasn't uncommon for students to choose to stay an extra year so that they could continue to learn. Sometimes they chose to do so in order to graduate in the same cohort as the person they had chosen as their future bonded partner. But to suggest that Doreen should be held back as punishment for her behavior was proof that the years of torment had bothered Kiely as much as they had Amelia. She was now out for blood. Figurative blood, of course. Kiely had already drawn Doreen's literal blood on more than one occasion.

Revered Jessamin smiled at her then. "Is that *all*, Kiely?" she asked playfully.

Kiely squirmed, probably trying to keep her welted skin from sticking to her skirt and nodded. Jessamin swept her long, gray-touched brown hair over her shoulder and sat back in her chair.

"Thank you, Kiely," the woman said, "for such a succinctly made argument. You have proven my forthcoming point for me. Allow me to bring forward the obvious, anyhow. You have a knack for words and a keen ability to speak directly to the heart of a matter. You understand who people are at their core and you know how to read them with the intuition of a Seeker, even without the mana distribution. I have been told by more than one of your instructors that they believe it will be you sitting this chair once I no longer warm it."

"Thank you, Revered—"

"I'm not finished speaking, Kiely," she said, her voice quiet but firm. "You see, Kiely, gifts only work if you use them. Words only matter if you mean them, and passion without temperance too quickly becomes violence. You will undoubtedly leave this place in a short time, and if you wish to leave the kind of legacy deserving of your talents and intelligence, then you must get your hot-headed tendencies under control. But, if you plan on hitting every mouth that makes you angry, well, you had better get used to the feel of a broken fist. If you wish to solve everything with violence, soon violence will be your only choice. You will have to learn to choose words as your weapons and accept that not every outcome will be as you wish." She paused to take a deep breath. "You are better than this. Do you understand what I am telling you, Kiely?"

Amelia's eyes darted back to Kiely, who was staring at her hands in her lap. "Yes, Revered Jessamin."

Revered Jessamin took a deep breath, and when she spoke again, her voice was softer. "Now, I do not tell you this next fact as a means of validating your outburst earlier, but rather as a measure of balance for the things that Doreen did say and do to Amelia earlier. In regard to your assertion that Doreen is unfit for service, that same conclusion had already been made by at least two of the instructors and the current Head of the Third Order," (the *ahem, me*, was implied). Kiely's head shot up. "She will not graduate with your cohort, but we will only hold her for so long, and she will become a member of the Third Order, just as you will. I suggest that the three of you make your peace, if only for the prospect of pleasant future interactions."

"Yes, Revered Jessamin," twin voices intoned.

"Now, Kiely," she said, by way of a dismissal, "please go and see if Revered Dahlia can set your nose and maybe calm the worst of your welts? Amelia, please stay behind." Amelia looked up and nodded.

Once Kiely had bowed and left the room, Revered Jessamin turned her full attention to Amelia, turning and moving to the edge of her chair.

"Are you okay?" she asked, her brow creasing.

Amelia thought of lying again, but Jessamin would see through it and push until she gave an honest answer.

"No," she said, shaking her head. "Why don't they understand that it's not my fault I was consecrated the way I was? I thought that after all this time, they would know me and they would at least start to treat me like a person, like a Vessel." Her voice was low and heavy with the emotion of six years' worth of mistreatment. "What's going to happen when I leave? Will other Vessels hate me because I'm a 'dirty river rat?'"

Jessamin exhaled loudly out her nose. "Don't you ever say that about yourself again, do you hear me?"

"That's what I am," Amelia answered.

"No. What you are is smart, kind, funny, talented, and incredibly powerful. And no, not everyone is as closed-minded as Doreen and her friends. Of course, there will always be purists, who believe that there is only one *right* way to become a Vessel. They will feel threatened by your ability and strength. But your ability and strength are exactly what prove them wrong, so what does it matter what they believe?"

She had shared this logic with Amelia before, and as always, Amelia tried to make herself believe it.

"More importantly," Jessamin said, her voice dropping, "Amelia, we both know what and *who* await you when you leave. You will have no choice but to spend your days with him. Kiely will not always be there to defend you."

Amelia felt the familiar dread that clenched her stomach at the mention of *him*. She had only seen him on rare occasions over the past six years, but he loomed like a constant, unwelcome presence in the back of her mind. The fact that she was already bonded to a member of the First Order pushed the rift between her and her classmates even wider, but that point Amelia could readily understand. They were correct when they voiced that there was something perverse about a grown man bonding himself to a young girl.

"I know," Amelia said.

"I know the two of you well enough to know that you are the mouth and Kiely is the fists," she said, a playful accusation in her tone. "I would never tell you to lose your voice, but perhaps you will also learn to use your words more wisely? Stand up for yourself when you must, but avoid fights when possible?"

"Yes, Revered Jessamin." Amelia knew that would be more difficult than Jessamin made it sounds. She wasn't a fighter, but she had honed a razor-sharp tongue as a defense instead.

Jessamin nodded, content that she had made her point.

"One more thing," she said. "We need to discuss matter of your chosen name. I know it's getting close to the deadline, and that you've had a difficult time choosing, but I want you know that this is important and that you shouldn't rush."

"Okay..." Amelia said, unsure of where the conversation was leading.

"It's just, I saw that a submission was made on your behalf, and I wanted to make sure that it was your choice, and not anther little prank. If it was you, there's no judgment! It is just a little...unusual," she finished.

Amelia smiled. "Yes, it is unusual. But that's it. That's what I want as my chosen name."

"Truly?" Jessamin asked, grinning.

"Yes," Amelia answered. "Kiely said it as a joke. We were harvesting herbs a few weeks back and she was picking them, and said that they reminded her of me, since I'm so sunny and bright," she said sardonically, motioning to her very un-sunny visage of dark hair and eyes offset by pale skin. "But I like it. I want to keep it." Every time someone spoke her name from here on out, she would be reminded of her best friend, no matter how far apart they were.

Jessamin's smile broadened and she scrawled her signature in approval of Amelia's new name in the Book of Names that lay spread out on her desk.

"Well then," she said and looked up. "I suppose you had better get used to it before you graduate. It is a pleasure to meet you, Revered Calendula."

Ten

April 24, 622

Nox

Nox stood from his chair, setting down the cool lemonade that had just been refilled by one of the many white-clad servers milling about the open-air dining space where he sat with Augustus, half a dozen bodyguards, and one of the city's elders.

"I'll be right back," he spoke low in Augustus' ear, who confirmed with a slight nod. The young man was confidently entertaining a tableful of important city elders, so Nox took the opportunity to slip away.

Weaving through the maze of linen-draped tables, and flower-adorned poles, he approached the expansive buffet with feigned nonchalance. There was easily enough food for the hundreds of participants in attendance for the multi-day ritual. His stomach growled, reminding him that he had barely eaten today, distracted as he was watching his quarry.

In the past three days, since their arrival at Old Roan, he had watched Brother Stokely and Revered Calen closely, trying to ascertain the nature of their relationship and decide whether or not Rosalind had been correct in her appraisal of the situation. So far, he had only seen them speak sporadically in short, tense conversations. It did not require a Seeker's distribution to notice that the way Stokely handled her was anything but gentle. His rough hands were often on Calen in one way or another. Did that prove that he was abusive? Not exactly. The most obvious fact Nox had observed was that the two were never apart for more than a few moments, usually when one of them needed the privacy of the washroom. Nox had not had a single opportunity to speak with her. Brother Stokely hovered around Calen like a possessive child with his favorite toy. Still, not a conclusive damnation.

But there she was, alone for the first time all week, kneeling before a ball of fluff in the general shape of a cat, feeding it cubes of cheese. As he watched, she nodded and shook her head, as if enjoying an unspoken conversation with the mangey animal.

"They carry disease, you know," he said, by way of introduction. Calen's hand stopped halfway through its journey to deliver another bit of food to her companion, and she looked up at him.

"Excuse me?" she asked, in a voice like velvet.

"Cats, particularly that one, it would seem, carry disease."

She mumbled something about him carrying disease and went back to her imaginary conversation.

"Meaning no offense, Mistress Calen," he clarified, "but at the very least, I have fewer fleas than she does." He smiled at her, but she leveled him with another flat glare.

"He," she corrected. "Purrseus is a tomcat, and I have not found a single flea on him. A tick, but no fleas."

This was not going well. Picking up a small plate, he began piling his own stock of cheese and flatbread. He used his mana-enhanced fingers to tap the bottom of the dish, and a piece of Manchego popped into the air and landed in his mouth. She did not look impressed.

"I was hoping that perhaps we could speak," he said. "That is, if you and Purrseus are finished solving all the world's problems?"

Calen rose to standing, dusting her fingers on her cream-colored dress.

"What about?" she asked, suddenly sounding nervous.

"First, allow me to introduce myself. I'm Brother Nox, of the First Order." He cleared his throat and met her eye. "I am here on behalf of Revered Rosalind," he said, watching as her eyebrows rose and she took a sharp inhale of breath. For just a heartbeat, the look on her face was one of anguish and longing, but then she pinched her lips together in a look of cold indifference.

"I cannot imagine why. Revered Rosalind is far too busy to be bothered by the likes of me," she responded, biting out every word before shoving a cube of cheese into her mouth.

He reeled back, puzzled by her response. That was definitely not what he was expecting.

"Well, she is busy, yes…but she seemed to think you were in need of some help," he said, pointedly looking past her shoulder to where Brother Stokely stood across the picnic area, looming over a young ritual worker. Calen followed his gaze, then her head snapped back.

"I'm not sure I know what you mean," she said, narrowing her eyes at him.

"Mistress Calen, I'm fairly certain that you do," he said. His stomach twisted at the idea of speaking so freely about her mistreatment, with them only having just met. But if his assessment was correct, they would only have a few minutes to talk and plan, if he was to actually get her to safety. Besides, if she was really in such a bad situation, she should leap at the offer of help.

Calen's disposition became even more frosty, and she stared off, seeing something that was not there. "But of course, she couldn't be bothered to leave the comfort of Whitehall," she said, placing her plate on the table.

"Please, Mistress Calen, if we could just talk for a moment—" he started, but she cut him off with a huff of mirthless laughter.

"Not only does she *not* come here herself," she said, "but she sends one of Stokely's fellow Brothers to check in on me? Unbelievable."

"Mistress Calen," he started again, but she spoke over top of him.

"Are you trying to tell me you're here to help? I think not, what did you say your name was? Brother Nox? But you *can* tell Revered Rosalind that I'll be fine, and she can go back to barely thinking about me, just like she has for the past few years."

"Is that what you think—"

"That's the truth," she interrupted. "And if anyone from Black Rock was interested in helping me, that help would have come five years ago. Clearly, it did not. So, I would appreciate if you could mind your own business."

He did not have a chance to speak up again before she turned and walked away, her wild hair bouncing behind her. He watched her retreat toward her table, catching the eye of Brother Stokely, who was no longer ignorant to their conversation. He stared at Nox with barely veiled anger.

"Well, that went swimmingly," he chided himself.

Back at his own table, he lowered into the empty chair beside Augustus.

"Any luck?" Augustus asked.

"No. It was...odd. She got angry when I offered to help."

Augustus' eyebrows pinched together. "That is odd. Maybe she gets grouchy after ritual work. Revered Rosalind told me some Vessels are like that. Seed blessings wear them out and they need a few hours before they are ready to celebrate."

The seed blessing.

It had been Calen's turn to participate today, along with two other members of the Third Order. They had spread out across a distance of roughly eight acres of flat, open farmland and performed the ritual in unison, which was commonplace for an area this large and populated. Nox had heard that Calen was powerful, but he had no idea she was *that* powerful. Her mana wave had carried enough strength that it met the limit of each of the other two ritual workers' mana and *kept going*. It crossed into their area and where the energies overlapped, it had danced upward, out of the soil and into the air, swirling and dancing in beautiful patterns like nothing he had ever seen before. He had been at the front of the crowd and the reaction of those who could see ranged from shouts of joy to tearful prayers of thanks. But when Calen moved out of the field, he could tell that she had been crying. Her face was drained of color and oddly filthy, and she clenched clumps of dirt in her fists.

In the five days of travel from the capital to Old Roan, Nox had pondered all the ways this week could go. Somehow, he had failed to predict anything correctly where Revered Calen was concerned.

"Perhaps she is tired," Nox said. "Or perhaps she does not need our help, after all."

He doubted his own words, even as he said them.

***

Calen

How dare he? No, how dare *she*?

She had not heard from Rosalind in well over a year, but their relationship had been deteriorating for the past five, ever since her visit to Black Rock and the disastrous events that had taken place there. The last letter she ever received from Rosalind had been all of three sentences, barely worth reading. Three sentences that Calen had since memorized, looking for hidden meaning.

> My Dearest Cal,
> I hope that this letter finds you well. My duties at Whitehall keep me busy, but I think of you often. Please know that I care for you now, and always will.
>
> Rosalind

Calen had eventually found the meaning in the words. They were a goodbye, and a poor one at that. Rosalind had been her closest friend, her chosen family, and her home, since she had been twelve years old, and it had all come to an end with three sentences. How dare she send someone to check up on her now? Of all nights, that tattooed brute would choose to approach her tonight.

"Sorry, Brother Nox, but you're a bit late," she whispered. "I'm no longer in need of rescuing."

She had planned and prepared tirelessly for the past two weeks for this very night, and she was not about to throw it all away on the hope that someone else was finally willing to listen to her pleas for help.

Calen sat down a little harder than intended, nearly tipping over the wooden chair but catching herself with the white linen tablecloth. The move shifted the floral centerpiece and six heads swiveled to look in her direction.

"Sorry," she said, looking at each of them in turn, and noticing Stokely approach the table. She needed him to stay close, for once. If everything went according to plan, this would be the last night she would have to spend breathing the same air as her tormentor, but he needed to be where *she* could control *him* for once.

She watched his approach in the setting sun, his athletic build obvious beneath his golden robe, set in contrast to the bold green of the oak leaves finally unfurling to hang lazily from their branches along the river. She could understand why people found him attractive. But to her, his strong hands had only ever delivered pain, his intriguing eyes had only ever searched out weakness. His full lips had only ever hidden sharp teeth meant for breaking flesh. A muscular body that was meant to protect her had only ever been used to overpower her smaller one. There was no part of him that would ever be beautiful to her.

The hanging lamps twinkled to life just as he sat down. She could hear the band starting to play low, slow music that would eventually build into a frenzy of instruments and voices in the coming hours. It was almost time.

"Who was that?" Stokely asked, leaning in too close.

"No one," she answered.

"No one?" he asked, his voice dripping disbelief. "Really?"

"He thought he recognized me," she answered, trying to not fidget. "Thought I was someone else."

Stokely rolled his eyes. "Not sure how he could make that mistake."

He was right on that point. He had hidden her away well enough that no one knew her anymore. Perhaps not even Rosalind.

"Sounds like the party is about to start. Should we head back?" Calen asked.

The look on his face turned to one of suspicion. She needed to tone it down before her forced ease ruined her plans.

"I just don't feel well after today," she clarified.

Stokely huffed, his eyes darkening. "Do you ever feel well, Cal?"

She ignored the insult and fought down the retort that came to her tongue.

"It is a little early," he said, leaning back and checking the timepiece on his wrist, "but I don't suppose we want to be down here when these idiots start getting drunk."

She wondered if there was anyone on this planet that he did not despise.

He stood then, nodding to each of the Order Members sitting at their table, flashing a smile that they did not seem to recognize as patronizing. Stokely made to leave without looking back, and Calen followed along behind him. His ever-present, ever-faithful shadow for just a while longer.

Eleven

April 24, 622

Nox

Nox took a long drag of amber whiskey and glared at the stairwell. The liquid left a pleasant heat in his throat and settled the jittery muscles full of mana that had begun to hum in response to his agitation. Nothing about this trip had gone according to plan, and Calen was about to slip through his fingers. He crumpled the handwritten itinerary that was no longer of use to him, given that she had fulfilled her duties. There was no telling what she would do, or where she would go from this point.

Which was why he sat in the common room of her inn, waiting for some sign that he was on the right path, and that this whole trip was not in vain.

Calen was hiding something, Nox was certain. Nothing about her situation made sense, and it had sent him on a spiral of questions, for which he had no answers.

If she was so powerful, why would she put up with abuse from her partner? Even if she was not trained as a warrior, she could use her mana to push back against Stokely. Or demand the attention of the Heads of the Orders, who were always eager to please the most gifted among them.

She had referred to Black Rock in their conversation. But surely if she had asked for help, his Brothers and Sisters in the First Order would have obliged? And if not, why refuse his offer of aid now?

A clean-cut young man delivered his long-awaited supper, but before he could even dismiss the kitchen boy, he was disrupted by a woman noisily tumbling halfway down the stairwell he had spent the past hour studying. She nearly lost her front teeth in the fall, but at the last minute, her hands shot out and grabbed ahold of the well-polished banister, saving her from the worst of her injuries.

Something about her hands struck a chord. It only took a moment for him to remember where he had seen them before.

It was Calen. As soon as she recovered her footing, she took off in a run.

He shot up from the chair, sloshing whiskey over his wrist. The kitchen boy reached to help him clean the mess, but he pushed the napkin-wielding hands away and took off after Calen, who had disappeared down the hallway behind the staircase. It was a service hall, with multiple doors and one exit, at the far end. She was nowhere to be seen.

The first three rooms yielded clean linens, the accountant's room, and a spare food pantry, but no Calen. As he stepped out into the hall again, she slunk from the last room on the right, then made a mad dash for the exit. That door led outside; he could not afford let her reach it.

"Mistress Calen!" he called. Habit prevailed and she stopped at the sound of her name, just long enough to look back over her shoulder, then she was running again.

"Calen!" he yelled once more, taking off after her this time. Her hair was tucked up tight in a knit cap, and she wore simple, brown cotton pants under a lightweight overcoat. There was no mistaking the dark eyes that had fixed him with a look of surprise, then irritation for that brief moment. It was her, in a flimsy disguise, and she did not slow when she hit the door.

He pressed his hands into the glass panels of the door and watched as she broke out into a sprint across the open expanse of grass behind the inn. In the moonlight, she disappeared in the shadows of the tree line.

Nox felt the pull of Augustus through the bond they shared, as if he had walked straight into a headwind and his muscles had met resistance. Augustus had sensed his distress. He groaned and leaned forward on the door. This night could not get worse.

***

"She bolted," Nox grumbled through clenched teeth.

"Maybe she was going for a night walk?" Augustus asked, lifting his shoulders in a helpless shrug.

Nox gave him his best 'you know better than that' glare from over the pack he was filling. If only that were the case.

"There was nothing casual about her departure."

"Okay. So...what do we do now?"

"What do you mean? She refused help. She ran away. If she wants to be alone, who are we to interfere?"

This time, Augustus glared at him. "We are the people who promised to find and protect her."

"How am I supposed to protect a woman who refuses my aid?" Nox asked, throwing up his hands. "You didn't see her earlier; she was angry that I would dare offer!"

"Nox, would you really just let her go off into the woods like that? Not try to help?"

Nox heard the boy within the young man and turned to face him. Augustus was teetering on disappointment, his face open and searching in a way that made Nox's heart ache. There were a lot of things in this life he could afford to lose, but Augustus' respect was not one of them.

"You're right, Augustus," he conceded. "I should go after her."

Augustus sighed in relief, running his hands through his short, textured hair. "Alright. What supplies do we need? I've never actually camped rough before, but this will be a good experience."

"It would be," Nox answered, "if I was letting you go. But I'm not."

"Of course I need to go," Augustus said. "We are in this together, remember?"

"You've never camped rough, remember? Chasing a runaway Vessel through the mountains is not the way to learn how to do it. We don't have enough supplies for us both to last more than a day in the mountains. And I need you to follow the pull of the stone to where I track Calen. If we need help, you will need to be close to a call center."

"I could be of help to you, tracking Revered Calen."

Nox stepped closer to him, lowering his tone. "Look, it's commendable for you to step up like this. I'm not saying that I don't need your help. I'm saying that I need your help *here*. I have no idea what state she'll be in when I find her, and I'll need a partner on the other side. Besides, you can help keep an eye on Brother Stokely. From a distance. From a *far* distance." Nox took the younger man by the shoulders. "Do you understand?"

Augustus stared at the ground for a moment. "Yes, that does make sense," he said, nodding his head. "You can take the stone so it'll guide me when the time is right. I'll try to follow your general direction, but I'll stay close to villages and call centers when I can."

Nox took the small, black, perfectly round Consecration Stone from Augustus, and placed it in the pouch he had attached to each of his belts for this very purpose.

Augustus had been practicing sensing the stone across longer distances, but he still could not do it with perfect accuracy. Regardless, Nox knew that was not the highest priority at the moment. What did matter was catching up to Calen. He still held out hope that he could find her soon and bring her back tonight. Augustus would not need to sense the stone across any distance, if Nox worked quickly enough.

"So then, what supplies do *you* need?" Augustus asked, glancing around the room.

Nox had not planned on taking a trek through the mountains. He *had*, however, planned on spending time with his sketch pad, pencils, and books, and had brought them in a waterproof, oilcloth bag. Dumping out the contents, he quickly rounded up matches, soap, two glass bottles of filtered water, a painting of the local terrain that would have to suffice as a map, and extra socks. He carried multiple weapons on his body at any given time, so there was no need to pack extra, and he would grab as many food rations as he could on his way out through the kitchen. That just left...

"A bedroll," he eventually answered Augustus. The two stood looking at each other, realizing there was not one handy.

"Will a quilt do?" the younger man asked, plucking one from the foot of Nox's bed.

"It'll have to, I suppose," Nox answered, taking it from Augustus and rolling it into a neat bolster before shoving it into his pack.

Nox begrudgingly realizing he would be living off of deer jerky and stale bread for a while. This had better be worth it. He slung the pack over his shoulder and laid his hand across the back of Augustus' neck, who returned the gesture. The two men touched their foreheads together, in the same farewell they had used for years.

"Be safe, Nox."

"You too, Aug."

Nox opened his mana, the power humming in his legs, and prepared to take off.

Twelve

April 24, 622

Calen

It worked. It actually worked.

Calen knew that it was far too early to consider herself safe, but she had put at least forty-five minutes and a few miles distance between herself and Stokely. This was the furthest they had been apart since they had started working together after she graduated from Grandview, and with each step her breathing became easier.

He would give chase, no doubt. Stokely would never let stand the indignation of her leaving him. She knew that he would come looking, if only to be the one to end her. If that was to be her fate, at least she would die standing on her feet, rather than cowering in a corner.

That fateful morning at the Graymount Inn, she had scrubbed her skin raw and planned her escape. She had very quickly decided that simple was best. The fewer the moving pieces, the less likely something was to go wrong. And she had told absolutely no one. She had not even written it down, but instead committed it to memory.

Step One: convince Stokely to drink his herb-drugged wine. Check.

It had not even been that difficult, in the end. The man might have looked down on others for being "drunken idiots," but he was not above imbibing himself.

Step Two: Leave on foot and head to the mountains. Set a few false trails. Check.

Two weeks had given her plenty of time to stockpile clothing and supplies.

Step Three: Travel to the border and cross over into Reclamation, beg for safe passage on the lie that she was visiting a dying father.

She would never be able to tell the Vessels manning the border that she was leaving to escape from an abusive work partner. She would be flagged for dereliction of duty and sent to Black Rock to file a formal complaint against said partner. There was no way she could face the indignity of revealing her most private humiliations to a room of starchy, stiff-necked First Order members only to be told, once again, that she was a liar and a prude.

Her entire identity would have to change before she arrived at the fort, and she would have to hope that there were no Seekers visiting sensitive enough to pick up on her mana. She had grown very adept at remaining closed off for long periods of time. Where her mana should be a shining beacon of her capabilities, it was a small bundle curled tightly on itself, barely present. It would have to remain that way if she was going to survive.

"Sorry," she whispered. A phantom fluttering tickled her belly.

The solution to successfully crossing the border lay tucked neatly in an inside pocket of her jacket. Courtesy of one Marjorie Millner, Calen had a sheaf of 'borrowed' travel papers that would effectively let her move about without raising suspicion. She knew nothing of the woman, other than the fact that she had been in the Southern Drift way station at the right time and matched the same general description as Calen.

With papers in hand, she would pass through Fort Vulhaven, and into her new life. It was not a foolproof plan, by any means, but Calen had had to work with what she had in front of her and find advantages where she could.

Stokely did not know the mountains the way that she did, and he would have a much more difficult time picking his way through them than she would. This was her native land, and she had roamed this very mountain range (though much further north) from the time she was old enough to walk. His physical fitness would count for little here when he had been raised on the open, flat land of the Fertile Plains Colony.

It did not matter that they had lived for the past eight years just an hour away from these very mountains. He had never taken the time to learn the native plants and animals like she had. Where she knew which wild foods were safe to forage, he would have to carry all of his rations and head back toward civilization when he ran out. Where she was as surefooted as a bobcat on the rocky terrain, he would have no idea how to spot loose shale that could slip underfoot and send him careening down the mountainside. Calen would have the upper hand for as long as she could stay in the mountains.

Once she left their safety and made her way across open country to the border, he could very easily overtake her. She just had to hold onto hope that she would put enough distance between them before that time came.

Her legs may have been accustomed to hiking mountains, but her pack was beginning to make her shoulders burn. It was nothing compared to the pain Stokely had inflicted, *would* inflict if he caught her, and that thought alone would keep her motivated on the long road ahead. Her shoulders could be rubbed to the bone by the straps of her pack and she would still put one foot in front of the other until he was contained within a pocket of time and space far away.

Calen could no longer hear the rush of the river she had followed out of Old Roan. She was already making her way through the foothills of the range, careful not to handicap herself with the full dark that loomed beneath the dense canopy of the old growth hardwood forest that blanketed the rock face in green. She would seek its protection at dawn, but no sooner. Nervous excitement pulsed through her, and she might not stop walking before then.

Despite her exhilaration at having successfully made it this far, a nagging remained in the back of her brain, like a small stone lodged in her shoe. Brother Nox.

Of all the people for her to run into along her escape, why him?

And was he truly planning on throwing his loyalty behind her, as he had implied? Or would he go run and tell his fellow *Brother* what he had seen? If he had gone to their room and found Stokely unconscious and unresponsive, that could be disastrous. She did not know his true intentions, could not know them. But Calen did know that she was wasting precious energy worrying about him. If only she could dislodge the worry from her mind.

She hoisted her pack up on her shoulders again, securing it more completely before climbing up and over a boulder that had fallen into the horse path she was following. Hopping down on the other side, she took a deep breath and refocused on the task ahead.

She was headed west.

Thirteen

April 24, 622

Nox

Nox was headed east. Following the dancing glow of tiny, turquoise dust motes through the woods, he was completely certain Calen had come this way. And with as strong as her trail was, he was not far behind her.

He had always been an exceptional tracker in his youth. His father and older brother had taught him all that they had known, and the three of them had routinely taken trips into the wild expanse that trimmed the norther border of Sun Grove Colony to hunt wild game. It was a skill that was further amplified when he had become a Vessel and had developed the ability to see mana trails others left in their wake, like a faucet that leaked for a time after being opened. However, he did not understand why Calen would be running around open. She had to know that with the aid of their Consecration Stone, Stokely would be able to follow this trail as easily as he could.

He passed through the dappled moonlight of a clearing and stopped on the other side, allowing his eyes to adjust to the darkness for a moment before looking around to regain his bearings. Following a mana trail with his eyes unfocused meant that if he was not careful, he would accidentally walk off of a cliff and never see the edge coming until it was too late.

Up ahead, he could make out the shape of a small building. It looked like an old hunting shelter, with its size and lack of windows.

He let his eyes lose focus again, and retraced Calen's trail, definitely leading to the shed. A few minutes later, he approached silently, circling the structure to take full stock of the situation. A dilapidated door hung crooked, connected to the door frame by a single hinge. There was one small window on the back, but the glass was missing, and the roof was moss-covered and half caved in. What could Calen be doing in there? Maybe she had hidden a supply stash and was packing up before taking off again?

"Or, perhaps," he mumbled to himself, "she was just out for a walk…"

He positioned himself so that if she tried to run out the front door, she would run directly into him. Then he lowered into a crouch, ready to intercept her, should that happen.

"Calen, it's me, Brother Nox," he said into the night.

There was no response.

"Calen, I know you're in there. I am here to help, but I need you to come out slowly so we can talk first. We can head back to Old Roan, work things out."

Silence.

Nox sighed. "Alright, Calen, I'm coming in. Do not attack me, please." It was not fear *of* the woman hiding inside that had him stalling, it was fear *for* her. If she rushed him, his well-honed fighting instincts would kick in and he had absolutely no desire to hurt her, even unintentionally. Noticing a fallen branch at his foot, he picked it up and used it to pry open the door to take a peek inside.

"A lamp," he said, ducking his head inside. "A lamp would have come in handy."

Calen was not there. No one was there.

He stepped inside the broken-down shelter, opening his mana and pulsing a small amount into the tips of his fingers. They instantly lit up a bold royal blue, illuminating the space enough for him to see that while Calen was not there, he was not alone.

"Mmmmmwwwwaaaaarrrrrrrr."

It came out as a low rumble that Nox registered as a warning. Slowly moving his hand to illuminate each corner of the shelter in turn, he found the source of the angry noise. What appeared to be a growling mound of fur moved its head and resolved into the mangey tomcat from back at the inn. It swatted and hissed as he approached, but he was also *swimming* in Calen's mana, so Nox risked squatting down beside him with his hand outstretched.

"Shhh. It's alright, big guy," he said, but the cat just eyed him and whipped his tail. He slowly set down his pack, searching for an acceptable peace offering. When he pulled out a small cube of cheese, the cat stilled, his eyes trained on the treat.

"Aha, something you and her have in common," he said, laying the cheese on the ground. "I'll tell ya what, fluff. You let me see what's tied around your neck, and I'll let you have this." The cat was on it in an instant, and Nox grabbed his collar just as quickly.

"There you go," he said.

Nox untied the small pouch hanging from its neck, mostly dismissed by the cat. Opening it, he dumped the contents into his palm, shaking his head.

Dirt.

More specifically, dirt from the seed blessing this morning. It was saturated in Calen's mana and it was undoubtedly the source of the trail he had been following.

There was no way she could have known about his gift; it was useful but would be dangerous in the wrong hands, and he kept it mostly to himself. There was no way for her to know that he would track her. Which meant this false trail was not set for him. It was set for someone else who could use her mana to find her. Brother Fucking Stokely. It was too much to hope that Rosalind had been wrong, and that he would be returning home soon.

"Clever, clever," he mumbled to himself. "How did she convince you to help her?" he asked the cat now licking his whiskers. Purrseus blinked slowly at him.

"Right, well my friend," Nox said, holding up the makeshift pouch,

"I may have another treat for you if you will let me reattach this." The cat seemed to agree, so Nox made the trade and reattached the bait to his collar.

He released his mana as he exited the shack. How many false trails would he have to follow before he found Calen? This one had cost him at least an hour, and that would be doubled by the time he made his way back to the inn. Even without meaning to, this woman continued to make his life difficult. There was no turning back from this mission, though, and he knew it. All he could do now was make haste and hope that this trap would also fool Brother Stokely, when the time came.

Fourteen

April 25, 622

Stokely

Stokely could feel the sun blasting his face as it screamed through the windows, unbidden by curtains. He sat up in bed, or at least tried to, but the immediate pounding in his head had him laying back down, groaning.

How much had he drunk last night?

Attempting to sit up a second time, this time much more slowly, he realized that it must have been a lot if he had not even changed out of his robes. They were a tangled mess of golden fabric that was choking him and reflecting an obscene amount of light. Needing to be out of them immediately, he ripped the fabric down the middle and wriggled his shoulders away from the destroyed neckline.

"Callie," he croaked. There was no response.

"Callie, where are you?" he yelled, but still no response.

She had probably gone out for a walk in the woods this morning. Despite his every attempt to teach her some sophistication, she still resorted back to her mountain troll ways every chance she got. The disgusting woman would often go out barefoot and track all manner of filth back into their room.

After bathing and scrubbing his teeth, he took a last look in the mirror, checking for imperfections that were not there, and emerged back into the bedroom of their suite. Calen still had not returned. He sighed his annoyance, then began rifling through her things to see what she had taken with her. That should have given him a clue as to where she had gone, but his search was fruitless. Her trunk was more disheveled that she typically kept it, but all her gowns were still there.

He clasped the consecration stone that hung from around his neck, pouring a small amount of pale mana in to awaken it, and waited for it to pull him gently the direction from which it could sense her. The energy within the stone shifted, but never settled. That was odd. Perhaps she was already inside the inn, and it simply could not decide which way to pull?

Stokely arrived in the common room to find it bustling with guests all eager to find something to break their fast before the day's festivities began. It had been like this all week, and even without a hangover, he had found the cacophony overwhelming.

Hard-soled boots slapped the smooth stone floor. The overpowering aroma of coffee and fried pork of every variety saturated the space. To top it off, after destroying his robes this morning, he had had to settle for wearing the only clean robes he had, which had been over-starched by inn staff and was rubbing the back of his neck raw. It all put him on edge, and he had to hold back from screaming into the rafters. Calen could be right here in this very room, and he would likely overlook her in the bustle.

**

An hour later, he had searched the inn, the grounds, the stables, and even the boundary of the woods beyond the grassy meeting area behind the main building. The Consecration Stone had first pulled him southward, then the sensation had faded out. Next, it took him east, but then went cold again. For some reason, it was not working, and he thought that he knew the reason. Without knowing *how* she had done it, he was confident Calen had broken the stone before she left him. She was gone. And he had no help finding her.

"Sir, did you hear me?" the guardsman asked. "She's not here."

Stokely adjusted his pale golden sleeve. He checked that each of the buttons on his wrist was pointing in the correct direction, with each glittering, golden *I* lined up in perfect parallel to one another, like soldiers standing at attention. It was an intentionally slow, methodical action meant to calm him down a measure, as well as to give the man in front of him time to stop being such an unbelievable idiot. It did not work on either count.

"Sir?" the man repeated.

Stokely glared at him.

The man flushed and shifted uneasily from one foot to the other. How had this man earned his title?

"Well, thank you for that," Stokely crooned in a quiet, deep voice. "Can you see that I am positively beaming with gratitude that your observational skills have allowed you to ascertain that the woman in question is, in fact, not here?"

Apparently unaccustomed to sarcasm, the guardsman actually smiled at the perceived praise. Stokely would have to have this man beaten.

"A job well done," he continued, "Congratulations are in order. You have adequately deduced what the rest of us here realized three hours ago, you imbecile. Perhaps now that you have caught up, you will bless me by turning your considerable investigative talents toward fulfilling the request I actually made of you?"

The guardsman seemed to hear the condescension this time, and Stokely watched as scarlet mottling climbed up past green eyes and all the way to the pale blonde hair under his cap.

"Sir? What is it that you want from me?"

Stokely would not have this man beaten, after all. He would beat the man himself. He bit down on the hot bile rising in his throat.

"Have you found any *actual* clues to where she may have gone?" he asked through clenched teeth. "A note? Prints in the mud? A giant sign stating, 'I've gone this way, please come and find me?'"

"No, sir. I did not." The man lifted his chin and met Stokely's eye. "She is your bonded partner, why can you not just use your Consecration Stone to locate her?"

Stokely adjusted the buttons on his right sleeve this time. It would be unacceptable to rip this man's head from his neck and kick it across the clearing. Satisfying, but unacceptable. Stokely had an image to uphold as a Brother of the First Order and that image was not supposed to include adjectives such as 'homicidal' or 'maniacal.'

"Are you a member of the First or Third Order?" he asked but did not wait for an answer from the guard. "No, you are not. And as such, you would not fully understand how our Consecration Stone works. Our traditions are none of your damn business. Now, do what your piddly little mind is capable of and follow orders. I better not see your pathetic, pale face again unless you are hauling the missing ritual worker to my side. Not one moment sooner, understood?"

This time, he waited for the guardsman to answer, knowing how sour the words would taste in the man's mouth.

The guardsman stared openly for a heartbeat, before schooling his face to calm. He appeared to focus on the space beyond Stokely's right shoulder.

"Yes, sir. Your will is mine and I do your bidding... Brother Stokely." Then he bowed and made a hasty exit.

It galled Stokely that even someone as lowly as a common guardsman would realize that he could not use his Consecration Stone to find his partner. They were supposed to be foolproof, providing a tether between partners to ensure that no matter what happened to one, the other would know of the danger, and where they had gone. He dragged his thumb along the smooth length of the milky-white stone, wondering how she could have rendered it useless.

He needed to move. The power coursing beneath his skin was a beehive, and his head pulsed with a hangover he owed to more than just wine. Striding toward the field of wildflowers growing on the southern end of the clearing, he listened to soft whooshing of the breeze moving through the knee-high, vibrant green stems to ease his tension. Stokely could smell the early blooms of chamomile, apple-sweet and light. He wished he were the type of man that this would calm. Unfortunately, he was the type to be more easily pacified by the harsh sounds of air squeezing out of a throat being choked than birds singing in the trees.

Opening his eyes, he spotted more guardsmen coming out of the hemlock grove at the end of the field of wildflowers. They were also empty-handed.

He stood with his chin high and his strong, well-manicured hands clasped behind his back. He would portray an air of cool confidence as always, even if he was seething inside.

How could she do this? He was certain now that her actions had been intentional. She had not been taken against her will; she had left him. No, it was even worse than that. She had drugged him and *then* left him. He would never be able to enjoy the smooth velvet taste of real wine again without remembering this betrayal. He would forever be relegated to drinking the disgusting fruit-wine swill commoners enjoyed. He scoffed. Just one more thing she had taken from him.

Almost worse than the betrayal was the knowledge that she had somehow plucked up the confidence to pull off such a scheme, and right under his nose. The woman had planned well. She knew how much he valued the gorgeous red vintage that was reserved exclusively for Vessels. She knew that the bold flavor would cover the taste of her soporific herbs. She had offered it up with all the charm she could muster, and it had taken every ounce of his considerable will to not chug the entire glass and weep with joy while doing so. One glass turned into two, turned into three…turned into him sleeping far past a dignified hour and waking with the taste of stale tannins on his tongue and drum beats in his head. He could not remember much past drinking wine with her, which meant he had not had the presence of mind to pull any mana from her last night. How had he gotten that drunk?

Searching his memories and rubbing his temples as if that would help, he remembered her pouring herself a drink and simply holding it. Holding the wine, but not drinking it as she watched him with those uncanny eyes.

Yes, she had planned this. He would not let her get away with it. For all her faults (and he counted many), she was a clever woman. He would have to be more clever *and* completely ruthless if he wanted to find her. Challenge accepted.

"Where have you made off to, my sneaky little fox?" he asked a hawk gliding across the azure sky, instantly regretting it as the sun struck his pupils. He closed his eyes against the pain flaring in his head.

Not only would he find her, but he would also make her pay. He was not a man to be disobeyed and he would make sure that she remembered that, before he ended her.

Stokely could think of so many ways to make her hurt and he would employ every...single...one. His mind filled with the possibilities. The pain, the tears, the humiliation...it would be so beautiful. His hands ached to dig into her flesh. He ground his teeth, imagining how her blood would taste, filling his mouth as her screams of terror filled his ears. There would be no escape for her, not after this.

He inhaled the fresh mountain air and found that he was relaxed, finally.

"I'm coming for you, Calen."

Fifteen

April 26, 622

Rosalind

"Yes, yes I see it now," Archmother Gwendolyn whispered to the air in front of her. "Of course, oh that makes so much sense!" She lifted her hands to her head, pressing the heels of her palms into her temples. Then she let out a child-like giggle and began bouncing on the balls of her feet.

"Mother," Rosalind said, taking the woman by the arms with gentle hands, "I think it would be good if you rested now."

She guided the Archmother away from the corner where the woman had been standing for the last thirty minutes, quietly talking to someone who was not there.

"No!" she cried out in protest. "Not yet, just a little longer, let me see just a little longer! It's so beautiful, Ros!" Gwendolyn shook her head furiously, her wide eyes swimming in dark sockets that had not seen enough sleep lately.

Rosalind could see the vibrant red of her mana dancing at the back of her pupils and wondered, for the hundredth time, how she could still identify the people around her while in this altered state of consciousness.

"Gwen, you really should rest now," she answered as tenderly as she could.

The woman's head bobbled back and forth, unable to decide whether or not to agree with the request. Rosalind steered her toward her bed, rolling back the lightweight quilt before tucking Gwendolyn beneath it.

"Are you ready?" Rosalind asked.

Even though this was her duty, and even though Gwendolyn occasionally refused, she would never forcefully use her mana on another without their express consent. The Archmother nodded, her face obscured by the halo of jagged, brown hair that had not been properly braided in at least three days. It was difficult enough for Rosalind to convince Gwen to bathe and run a pick through her hair, any further grooming would have to wait until she made it out the other side of this fit.

The Archmother was a woman of astonishing beauty, but when her mana ran wild and suffused her brain in ways it was not meant to do, she spent her days, as she put it, "learning about the secrets of the universe and simply didn't have time to indulge her beauty." Regardless, Rosalind would wait until she had slipped into a deep slumber and gently fold it into a simple plait to keep it from becoming a tangled mess while she slept.

Receiving permission, Rosalind prepared. Her coral-hued mana was already open and ready to work, so she rubbed her hands gingerly to warm them, then laid on either side of the Archmother's dark brown face. She coaxed her power from her core, across her chest, down her arms and out through her palms, into Gwendolyn's tense face. The skin around Archmother's eyes went lax, and she released a sigh.

"Song's beautiful, today," she mumbled.

"Just for you," Rosalind said, and smiled. She had no real control over the musical aura of her mana, but it did not always sing for the people she healed. It always sang for Gwendolyn.

Her power met the other woman's and wrapped tiny tendrils around the bolts jumping from one part of her brain to another. The red mana slowed and wrapped itself around the coral. With a practiced concentration, she guided them both away from the Archmother's mind. The red came more easily than it had in the past. Rosalind had the distinct impression that it had begun to recognize her mana, and knew it was okay to follow. The bold light slowly drained from the Archmother's pupils, and her lids drooped, no longer strung tight by the frenetic energy of a moment ago. Once eased from her brain, Gwendolyn's mana let go of Rosalind's and flowed back into her chest, where it mostly lived these days. It made a swirling cocoon around her heart, then stilled, and Gwendolyn laid both hands atop her breast, as if cradling a new babe.

"Gwen, are you okay?" she asked, just above a whisper.

"Mmmm. I am always 'okay,' Ros. But it's only me in here now, if that's what you are asking," she answered, with eyes closed. Then, just before succumbing to sleep, she whispered, "It will be so beautiful, Ros. Just wait."

She always wondered what it was the Archmother saw when she had visions. Over the years, since the fits had first started, Gwendolyn's behavior had morphed. In the beginning, she would lose herself to the fit, screaming and crying and begging for it to stop. Gradually, the episodes began to send her into fits of ecstasy that would end with violent seizures. Now when she had an episode, she would carry on as if she were talking so someone else who happened to be sharing her mind. Sometimes, it sounded as if the 'two' of them were formulating a plan. Other times, like today, Gwendolyn was being shown something. When Ros would ask her what she had seen, she was redolent to answer. "It doesn't make sense yet," or "I don't have the words to explain it," were common responses, often followed by a sharp change of subject that told Rosalind she would not find the answers she sought. So, she continued to do her job and pull Gwen back from the brink of oblivion with the hope of receiving answers someday.

She stood and walked to the window, propping it open to let in fresh spring air that held the scent of a light afternoon rain. The fields just beyond that very room were being seeded in preparation for the big May Day festival blessing, less than a week away. The farmhands would have to stop their work soon or risk damaging the soil with their heavy footfalls once the rain started in earnest.

Rosalind felt the familiar pull at her core in the same moment that she registered a light knocking on the door, both of which signified the arrival of Freddie with her mid-day meal.

Just in time. She was absolutely famished from working. Contrary to popular belief, working minuscule amounts of mana was actually far more difficult that working large amounts. The level of precision required to do her work necessitated extreme control that drained her energy at a surprising rate.

She checked a sleeping Gwendolyn once more before joining Freddie in the gathering room just outside.

The room was tastefully furnished, with large fresco-style paintings that adorned the spaces between the floor-to-ceiling windows facing the northern expanse of the Whitehall Homestead. They were vivid and detailed, but somehow had the effect of highlighting the beauty that waited just outside, rather than detracting from it. A large portrait of the current Archfamily had been commissioned last year, during one of the Archmother's periods of lucidity, and it hung on the wall that separated the dining hall from the master bedroom from which she had just emerged. In the center of the room was a round, solid oak table, stained and varnished to highlight the natural wood grain. Around the table were ten matching, high-backed chairs that were deceptively comfortable and were as likely to host the Heads of the Orders as they were the young children of the Archfamily. Today, it was set only for two, and Rosalind wasted no time in taking her seat and making a plate.

The platter before her contained hard cheese, fig preserves, fresh, warm flatbread, smoked ham, crispy greens, and even sugar-preserved lemons. The offering brought back a memory of being in this very room, presented with a meal very similar to this one. The main difference between the two was that meal had also contained small, rich fruit called olives. They had come from the continent to the east whose name translated roughly to Blessed Mother Land, a nod to the fact that when the meteors had struck, the largest had landed smack in the middle. It had bestowed them with the largest supply of mana, and they believed that marked them as special. In reality, what it had actually brought them was the greatest amount of infighting and bloodshed during that tumultuous time in human history.

While they had suffered the greatest casualties in the wars that raged for decades, they had also recovered relatively quickly, once the fighting had stopped. They were the first to venture back into the oceans with barges and sailboats, and had sought to reestablish transoceanic trade routes. The olives, along with other foreign delicacies, had been brought to the New Colonies on a shipment intended to help establish those new trade routes. Ultimately, the Blessed Mother Land had decided that the requisite trips were too costly and dangerous to continue with so little return on their investment. They abandoned the trade route, but not before offloading a stockpile of exotic foods and goods.

A mere eighteen months after leaving Grandview Academy, Rosalind had been summoned here and pressed upon to lend her exceptional gifts to the Archfamily. To help entice her, the cooks had included some of the decades-old, salt-packed olives with dinner that night. Rosalind had already decided to take the position, but she enjoyed the intense, pungent flavor of the olives all the same.

Even without the olives, Freddie had outdone himself, including most of her favorite foods in this meal, and she looked at him pointedly.

"You have news, don't you?" she asked, shoving a bite into her mouth.

"I do," he answered, not looking up from her cup as he filled it with chilled water.

"And?" she asked.

"Eat first, Ros. I know you're hungry," he said, sitting down the pitcher and starting on his own plate.

"How can I eat when—"

He stopped her by holding up his hand.

"She's alive, and nothing is going to change in the next ten minutes," he said in his usual, unhurried way, "so please eat."

He was right. She could not focus with an empty stomach, anyhow. The two ate in companionable silence for as long as it took her to clear her plate and down a mug of water. She wiped her hands on her linen napkin, then folded them in her lap to keep from fidgeting.

"Okay, I've eaten. What's the news?" she implored.

"Thank you for the lunch, Freddie, that was delicious," he said into his mug.

She sighed. "Yes, thank you for lunch, Freddie, it truly was delicious. You are a gift I do not deserve."

He smiled at her. "Oh, you are very welcome, Mistress Rosalind."

"Freddie, please. You are killing me right now."

Freddie ripped off a piece of flatbread, shoved it into his mouth, but thankfully answered her at the same time.

"I've had a call from Augustus," he said. Rosalind leaned forward in her chair, her now-full stomach fluttering. "They were able to find Calen and Stokely, but I guess it didn't go well. Nox apparently approached her, but she refused his offer of aid."

"What?" Rosalind asked. "What do you mean, *refused*?"

"I mean she did not want his help. She did not want anyone's help."

"That doesn't make any sense." Unless she was wrong. Unless Calen was fine. Unless...she had someone else to help her, now.

"I'm too late. Freddie, she has someone else to help her. I left her, and she found someone else, and I'll never be able to make amends for...for..." Oh, blessed Vessel. She may have actually lost Calen. How did she let this happen? Surely, it was not entirely her fault. Calen stopped reaching out for her, too. The ache in her chest deepened. She could feel Freddie looking at her. "What?" she asked, "Is there more?"

"There's more," he added somberly. "Two nights ago, after Nox approached her and offered to help, she...fled."

Her shoulders dropped and she slumped back in her chair.

"Fled?" she asked.

"Yes. Nox was watching from the common room at their inn and happened to see her sneak out. He checked in with Augustus before pursuing her on foot. Aug waited to see if they would return quickly, but he hasn't heard anything since that night. He says that the bond still pulls at him. So, we know that Nox lives, at least."

Each word ate away at the hope that Calen would be returned safely to the capital.

"Is Augustus still in Old Roan?" she asked, her mind working.

"No, he is following the pull of Nox to the southwest. He waited to see what Brother Stokely would do, and when *he* left the next day in a carriage with a handful of guards, Augustus left as well."

"Southwest? Where could she be going?"

Calen's family lived in the mountains northwest of Old Roan, but Rosalind did not think she had spoken to them in years. The capital was northeast, but she would have contacted Rosalind if she were coming there, right?

Not if she had someone else.

"Ros, you know that odds are, she's just headed away from *him*. Maybe she has a plan, but maybe she's just running scared."

"And he left with a carriage and a handful of guardsmen," she realized, panic climbing up her throat. "Oh, Freddie, he is hunting her! All that's missing is a pack of hounds."

Freddie took a deep breath, leaned forward, and took her hand.

"Ros. Calen is strong and smart. She grew up in the mountains, right? She has half a day's head start on Stokely. Nox will catch up with her, and help get her to safety. You sent him because he is reliable, so rely on him."

"Yeah, you could be right," she conceded.

"Augustus will be near a call center again soon, and Nox will figure out how to get a call to him. We just have to be patient."

"Ha," she barked. "You know patience isn't one of my strongest virtues, Freddie."

"Well, unless the Archmother magically emerges from this episode," he said, plopping another piece of ham into his mouth, "we have no choice but to sit tight and be patient."

***

After sitting with Freddie for another twenty minutes, the two picking at the bits of food left on the platter while catching up on other important business, she excused herself back to her work. Gwendolyn did not tend to sleep long during these phases, and Rosalind was always there when she awakened.

Gwen was leaning against the windowpane, welcoming the misty breeze blowing through her hair. Her face was relaxed, her eyes closed and a slight smile playing on her mouth. At the sound of the door opening, she turned toward Rosalind.

"My dear Ros, what are you still doing here?" she asked, genuinely puzzled.

"I figured I should check in on you and make sure you were resting peacefully," Ros answered.

"No, I don't mean, what are you still doing in my room?" she explained, smiling wider. "I mean, what are you still doing in the capital?"

"Mother, you remember what was happening this morning?"

"Of course, I do, Rosalind. And I know that you take your duties very seriously, but you shouldn't be here."

"I'm confused. Where else would I be?"

"With her."

Rosalind's steps slowed. "With whom?"

"With *her*. The dark-haired one. She needs you, and you know it. You saw what happened. Now, send for my husband and get busy packing. You won't want to be loading up the carriage when the rain comes. I'd say you have, mmm, twenty minutes."

There were no words for the confusion Rosalind felt. She stuttered out a few choked sounds but could not form the question in her mind.

"My dear Rosalind. I know you want all of the answers, but I cannot give them to you. Not yet. And I know you don't understand my gift, so I need you to just trust me." The Archmother stood and walked to her, placing her hands on Rosalind's shoulders. "You need to leave, now. Find your friend, and don't return until you can bring them all home safely."

How could the Archmother possibly know about Calen? She was certain that she had not spoken of her troubles to Gwendolyn, choosing not to involve her in the conflicts of others when she so clearly had her own to fight. Rosalind was also certain that she would not remember the last time Calen had visited the capital. Gwendolyn and Calen had only met once, and that was at a dinner party where at least a few dozen people were in attendance, with the Archmother as the guest of honor.

"You want me to leave?" Rosalind clarified.

"Yes. Now."

"And bring her back?"

"Bring them all back."

"All?"

"All. Trust me."

"But…I can't just leave you, what if—"

"I will be fine, Ros. I have seen everything I need to see, for now. I will be well until you return."

"You are certain?"

"Absolutely. Now, I've not let my husband in my presence for two weeks, and I very much plan to make up for lost time. Could you ask Carina to send for him while I bathe?"

"Yes, Mother," Rosalind said, bowing before turning to the door. Without knowing why, she asked, "What if she doesn't want my help?"

"She will," Gwendolyn answered. "She will."

***

Gwendolyn had been right on one count, at least. Twenty minutes later, the skies opened up and released a deluge of water a far cry from the light shower Rosalind had predicted. Fortunately, in that time, Rosalind had found Carina, then Freddie, and packed as frantically as possible. Their unmarked carriage was making its way through the gate at the side of the large garage, and as they emerged into the rain, the driver released a string of curses before stopping mid-stream to apologize.

"Mistress, Brother, it's going to be slow-going in this rain, but I'll do my best," he said over his shoulder.

"It's alright, Donal," she answered, patting the man's back.

"Where, exactly, are we headed, Ros?" Freddie asked.

"Well, I figure that our best bet is to head in the direction Augustus indicated. It will take a few days on the road to get there, but with them on foot and us in a carriage, I'm thinking we can catch up quickly enough." She dug through the satchel at her side and pulled out a small travel map. "I'm counting on Nox to find and steer Calen, if she will let him. And you know him, he will insist on taking refuge at his favorite inns."

Freddie grinned. "Yeah. He's not one for humble lodgings."

Sixteen

April 28, 622

Calen

Calen awoke with the dawn, rolling over onto her back and stretching her arms over her head into the cool, damp morning air. The night had been brisk, but she had stayed warm enough in the cocoon of her own body heat. The first rays of sunrise were pushing against the velvet blue of night, and she actually felt rested.

"What a lovely morning," she said to herself.

"Can't say I agree," said a voice. She shot up, the bedroll pulling tight against her legs, and turned toward the speaker.

"Please, stay calm. I'm not here to hurt you," he said, quietly.

The fog of sleep cleared in an instant.

"Brother Nox?" she asked, fear and incredulity making her voice wobble. She began backing her way out of her bedroll, kicking at the thick fabric.

"Calen...it is okay," he said, eyeing her with suspicion.

"No. No no no no," she mumbled, opening and closing her fists. None of this was okay. She searched the ground for something to defend herself, scooping up a rock.

"Calen," he warned, "please don't do anything stupid."

She hurled the rock at his head and took off in the opposite direction. He cursed, but then she heard his pursuit. Within seconds, he had caught her by the elbow and spun her around. She swung her arm wide, hoping to connect with his face, but once again missed. His blue mana whirled in her vision as he grasped her with both hands and pinned her to a tree. Her stomach gave out.

"Calen, please—"

This time, she did not miss as she brought her knee up between his thighs and made solid contact. He dropped her with a groan and stumbled backward, his arms still racing with mana as he groped at his abused groin. Calen landed on her feet and lowered into a crouch.

"What the fuck?" he squeezed out.

"Get away from me!"

"I'm trying to help!"

She backed away, looking once more for a weapon. "Liar!"

He straightened. "Are you serious? What possible reason would I have for following you into the mountains! Do you know how much I hate hiking? I've lost more blood to mosquitos these last few nights that I have in all my years fighting!"

"Stokely put you up to this, didn't he?" she shot back. Her arms and legs were shaking, but she tried standing anyhow.

"No! I told you, I'm here to help you! Rosalind sent me! Although, I'm starting to wonder if I did something to piss her off and this is actually her revenge."

She began pacing, trying to shake away the heat coursing through her limbs. Maybe he was telling the truth. Trying to think through her next moves, she focused on her breathing. That always helped.

"You are really here to help?" she asked.

"Maybe," he answered. "I might need to head back down the mountain and find a healer to locate my left testicle after that little stunt."

"I'm not apologizing."

"Of course, you aren't. Why would you?" he asked sardonically.

"What the hell were you thinking? That's the worst possible way you could have announced your presence."

"Yeah, I realized about five seconds too late. But I figured you would find it unfavorable if you woke up and I was just sitting there, watching you sleep, like an absolute creep."

"You were just sitting there, watching me sleep?"

"Yes, like an absolute creep. But in weighing my options, I realized that if I went to sleep, you could crush my head with a rock, should you choose to. I'm now pretty certain you would have chosen to, considering recent events. So, I watched instead of sleeping. And now, here we are."

The pace of her heart had slowed, and she suddenly felt dizzy. Cutting through the trees, she made her way back to the small camp. She was even more disheartened when she realized that their little scuffle had only taken them a few yards from where they had started.

"Sure, Calen, let's head back to the fire I built and make some breakfast," he said to her back.

"How did you find me?" she asked, when he did seat himself across the pit. "I've been climbing to scout every few hours, and I have not seen you following me."

"I'm a very good tracker," he said, shrugging. "Not that you made it easy. That was a pretty clever trap you laid."

"So, it worked?"

"Yes. While I was tracking your mana, it did."

"Which one?"

"Pardon?"

"Which trap did you follow?" she clarified.

"The one with claws. And most likely, fleas," he answered, cringing.

A smile tugged at her lips. "He's a sweet boy and you will not talk about him that way. He definitely has claws, but no fleas, as I already told you. How far away did he lead you?"

"About a mile and a half through scrub brush and steep woods, to an abandoned hunting shack."

"Wait, how were you tracking my mana?" she asked, rifling through her pack for something to eat.

"I have a unique ability that I share with only a handful of other wielders in known history. When a Vessel uses their mana, it releases a stream of tiny particles, even for a little while after they have closed off. I knew your signature from the seed blessing earlier that day, and I used my gift to follow the trail your 'sweet boy' left a few nights back. But when I realized that it was a false trail, I backtracked and used more traditional methods to find which way you had gone. I came upon you shortly after you had fallen asleep last night. And by the way, you snore loudly enough to wake the bears, so maybe we should find a better hiding spot tonight." He waved his hand to indicate the hollowed-out space at the base of the grandmother sycamore tree where she currently huddled in her blanket. "Not a bad spot, but way too easy to pick you off in your sleep."

"I don't snore," she corrected him. "And there is no 'we.'"

"You're right, it must have been the tree making all that noise. And I count two of us here, so that constitutes a 'we.'"

"I do not need, nor do I want your help. You can tell Ros that you did your best but...just leave me alone." She punctuated the last three words by slamming her fist against the tightly rolled fabric of her blanket, jamming it into her pack with more force than necessary. Belatedly, she remembered that her water skin was still inside, empty. She growled, then began emptying her pack once more.

"Sure, okay." Nox said nonchalantly. He bit into what looked like a piece of dried meat and chewed slowly, watching her.

"I mean it, Nox. Just go, this doesn't involve you," she insisted, pinning her water skin under her chin while she repacked her bag. "I've made it this far alone, I'll be fine."

"Yeah, of course. I'll head back soon. It's just that..." he trailed off when she fixed him with a glare. "Well, I've never really traveled the mountains like this before. Maybe hiking is growing on me. At the very least, I should give it an honest shot before I give up. I figure, I've already made it this far, I might as well keep going."

She stood. He did the same.

"You're just going to keep following me, aren't you?" she asked, ignoring the sting of pain as she slung her bag over her shoulder. "Even after I've asked you not to?"

"Nope," he said, picking his own pack up off of the ground and kicking clumps of dirt on the fledgling fire. "I'm just going to enjoy a nice walk through the mountains."

"Great, well, enjoy your hike," she responded, saluting him, and climbing the roots clinging to the hillside that led back to the trail. "I hope it grows on you." Just as suspected, he followed. Calen walked another hundred feet before she gave into the urge to release the torrent of irritation he had stirred.

"I don't need your help" she yelled, turning back to him. "No one has ever been there for me, and you will be no different! You know what, I don't care what you tell Rosalind. You can both sit in your lap of luxury, back at the capital, with your feet up, reminiscing on all the times you came to the aid of worthless mountain trash! Pat yourselves on the back and celebrate your heroics! Just leave me alone!" Her face heated with frustration. She knew from experience that he would be a formidable foe, if he chose to be, and that her outburst might incite his anger. But she had made the decision weeks ago that she would no longer make herself small in hopes of avoiding dangerous men. Instead, she raised her chin and fixed him with a glare.

"Well," he said, rocking on his heels. "Feel better?"

"Fuck you."

"Temper, temper."

"I'm serious. We've known each other for all of three days and you expect me to just trust that you will help me when I need it, but what on earth does that even mean? Help with what?" she yelled, throwing her hands in the air. "I know my way to where I'm going, I have a plan for when I get there. I know how to find food and clean water. I know how to handle wildlife if I should encounter it. How are *you* going to help me?"

He took the wind from her storm with one word.

"Stokely." The look on his face said he was no happier about the prospect than she was.

"Stokely?" she asked, her eyebrows shooting up.

"Yes," he said calmly. "Last night wasn't the first time I watched you.

Back at Old Roan, in the three days I observed the two of you together, he could never be away from you for more than a few minutes. I think we both know he's going to come for you. No offense, but I've seen him fight before, and I don't think you will be stopping him with a cheap shot to his manhood."

Calen stared in disbelief. Then a completely inappropriate bubble of laughter rose in her chest. She doubled over in near hysterics.

"I'm sorry," she said, after the bizarre need had passed, "but you want me to believe that if and when Stokely finds me, you will be there to protect me? You would fight your own 'Brother' should he raise his hand to hit me? Or pull him back when he pins me down and tries to choke the life from me? You would dare break the sacred bond that all of you First Order shitheads swear to one another? No, I don't believe you."

Nox took a few steps toward her, not entirely closing the distance. Her shoulders tensed in anticipation, and to his credit, he noticed. He stopped walking and held his hands out like she was a startled animal he did not want to scare.

"Let me be perfectly clear, Calen. If he should raise his hand to hit you or pin you down to end you, he is no longer my 'Brother.' He is a disgrace to our Order, and to men everywhere, for that matter. I will put my own sword through his chest before I let him lay a hand on you, I swear it."

Calen studied him for a long time, the jovial man from a few minutes ago replaced entirely by one of intensity and intention. She could see the sincerity in his eyes and she wanted so much to believe him, because he was right on one point. If Stokely found her, she would be all but defenseless against his physical ability.

"Yeah, well, we'll see, I suppose. You can say that now, but when push comes to shove, you all have each other's backs. That's been my experience, anyway," she said, lowering her eyes.

"Look," he said. "I will be honest with you, Calen. I didn't want to come here. I didn't want to do this. Rosalind...Rosalind had to twist my arm to make me find you. I personally think that this is something you should take to the Head of the First Order. But I'm here now. And if things are as bad as you say they are, I want to help."

She openly examined him, tip to toe, making mental notes of the myriad weapons strapped to his warrior's body. Boots that weren't appropriate for walking the miles that lay ahead of them, but clothes that looked warm and clean. Her eyes stopped on his pack.

"What's in there?" she inquired.

"Supplies. Some rations, water, matches, socks, map, quilt."

"Quilt?"

"Not all of us were in on the plan, so not all of us are entirely prepared," he said with a grin. Calen was convinced the man could not remain in a serious mood if he tried.

She narrowed her eyes at him and took a tentative step forward.

"Just know this, *Brother Nox*. I am not completely helpless. So help me, if you even think of betraying me, I will find a way to make you pay."

"Yes, as demonstrated," he said, and shifted his pants uncomfortably.

Calen inhaled deeply, then blew out a long breath between her pursed lips, turning back to the trail. "Well, come on then."

Following the light burble of a stream further down the trail, they took a short detour to refill.

"We're not all shitheads, just so you know," he said, watching the water fill his bottle.

She shot him a sidelong glance, taking a big swig from hers. She had run out of water the previous evening and had not trusted herself to find the stream in the dark. The water was bitingly cold and coppery, but she kept drinking until her belly was full and her thirst quenched.

"Yeah, I guess we'll see about that, too," she said, dipping her water skin back into the stream.

Nox chuffed a small laugh. "I can see why you two get along so well. She likes to give me a hard time every chance she gets."

"Us two?"

"Yeah, you and Ros. I imagine the two of you together are quite the force."

She felt the gut punch that always accompanied the mention of Rosalind. It was anger, but also longing, and a deep, painful loneliness that filled her. She tried to feign indifference, but it was pointless. The truth was, Calen did not know how describe the way she felt toward Rosalind. But apathy could never truly find a home in their relationship, no matter the time and distance between them.

"How is she?" Calen asked the stream. Nox started to answer, but she cut him off. "Never mind. It doesn't matter. We need to get back to the trail."

***

Nox

Rosalind had better wipe his slate clean after this little 'favor.' He had known this mission was likely to be challenging, but he was now on day three of hiking through some of the roughest terrain on the continent, accompanied by one of the most difficult women he had ever met.

She was not difficult, she was tough, he had to remind himself.

Despite their tentative truce, she showed no signs of warming to his presence and seemed to be intentionally challenging him. Every attempt at conversation was met with a short, sarcastic remark and the few times they had stopped to relieve themselves on opposite sides of the trail, she somehow emerged first and continued on without waiting for him. The last time, he had to jog to catch up with her.

Now, she was suddenly headed off the trail, making her way into a crevasse in the mountain. He could already see up ahead to where the space narrowed and emptied out through a small hole at the base of the rock, thanks to an enormous boulder that had fallen and wedged in the space between the two walls of the crevasse. He would never fit through.

It was a clever attempt, but she would have to try harder if she wanted to thwart him. Last year's fallen leaves crunched loudly beneath his boots as he opened his mana, focused on his legs, feet, and hands, and took a running leap. He launched skyward, landing ten feet up, atop the bolder, before deftly jumping off the other side, landing just as

Calen was crawling out from underneath. She stood, brushing off her knees, and shot him a look of pure annoyance.

"Really? Was that necessary?" she asked.

"How else was I going to get to this side?" he asked.

She had taken off the knit cap a while back, and he reached for the small stick that had lodged itself in the hair just above her ear. The act was meant to be innocuous, but Calen leapt back, flattening herself against the boulder. The annoyance on her face was quickly replaced by terror.

"Hey, hey," he said gently, holding up his hands. "It's okay, I was just getting that stick from your hair."

Her cheeks colored in embarrassment and she looked down at her feet.

"I'm sorry. I'm not...used to..." She looked up then, and he could see confusion warring with anger. "Just, back up," she mumbled.

"Sure, okay," he conceded. He had never seen someone so frightened by the prospect of human contact, and a growing feeling told him that maybe Rosalind *had* been correct in her assessment of the situation.

Calen edged forward as though she wanted to get past him, so he moved to the side and allowed her to take the lead again. He graced her with a moment to regain her composure before catching up, matching his long strides to her shorter ones.

"So, how many did you set?" he asked, hoping to tread on safer ground.

She pinched her lips together but said nothing. "Huh?" she finally asked.

"Back at camp, this morning. You asked me which false trail I had followed. I assumed that meant you had set more than one?"

"Oh, yes. Three total. You met Purrseus."

"A name he is mostly undeserving," he added.

"He is entirely deserving of being named after a hero."

"And the other two?"

"The second was a young doe who was ready to move her fawn back into the herd. And the third was a rabbit whose regular trail passed through the meadow just before the woods. I asked him on my way out. They all agreed to carry a pouch of dirt for me."

Had he just heard her correctly?

"They *agreed*?"

"Yes, how else would I have attached the pouches to them if they hadn't been willing? They would have run off if they hadn't wanted to help me," she said, her inflection implying that he should know this already. Perhaps she did not realize she was speaking nonsense.

"And... how did you get these animals to help you, exactly?"

"I asked them. I just said that," she answered, actually starting to sound annoyed.

He watched her face to see if she was joking, but her face remained a mask of mildly irritated calm.

"What?" she asked after several moments of his silence. "You just jumped ten feet straight up into the air like it was nothing, and you admitted to having a rare talent of your own. Is it so odd that I can communicate with animals?"

"Well, any fourth year at Black Rock has trained with their mana enough to be able to do what I did with the boulder. And my other gift is just that, rare. But speaking to animals? I've never heard of anyone being able to do that. Is that a specialty of ritual workers?"

"Well, it's not common. But it's not difficult, either," she answered, but then said no more. This was the most exciting thing to happen in days, and she seemed utterly bored by it.

"Use more words, please?" he prompted.

"You actually want to know how my gift works?"

"Yes. Doesn't everyone?" he asked. Nox was so certain that other people would want to know about her gift that he was already making a mental list of academics who would be willing to write a paper based on her knowledge.

"Most people don't know about it. Most people don't... I don't really get to spend a lot of time with other people," she finished sheepishly, tucking a stray lock of hair behind her ear. "It doesn't work all the time. The animal has to have mana of their own. I don't really know how that happens, but I assume they draw it in from the environment. A stream with mana that has leaked from the Well, or maybe even a smaller meteorite. Anyway, I'm not completely sure how they gain it, but they have to have mana of their own. It's how we connect," she said, winding the fingers of both of her hands together to demonstrate.

"I've wondered how it happens, too," Nox added. When she looked at him questioningly, he explained, "I can see their trails as well. I've always wondered how that happened, but no one really seems to know."

"Right," she said, nodding her head. "Anyway, when I open, I can kind of…I don't know how to explain it… 'go into' my mana and connect to them through theirs. Then, I just think of what I want to say to them and if they feel like speaking to me, I can hear them in my head." She smiled, then. A big, genuine smile.

"Calen, that's incredible," he said. "How long have you been able to do that?"

"Well, honestly, I have always had a strong connection to wildlife, even before I became a Vessel. I guess I'm like you, and it just sort of came along with the territory. The first time it happened, I was actually lost in the woods!" she exclaimed, growing more animated as she continued. "It was back at Grandview, and Rosalind and I were playing this game where we would run in opposite—never mind, that part doesn't matter. We were playing a game, and I got lost. Then as I was wandering aimlessly, I felt a strange pull toward this little black squirrel that had been following me, and somehow, I just knew that I could talk to him if I tried. It took me a few attempts, but I got it. He was rather cheeky, if I remember correctly. But he helped me find my way back."

He listened to her story and realized he was looking at a version of Calen that was happy.

"You must have some pretty amazing stories," he said.

Her smile faltered, then fell altogether.

"Not as many as you might think," she mumbled. And just like that, her high spirits were gone.

That was well done.

Rotation #6 had been Nox's least favorite obstacle course at Black

Rock. The traps were constantly changing, and you never knew when a floor tile was going to fall out from under you, or blunted knives would fly out from a hidden door. He still bore a large scar on his left rib cage where a jagged log had come swinging across the beam he was traversing. He had moved to dodge it, but not before earning a giant gash that had taken two weeks to recover from. Talking with Calen was lot like that obstacle course. He had no idea where the pitfalls were and how to avoid them.

***

The melancholic fog that had settled over them was in stark contrast to the gorgeous spring day. With the exception of an occasional warning about a slick spot, or an offer to share rations, they walked in silence. Calen had stopped challenging him, though, and their conversations were short but soft, so he felt they were still headed in a good direction.

Evening was setting in as they worked together to set up a simple camp in a well-hidden spot. They had built a small fire to cook the fish he had caught, which they ate with boiled fiddleheads she had foraged. Over the quiet crackling of flames, she cleared her throat.

"Can I ask you something?"

"Yes?" he drawled.

"I thought you were in charge of protecting the Archson?"

"That I am. Along with half a dozen guards when we travel. Plus, we are supplied with additional protection by the locals wherever we happen to be visiting."

"But you just left him back at Old Roan and chased after me?"

"Yes. Before we left the capital, we had both agreed upon a plan to find and help you. Before I left Old Roan, I let him know that the plan had changed and that I would come after you on foot. He was to stay back and provide support as needed."

She crossed her arms and sat back. He did not like the eerie feeling of being studied by her dark eyes.

"Why would you go through all that trouble just to help me? Really?

There have to be hundreds of people, if not more, who could use that kind of help. I'm not that special."

He leaned forward, holding his hands out to warm them by the flames. "I told you why. I did it as a favor to Rosalind." That same array of emotions played across her face. Longing, anger, hurt, forced indifference.

"And who is she to you that you would chase someone across the Green Ridge Mountain Range just because she asked you to? Who owes someone that kind of favor? Either you did something truly terrible, or the two of you are—" she stopped short, looking injured. "You know what, never mind. I don't want to know the answer. Good night, Nox." She shifted into her bedroll and put her back to him.

He could hear her trying to school her breath to calm but failing. Steepling his fingers between his knees, he decided to answer her anyway. How many times would he have to explain this before she believed him?

"Calen, I know it's difficult to understand. I myself have questioned what I'm doing here and how I got roped into this." He shook his head, still not entirely certain of the answer. "But here is the truth. To me, Rosalind is a dear friend. We work together at the Homestead of Whitehall. We both advise the Archfamily in our own respective ways. She is a dear friend and a work companion, and *nothing more*." He did not fully understand what had passed between the two women, but if his guess was correct, Calen's anger was at least in part due to a broken heart.

"I'm not a terrible person, and I haven't committed some kind of unspeakable atrocity. I'm not beholden to her that way, or any way, for that matter. She needed my help, and I gave it." He paused, her body unmoving across the fire. "You asked me earlier how she was. Last I saw her, Rosalind was lonely, and frightened for you, and torn between her duty to the Archmother and desire to help you. I don't know your history, but I know that I've never seen her want something as badly as she wants you to be safe and whole. That's the truth."

She remained still, but he hoped he had gotten through to her. When he crawled into his own blankets and looked across the fire to her once more, the jerky movements of her silent sobbing told him that maybe he should not have.

Seventeen

May 1, 622

Rosalind

"We will find them, Ros," Freddie said, marking a tidy *x* on the small map that was quickly becoming a tattered mess. Being opened, closed, and marked several times a day will do that.

"What if we don't?" she asked around the thumbnail she had pinched between her front teeth. "What if Stokely finds them first. How could I let this happen!"

"For the hundredth time..." he said, "this is not your fault. You did not turn that man into a monster."

"No, but I let him shove me out of her life."

He sighed, letting the argument go, and for that, she was thankful. There was only one path to absolution for her, and it was not through Freddie. She had spent every night on the road replaying the past eight years. Every night, remembering how hard she had fought for Calen in the beginning. And recalling, with a disturbing amount of shame, how their communication had dwindled toward the end. How, even though Calen was alive and vivid in her heart, she convinced herself that her business in the capital was more important than anything else. Not only was she responsible for the wellbeing of the Archmother, but she had also spearheaded an effort to pull Vessels from all Orders together and work for positive changes for that would make their lives safer and more productive. There were, of course, benefits to being an important person in Whitehall. Life had been luxurious, soft, and full of every kind of joy for her. It was somehow only occurring to her, *truly* occurring to her, that Calen was living a very different life all the while.

The worst of the nightly torture, though, came in the form of fantasies. What if she had fought harder? What if she had somehow helped Calen leave that partnership and find a life closer to Whitehall? What could they have created together, with all those days? How many precious moments could they have shared?

"You are going to chew it down to a nub," Freddie said, interrupting her reverie. She pulled her thumb from her mouth and examined it.

"Why don't they teach you healing at Black Rock?" she asked.

He looked at her as if she *had* chewed her thumb down to a nub. "You know that's not how it works, Ros."

"In practice, they don't teach it. But hypothetically, it could work. You could learn to use your mana that way."

"Yes, but if I'm busy using my mana to heal your nub, who's watching your back on this little jaunt we find ourselves on?"

"Good point. You can heal me, and I'll borrow some of Augustus' guards when we see him tomorrow. I really hope he can sense Nox more accurately. I worry that we are making too much noise, riding from one place to the next, asking after them."

"Do you have a better idea?"

"No," she conceded, looking out the window at the swiftly passing landscape. They had been on the road for the better part of five days, checking the typical inns they frequented when on the road with the Archfamily. Nox was like a rabbit when it left the warren. It may travel long and wide, but it always took the same path.

"We will find them," he repeated.

Eighteen

May 3, 622

Calen

Morning pushed through the weak light of sunrise under a blanket of clouds and the sensation of fat drops of rain landing on Calen's forehead. She blinked away the delicate crystals that had crusted on her eyelashes in the frigid air and sat up, pulling her bedroll along with her. They had crossed the threshold into May a few days back, but the mountain did not read calendars, and late spring cold snaps were commonplace. She had known to expect malleable weather and had planned accordingly, but she also felt a sinking disappointment as she looked around at the half-frozen puddles dotting the ground of their makeshift camp.

Nox was waking up just as she was, and she watched him across the cold pit where their fire must have gone out sometime in the night. He let out a curse aimed at the sky and began rolling his shoulders, wincing as they popped. Apparently, she was not the only one feeling rough after nine nights of sleeping on the rocky ground.

Nine nights.

It was simultaneously a lifetime of freedom, and also not nearly enough time at all. Nine nights away from Stokely, but only a small fraction in comparison to how many nights it would take to reach true, lasting peace. She just hoped that the sun would rise and aim enough of its growing strength to burn off the clouds threatening to slow their progress.

Nox rummaged through his bag, letting out an exasperated sigh as he revealed his water bottle, the liquid inside trapped by a thin layer of frozen slosh.

"We'll have to make a small fire," he said, glancing around the camp for any kindling that might have been spared. Calen knew none had been.

"We don't have time for that," she answered, her voice groggy from too little sleep. "We just need to get up and get moving." He looked at her with decided annoyance, the first negative emotion he had displayed in the seven days they had traveled together. Then, he rolled his neck, popping it to each side with eyes closed, and took a deep breath.

Just like…

No, she would not let her mind go back to that night. She had put too much distance between herself and that place where Stokely had hurt her in so many ways. She would not let those thoughts intrude on her now. She needed to focus on the man in front of her. He was no Stokely, but she still had the feeling he was about to explode.

But he did not lash out. When he did open his eyes and speak, his voice was even, if irritated.

"Calen, I know that you want to get to… wherever it is that we are going, but I think it would be prudent to warm up before we head out. I don't know about you, but every joint in my body is sore and I can't feel my toes." She could see his feet moving beneath his blanket as if he was trying to wiggle warmth back into said toes. "Our water is mostly frozen and we won't make it far without anything to drink."

No matter how badly she wanted to get moving, he was right. Her toes were numb, and she was already thirsty.

"Plus," he added, "he has to be out in this weather, too. It's just as likely to slow him down as it is to slow us down."

"Not necessarily," she said. "He would never travel on foot, unless every horse and carriage in the Colonies suddenly disappeared. He's not one for doing things the hard way."

"All the more reason for us to get off to a good start," he said, ducking his head into his pack, presumably to look for matches.

Calen dug into her own pouch, pulling out the knit cap and dragging it down over her ears, the shells of which were frigid against her head. Then she emerged from her bedroll and started to look for something to burn.

***

Five hours and several difficult miles later, the rain had yet to let up. It was coming down lazily, and Calen thought it might have been peaceful, had she not intended to spend the entire day hiking through it. The clouds had only released the bare minimum, but the shift in temperature that had accompanied them had turned the thin mountain air icy. Every inhale pulled shards across the back of her throat, and she had to blink constantly to keep her vision cleared.

One would have no clue that Nox was breathing the same uncomfortable air. He had regained his formerly chipper mood and was actually *whistling*.

"Do you mind?" she asked, rounding on him.

He stopped in his tracks. "Mind what?" he asked, with what she was beginning to recognize as unwavering sincerity.

"The whistling?"

"The whistling. What about it?"

"Well, in case you hadn't noticed, it's a bit loud. And in case you had forgotten, we are on the run. Trying to be inconspicuous?"

"Right. Well, in case *you* hadn't noticed, we can see for miles, and there is no one around," he said, throwing his arms wide to indicate the forest around them. "Unless you are worried that circling hawk back there is going to give us up? Maybe the squirrels? I hear they like to gossip."

She rolled her eyes at him and started walking again.

"Wait, can Stokely talk to animals, too?" he asked, sounding genuinely curious. "Did you two share abilities? Is that a possibility?"

"No. At least, I don't think so," she answered. "He's not exactly an open person. I know he has some pretty dark secrets that he keeps, and he guards his privacy fiercely."

"What do you mean by that?" he asked, his grin slipping.

"Well, he's not exactly 'standard issue' First Order."

"And what do you mean by *that*?" he asked in the silence that followed.

"He has...abilities. Nevermind, I don't want to talk about that. About him," she mumbled.

Nox had a disarming disposition that made her *almost* feel comfortable enough to open up to him, like maybe they could have been friends in a different life. He was honest, answering any of her questions freely and fully. He was helpful and polite, carrying his own weight and then some. And since the incident with the stick in her hair, he had been careful to keep his distance. At this point, she had accepted the fact that he wanted to help, and she was actually thankful for his companionship on this journey. Even still, there were certain things about her past that she simply was not ready to reveal to anyone.

They walked on, and he did not whistle anymore, but he did stay at her side instead of falling back as he had for most of the trip.

"So, how about this weather, huh?" he asked deliberately, holding out his hand to catch the now-pouring rain.

"How about it? It's mountain weather," she answered.

"It's *cold, rainy* mountain weather," he said. "And it's not letting up."

"So, we can build a bigger fire when we stop for the night."

"Sure. We can hope that no one sees the giant fire, and that we don't catch the forest ablaze."

She glared at him. "We will be fine, Nox."

"Or. Just a thought. We will freeze to death."

She walked on, ignoring his dramatics, and hoping he would let it go. He did not.

"*Freeze* to death," he repeated.

"What are you getting at, big guy?" she asked.

"One, thank you for noticing. And two, I have an idea. Hear me out," he requested, holding his open palms toward her. "There is a village..."

"No."

"...that we are going to skirt..."

"No."

"...where we could stop for the night..."

"Absolutely not."

"...and stay warm enough to *not* die. Yes?"

"Did you not hear me?" she said, shaking her head. "The answer is no. It's too dangerous."

"No, Calen, sleeping in the mountains, in a freezing rainstorm, with no cover, is dangerous."

"Rainstorm? You grew up in the south, didn't you?"

He let out a sigh but did not take the bait. "Draining our energy sleeping in this cold, wet weather, making ourselves weak, that is dangerous. What if something does happen and we need to fight? What if we need to run?"

"We will definitely have to fight and run if we are spotted in that village and someone tells Stokely!"

"Not necessarily," he said, pointing down into the basin of the mountain valley around which they were currently carving a path. "I know that village. That's Sandria. I have stopped there every time I've traveled to visit my family at the border. I've known most of the people in that village for most of my life, and we can trust them. We'll be safe there."

She refused to meet his eyes and continued to walk, trying her hardest to ignore the painful ache in her fingers.

"What's more," he continued, "I should make a call to check in with Augustus. He knew that my plan was to follow you, and I'm sure he has done his best to remain patient, but he hasn't heard from me in nine days. Even if he can sense me with our stone, he will be waiting for a call. If I don't check in soon, he might get spooked and send out a search party."

If the Archson sent people looking for them, it would be disastrous. He had the Consecration Stone, and he could find them fairly easily. Odds were good that Stokely had paid close enough attention to notice that she and Nox were both missing, and he would presume them to be in league. An Archfamily search party scanning the mountains would be like a giant arrow pointing straight at them.

"What's even more," Nox said, his voice pitching upward, "I should check in with Rosalind. She's undoubtedly aiding Gwendolyn in the capital, worn out and worried sick about you."

She expected to feel the familiar flush of anger and betrayal that had accompanied that name since she had received that awful letter, but it did not come this time. The lonely ache still blossomed in her chest, but Calen had spent a significant amount of the quiet that stretched out each day on the path thinking about Rosalind, and she was finding it more difficult to summon the resentment that had shored up the crack in her heart for so long.

Deep down, Calen knew that Stokely had interfered, putting a stop to the communications between her and Rosalind at some point. Rosalind was not to blame, Stokely was. He was possessive and cruel, and it did not serve his ends to allow Calen contact with someone who had loved and protected her as faithfully as Rosalind had. Still, there was one thing she could never reconcile. Why had not Rosalind come to Black Rock to defend her all those years ago?

"Hey," Nox said, waving his hand in front of her face, "you in there? You went radio silent there for a minute."

"How did she know?" Calen asked.

"How did who know what?"

"Rosalind. How did she know that I was in trouble? Why did she think I needed help? Or did she just wake up one day and remember that her best friend had been saddled for the past eight years with a monster?" She felt heat creep into her cheeks, but she bit down on her embarrassment. There was no way she would cry in front of Nox.

He watched her for a moment before answering. "Well, you probably won't believe it, I know it was hard for me to wrap my mind around. Although, a few weeks ago, I wouldn't have believed it was possible to communicate with animals, so..." he trailed off, lifting his shoulders in a shrug. "She said she had a dream of you a couple of weeks back. A dream, but not a dream, I guess? She said..." He paused again, looking away from her. "She said that she could see him hurting you. Rosalind said...she spoke to you...and she thought that you could hear her."

Well, there was the gut punch. She came to a stop, looking up into his deep green eyes. "What did you say?" she breathed out.

"I know, it sounds wild," he said, running his hand through his thick, dark hair. "But she was right, wasn't she?"

Calen nodded. "She told me to run. I tried, but—" She had to stop, emotion suddenly clogging her throat. Her legs felt weak beneath her. Making her way to a large boulder, she swept off the mat of old, wet oak leaves and sat, resting her head in her hands. "She...saw?"

"That's what she said," he answered.

What a beautiful gift to be given, only for it to be tainted in such a way.

"She saw."

Nox squatted down in front of her, setting down his pack. He opened the top flap and removed his water bottle, as well as two pieces of deer jerky and two small, hard apples. He offered Calen her share, then tore off a big piece of the dried meat, working it between his back teeth slowly. She began eating her own meal, thankful that he had brought something to compliment the dried flatbread and raisins she had scavenged from the inn's kitchen before leaving. They had not found much to forage in the past few days, and her rations were growing scarce.

"So, you know?" she asked him, the heat in her cheeks deepening.

"Not everything, I suspect," he answered, "but enough. So, it was all real?"

Calen nodded again, toying with the small stem still attached to the apple.

"Are you okay?" he asked, the tenderness in his voice surprising.

A pause.

"I guess. As 'okay' as I can be." She looked at him then, but he just chewed and looked back at her.

"You wanna talk about it?" he asked between bites.

"No," she answered briskly.

She watched him lower himself onto the frosty ground, leaning back on his hands, content to wait. He ate the apple in three bites, chucking the core into the forest, then spoke again.

"Calen?"

"Yes?" she said, still struggling to regain control over her emotions.

"We need rest. We need hot food and warm baths. We need to let people know that we are okay. I promise, we will be safe in Sandria." He lowered his head to meet her downcast eyes, but she looked away.

Her body sagged with exhaustion, and the mention of rest, hot food, and a warm bath did her in. They could be smart and quick, and hopefully they would be in and out before anyone even noticed they had visited the large village.

"Yeah, okay. We can go."

Nox smiled and hopped back up to his feet, extending a hand to help her up off of the boulder. "You are going to love Sandria."

Nineteen

May 3, 622

Calen

She hated Sandria. There was nothing wrong with the village, exactly, but being within the short walls made her feel trapped and anxious. Queasy and weak, her entire body racked with tremors as she tried to remember how to walk like a normal person. Worse, Nox was not even attempting to be inconspicuous. Yes, he checked down alleyways before they crossed, and discreetly looked over his shoulder once in a while, but he also walked straight through town as if he were the village elder.

"I don't like this," she whispered, again.

"We will be alright, Calen," he said, his voice as calm as the rain that still fell. "The call center is just down that road. Pull your hood forward a bit more, and your face will be entirely concealed."

She followed his instructions, but it did nothing to quell the feeling of being watched. Every time she looked over her own shoulder, she could swear there was a tall, lanky, red-haired boy following them. But then, he would cross the road or pretend to look into a storefront window.

"We are being followed," she said.

"That is possible," he agreed. "But it is also possible that you are afraid, and it is making you paranoid. Just walk like you belong. We can make our calls and find a place to stay."

"I don't like this. We should make the calls and leave."

"Calen, we will be okay. Just follow my lead."

He adjusted his cloak and stood straight, walking across the thoroughfare with what Calen considered to be entirely too much confidence. There was no way for her to follow that lead. Doing her best, she pulled her jacket around her and walked, holding the straps of her pack. What she would give to be able to put the damned thing down.

"How do you know he will get the call in time?" she asked. "We really cannot afford for him to send a search party. That would lead Stokely to us."

"He is particularly gifted with our stone," he answered, keeping his eyes on the path ahead. "He is probably close by. He knows my favorite inns, because they tend to be his as well. We also have a plan for him to be checking for messages from every Colony, in the event something strange happened, and we ended up on different paths."

"Good, that's good," she said, looking behind them once more. "And...what about Rosalind? What will you tell her?"

"Is there something you would like me to tell her?"

"Anything I have to say would be for her ears only."

"Really?" he asked, turning to grin at her. There was something in his expression that she did not understand.

She sighed. "What do you plan to tell her?"

"Well, for one, she was under the impression you would want to come back to the capital, to her. She needs to know that is no longer the plan. Would you like to clue me in to our final destination?"

She would *not* like to do that. Not yet. "No. If you are along for the journey, you will find out soon enough."

"Okay," he said, annoyance edging his voice. "Secondly, I will need to let her know that you are okay, and that I plan on staying with you until we get to wherever it is you are leading us. You understand this means that you are dragging the Archson across the Colonies blindly, don't you?"

"Yes," she conceded. "I am sorry about that. And I'm sorry that you got thrust into the middle of my mess. But...but I am glad you are here."

She risked a glance at him, her cheeks hot with embarrassment. He smiled. It was not his typical mischievous grin, but a soft, warm smile.

"We're here," he announced.

Pulling the door open for her, he stepped back and scanned their surroundings once more, and she could see the smile slip as she passed in front of him.

"We are being followed, aren't we?" she whispered.

His nod was quick and terse, then he swept her inside and followed.

"Nox, we have to leave."

"No, Calen. It's not Stokely. Think about it. Is he the kind of man to be skulking about a village like Sandria, peeking at us when we're not looking? Or would he be waiting at the gates, as dramatically as possible? Whoever that is, it's not Stokely."

That made sense. He was undoubtedly angry and ready for retribution. He would not be waiting quietly in some dark tavern corner. He would be impossible to miss.

"So then, who would be following us?"

"Probably an unclaimed mana wielder looking to pick our pockets."

"Unclaimed mana wielder? Is that what you call a stray?"

"I will be right with you," the call center attendant announced, emerging from a room at the back. "Not many folks out in weather like this, I'll need to get a line open for ya."

"No problem," Nox said. "We would appreciate a private room, if you've got one available."

The attendant smoothed his hands down the front of his shirt and nodded, disappearing into a small side room off the main waiting area.

"Yes, that is what I call strays. I find that term to be a little unfair. This place is a haven for them. A lot of the shop and inn keepers try to find useful ways to employ them. It provides a sense of dignity and allows them an outlet for what power they have. Unfortunately, they don't all get an opportunity, and some of them turn to less savory means of acquiring what they need."

Great. They had to worry about criminals on top of maniacs.

"Line's open," said the attendant, peeking out from the room, "come on back."

They made their way down to the room, but Calen stopped outside the door. "You go ahead. I'll stay out here and keep watch."

"You sure?" Nox asked.

"Yes," she assured him. "Go ahead and make your calls, then we can find somewhere to stay." The truth was, if she had a chance to speak to Rosalind, to send her a message, she did not know what she would say. I hate you? I miss you? How could you abandon me when I needed you most?

No, it was best she left those words unspoken.

PART THREE

June 20, 614

Revered Calendula

In the six years she had studied at Grandview, Amelia, *Calendula*, she reminded herself, had never been allowed inside the walled garden that lay tucked in the back corner of the grounds. Everyone knew about it, and students perpetually attempted to break in. But it was guarded by Vessels and mana alike, and no one ever succeeded. At least, not since she had been there. It had been a constant source of frustration, knowing that there was something so close that she was forbidden from exploring. She had even tried convincing a fox kit to sneak inside and report back, but the explanation he had given was jumbled and nonsensical. It had made her want to break inside even more.

But now...now that she was walking through the massive, arched gateway and into the garden, as an invited guest, she was grateful she had been thwarted. There was no way a stolen view in broad daylight could compare to the ethereal wonderland she was being welcomed into tonight.

The walled garden was, of course, a ritual space of the highest order. Tonight, upon their official initiation into the Third Order, her entire cohort had been dressed in ceremonial gowns and walked to the sacred place at dusk to take their vows. She was not sure she would be able to speak when the time came, being breathless as she was.

The archway itself hummed with energy that was welcoming and warm, and a thousand strange and beautiful voices sang to her from the stones leading to the central court. Her bare feet grazed the path and with each point of contact, a new layer was added to the harmony. The smell of summer lilacs floated and mingled with the crisp notes of running water, and she looked around for the source. A stream babbled and weaved beneath a footbridge just ahead. As she crossed it, some sort of long, orange fish darted between lily pads, and she jumped back in surprise, giggling. Across the bridge, the path passed under the bent frame of a willow, hushing in the night breeze. She reached out and brushed her fingers along the delicate branches, the lance-shaped leaves tickling her palm. Kiely, no *Rosalind*, squeezed her hand, and when Calen turned to her, the wonder in her friend's eyes stole what little breath she had. They were pools of emerald, wide, and rimmed with joyful tears.

"Look up," she whispered, and pointed an elegant finger skyward. Dancing within the canopy of the willow were small globes of light, in every shade of the rainbow. "Mana lights," Rosalind said, then placed her hand across her mouth. "For us."

They followed the gently moving tide of cream gowns beyond the willow tree, to the central courtyard. Once in the clearing, she could see that it was enclosed on all sides by willow trees, all twinkling with mana lights. The stone pathway created a circle, and in the middle lived the largest birch tree she had ever seen. Her fellow initiates spread out around her, but Rosalind held her hand tight and stood close enough that their arms touched.

"Welcome," intoned Revered Jessamin, from where she stood at the base of the birch tree. She spread her hands wide and smiled at the group. "Tonight, you are reborn into your new lives. You bring with you all that you have learned, all that you love, all that you are. You take with you all that you must protect, all that you must bless, all that you must be. Those of you prepared to take your vows and serve The New Colonies as members of our sacred Order, please prepare your offering and step forward."

They had not known what the words would be, but they had known what would be expected of them. One by one, the initiates of Calen's class lifted open hands and filled them with mana from deep inside. Rosalind's hand slipped from hers, and she did the same. Calen opened, her mana glowing bright and beautiful. It was really happening; she was joining her Order. Her mana swam down her arms and emerged from her palms. She marveled at it, wondering what it would be like to finally bless a field, or to heal an injury. What lovely gifts she would give.

When her turn came, she walked before the great birch and placed her power-filled hands flush to the trunk.

"May I?" she whispered.

You may, her mana answered within her mind. She pressed her hands and released the offering she held. It climbed beneath the bark and into the heartwood of the tree. Calen could swear the tree sighed, a delighted sound, and grew a small fraction. She was giddy with her own joy as she stepped back and rejoined Rosalind.

After the last of the newly minted Third Order Vessels finished with their offerings, the group gathered around Revered Jessamin once more.

"Congratulations, my fellow Vessels. And welcome to the Third Order."

Jessamin led the procession thrice around the birch tree, in silence save for the celestial voices that sang to them in turn, then they moved out of the garden on the path opposite the one they had entered. Beyond the exit gateway, a large crowd stood gathered, expectant. When she and her cohort stepped outside that sacred space, the throng erupted in cheers and clapping. Calen could hear Rosalind's laugh above it all.

"We did it!" she shouted, wrapping Calen in a hug. She buried her face in Rosalind's cinnamon hair, knowing it might be their last chance to embrace for some time. Rosalind had chosen her bonded partner, a tall warrior scholar from the First Order who, to Calen, seemed a bit aloof. If Rosalind had not been a decent fighter herself, Calen might have worried for her safety. After their stone ceremony later this evening, they would be headed with a large group of Vessels back to the capital, where Rosalind was hoping to find work as a healer. Calen would not be participating in the stone ceremony or leaving for the capital after.

Rosalind pulled away, waving to someone behind her.

"My grandma made it, Calendula!" Rosalind said. "Let's go say hello."

"I'll give you two a moment," she said, and sent Rosalind off with another quick hug. She scanned the crowd, hoping against all odds that maybe someone from her family had made it. By the looks of it, they had not. Her disappointment should not have been as potent as it was. They had not spoken to her since her arrival at Grandview, with the exception of a few letters her sister had managed to smuggle into town.

Someone *had* shown up for her, though, and he was sauntering toward her with a grin she could not read.

"Well, you've grown up," Brother Stokely crooned, examining her from head to toe in a way that made her feel as though she were being catalogued. Each piece of her assigned a future use.

"Brother Stokely," she said, making a small bow. It would not be ideal to draw attention to herself. Well, more attention. Their pairing was more than a little odd, and at least a dozen pairs of eyes were already watching the strange tableau.

"Are you prepared to leave?" he asked. "We are expected in Fertile in three days' time. We can stop in a few hours at a decent inn and stay the night."

"Tonight?" she asked. "But I thought we could stay for the stone ceremony. And there is to be a large breakfast in the morning to send us off. My friend..."

"Breakfast? You have just vowed to serve the Colonies and to honor our partnership as a Vessel, and you want to delay your duties for *breakfast*?"

So small and so young. Always so small and so young in his presence.

"I apologize," she said, blinking against the embarrassed tears that stung her eyes. "I can be ready to leave. Please, at least let me say goodbye to my friend." No matter if it made her sound immature, she would not leave without saying a proper goodbye to Rosalind.

"Be quick," he clipped out, then tugged at each of his sleeves to straighten them.

Calen turned away from him, trying to enjoy the merriment still ringing out around her. She wove through the crowd, smiling at the few friendly faces she saw, and ignoring the rest. Rosalind was waiting with her new partner at the edge of the lake that hedged in north side of Grandview. Someone had placed a flower crown on her head. Calen was struck by how uncomfortable she felt approaching, as if she were intruding. *They* were the pair now, or would be soon enough, and she was the odd one out.

"Brother Frederick, it is nice to see you," she said.

"And lovely to see you again, Revered Calendula," he said, with his voice like a boulder tumbling down a hill.

"Please, I think I just want to be known by Calen."

Rosalind giggled. "Still cannot believe you took that name."

"I'll be reminded of you every time someone addresses me."

The amusement on Rosalind's face slid into some other emotion, and she lurched, throwing her arms around Calen, who immediately returned the gesture.

"I'll see you at the ceremony," Frederick said, then slipped back toward the celebration.

"I'm going to miss you so much," Calen whispered, squeezing tighter. "I can't believe I'm going to be so far away...with him. And you will be in the capital. You are going to meet so many amazing, new people. Please...please don't forget me."

Rosalind pulled away enough to cup her cheeks and look into her eyes. "Hey, don't say that. You need to know that there is no one in this world like you, Millie." She smiled. "Sorry, *Calen*. I could meet every single person in every single Colony, then travel the world and meet every person on every continent. I could put them all together, and everything they would have to offer could not compare to one day spent with you. There is *nothing* that could come between us, do you hear me? Nothing."

Somewhere in the middle of the speech, she had begun to cry. "I hope that's true, because you are my best friend, and without you, I'm pretty sure I'm lost."

"You will never be without me. I will always be there for you."

They resumed their tight embrace, both sniffling.

"Don't play Run of the Trees with anyone else, do you hear me?" Rosalind finally whispered.

Calen laughed. "As long as you promise not to hum Frederick to sleep."

"Oh, no," Rosalind moaned. "I will have to share quarters with him, won't I?"

"Let's just hope he doesn't snore."

"Or fart."

"Or sleep naked."

The mention of nudity charged the air between them, and that strange, new sensation hummed beneath Calen's skin. Judging by the way Rosalind blushed, she had felt it too.

"Well," Rosalind said, "I guess I'll just have to lace his sheets with stinging nettles if he decides to sleep in the buff. That will cure the problem right away."

They both laughed, and the tension between them released. Rosalind's eyes caught on something behind her, but before Calen could turn, her friend spoke.

"He's here for you. I know you probably aren't staying, so this might be the last time we see each other for a while. Calen, I..." she trailed off, running her hands down the back of Calen's arms to take her hands. She took a deep breath. "Remember what I said. Anything you need, I'm yours."

"And I'm yours."

"Forever."

"Forever."

Twenty

May 3, 622

Nox

"Is that hot enough, sir?" the young man asked, shaking the water from his arms.

"Yes, that's perfect…"

"Fil, sir," he provided.

"Thank you, Fil," Nox said, pulling his own hand from the water and nodding to excuse the young man who had just used his hyperthermogenic mana to warm the bath. As much as he supported the gainful employment of unclaimed mana wielders, it was still a little uncomfortable to watch Fil's arms heat like glowing coals beneath the water and send steam up enough to fill the bath chamber.

His soft spot for unclaimed mana wielders was actually what had led him to this inn many years ago. Bastian, the innkeeper, took them in and found uses for their unique talents. The man had been born missing the lower half of his left leg but had refused to allow that fact to define him. He imprinted that spirit into the young people who made their way here. Nox had no doubt that the inn had ready access to running hot water but allowing Fil to work meant one more full belly and one less pickpocket on the road.

Once Fil had closed the door, Nox dropped the fluffy cotton towel from around his waist and stepped into the tub, sinking in up to his chin, immediately grateful to Calen for agreeing to stay. The water steamed where it met his still-chilled skin, and he could feel the warmth already seeping into his muscles. Once this was over, he was never leaving the comfort of the capital again.

Unlike his private bathing chamber at the Homestead, this one had multiple bathtubs and a steam room that were shared among the patrons at Bastian's Inn. There were actually two separate chambers, but no hard, fast rules for who could use each. Since they had both been empty at his and Calen's arrival, they had decided to part ways long enough to get cleaned up and dressed before meeting for dinner.

After taking an indecent amount of time to soak in the tub, Nox had finally climbed out and gotten dressed, then made his way down the hall that led to the center of the inn, where the entry hall and check-in desk were. The inn was set up with two long wings leading from the central chamber. The east-facing hall held the bathing chambers, a large kitchen, and a small common room where patrons could take their meals if they did not want to eat in their rooms. The west-facing hall held ten single rooms and five double rooms that were almost always occupied. He and Calen would each get a single, which was not ideal, but anything was better than spending the night in the cold rain.

Nox ambled slowly toward his room, where he was to meet up with Calen. The sleeves of his loaned shirt were supremely bothersome, being entirely too short and a bit snug around the biceps. He fought the urge to flex and move, not wanting to destroy the clothing Bastian had so generously provided from his own personal stash, but there was only so much a man could take. If he did find himself presented with the need to defend Calen, this shirt would be shredded in the process. He had been extremely thankful to be out of his muddy, wet clothes for the night, but he would be even more thankful when his freshly laundered clothes were returned to him in the morning.

Looking up from the interminable buttons that he couldn't seem to push through their loops, he spotted his traveling companion standing in the entry hall, a tension in her posture.

"Calen?" he asked.

Her hair was damp, and her clothing changed, but she stood eerily still, one foot in front of the other as though she had stopped mid-stride. He quickly followed her gaze to where it landed.

"Rosalind?" he heard Calen whisper.

Rosalind, who was never at a loss for words, stood ten feet away, just inside the front door of the inn. Her right hand pressed firmly into her stomach and her shaking left hand covered her mouth, looking every bit as transfixed as Calen as she nodded.

"I can't believe I actually found you," Rosalind managed to get out, her words sounding oddly choked.

Neither woman made a move. They just stared wide-eyed at one another across the weighted distance. Nox could not decide if it would be better to stay or go.

"Found me?" Calen asked.

Another nod from Rosalind. Fat raindrops clung to the cloak that rose and fell with her breath. She had only just arrived. Movement drew his attention back to Calen who had begun a slow, tentative march toward the other woman. They were merely feet away from one another when she stopped. Rosalind looked as anxious as he felt, the anticipation in the room reaching a fever pitch.

Then Calen closed the distance, throwing her arms around Rosalind's neck and burying her face in the loose, cinnamon-colored locks flowing out of the hood of her cloak.

"Oh, Calen," he heard a muffled voice utter, then Rosalind returned the embrace, wrapping her arms around Calen's waist.

"Did I seriously just travel all this way," he asked to no one in particular, "sleep on the ground, and put up with a week's worth of verbal abuse just to be outdone?" He threw his hands up. At least he would be able to go home now. "If anyone needs me, I'll be getting very full and very drunk in my room."

"Not so fast, you grumpy oaf," Rosalind said. "You can put those ridiculous biceps to good use and carry my bags to my room."

Nox thought about complaining, but he was fairly certain he would incur the wrath of both women if he pointed out that he was not, in fact, her servant. So, he settled for letting out an annoyed sigh before crossing the room and picking up the duffels.

"My biceps aren't ridiculous, these bags are," he muttered, and earned a small laugh from Rosalind. "And where will I be taking these?"

She fished in the pocket of her cloak for a key that she held out to him. "Room Five," she said, pointing down the hall. "It's the double at the end of the hall."

"I think you're right across from us," Calen said, her face emerging from the curve of Rosalind's neck. Strands of silky hair clung to her cheeks where he could see she had been crying.

"I'm just happy to be anywhere close to you again," Rosalind responded tenderly, brushing the hair away from Calen's face.

"Well, then," he mused. "What a happy reunion."

***

Sitting across the table from the two women, watching them talk animatedly, Nox never would have guessed they had spent years apart. After the initial shock had worn off, and they had come down from the emotional high of their reunion, Calen and Rosalind had settled quickly into a comfortable pattern. They spoke of the places that they had been since their last visit, and caught up on matters in the capital, all while setting the antique table of Rosalind's suite in preparation for dinner, which they had decided to take there. They worked together in a kind of dance, placing wine glasses and dishes, rearranging the seats and napkins and candles in unison, as if they had done this hundreds of times before.

It had been his job to get the fire going and as he watched from his station by the large, stone fireplace, he could not help but notice how the women unconsciously touched one another every time they were in a close enough proximity to do so. A quick grasp of a hand, a brush of hair of off a shoulder, a gentle stroke of a cheek. The affection was in stark contrast to that first day when he and Calen had traveled together. He had benignly reached toward her, and she had reacted as though he held a rattlesnake in his hand. Now, here she was, leaning halfway out of her own chair so that she could keep her hands intertwined with

Rosalind's on the tabletop as they awaited the delivery of the previously promised hot meal.

It was not jealously that tinged his thoughts, regardless of how he had joked before. He had not known Calen long enough to have forged that kind of bond with her. No, it was not jealousy, it was wonder. Rosalind had hinted at the type and severity of the abuse Calen had suffered as Stokely's partner, and he was amazed that she still had the capacity for the fondness that was on full display. That level of closeness was hard-won, and he thought he understood Rosalind's desperation from that day in the capital, when she had asked for his help. It felt like he was watching soul mates in motion.

He was also fairly certain they would not need a second room for Calen that night.

"I'm still a little confused," Calen said, unclasping a hand to reach for her water glass. "How did you actually find us? We hadn't originally planned on stopping here. We only came in to get out of the cold and make calls."

"Well, we had known your general direction and location by checking in with Augustus," Rosalind answered. Her gaze shifted to Nox. "He really is getting quite good with that thing. Your stone pointed us to this area of the mountains, and from there, Freddie and I did the math during the carriage ride. We knew you would be on foot. We knew you had been traveling for six days at that point, and that you would stick to the lower altitudes of the mountains to avoid wearing yourselves out too much. Once we homed in on an area we believed you would be, it was just a matter of retracing the path taken anytime we've all traveled with the Archfamily. You really are quite predictable, Nox. And for that, I'm thankful."

He smiled at her. He may not have had the incessant need to share her breathing space the way that Calen did, but he was happy to see his friend, nonetheless.

"Even still, it's pretty amazing that you actually found us," Calen said.

"Trust me, this wasn't our first stop. Brother Nox, here, insists on only staying where he can be absolutely certain he can trust whoever runs the place. He would never endanger the lives of Archfamily. We have been stopping at as many of our tried-and-true lodging sites and asking around, discreetly, to find out if anyone had seen you. No one had, so we kept trying. This inn was not our first stop on the 'needle in the haystack official tour,'" she finished, flourishing her glass in an arc to take in the whole room.

"Did you happen to see Stokely at any of those stops?" he asked, sipping his bitter ale.

"No," she answered, fidgeting. "But Augustus said his caravan was spotted in the vicinity. They were sticking to horse paths along the base of the mountain range, so they were harder to track. I was getting really nervous they would find your first."

"But they didn't," Calen said.

The creaking of metal grinding turned their heads to the door in unison. It stood ajar by a mere inch. Nox was up in an instant, flattening himself against the wall, his favorite dagger held firmly in his palm hovering at shoulder height. His muscles vibrated with mana, ready to react. He spared a quick glance at both women, frozen in place, just before the door flew open to reveal Brother Frederick advancing quickly inside, a hori hori knife raised in his left hand. He reached for Nox's collar just as Nox swung his left arm across his body into a defensive position, blocking the knife before it had a chance to advance. He and Frederick locked eyes in time to register that they did not, in fact, want to stab one another. They both stopped moving, but neither lowered their weapon.

"Boys, boys, you're both big and strong and very special," Rosalind said patronizingly. "Now, put the weapons away before one of you pokes out an eye."

Nox relaxed, lowering his arms, and closed off.

"A gardening knife? Really, Freddie?"

"A gardening knife will still make you bleed," Frederick rumbled.

Nox chuckled. "It's good to see you too, Fred," he said, and pulled the man into a one-armed embrace.

Frederick quickly returned the affection, then leaned out into the hallway to pick up the basket he had apparently discarded before entering the room. He offered it up for Nox to see and waggled the gardening knife with his other hand. It held stems with bright green leaves and small clusters of flower buds at the tips that had yet to open.

"Wild feverfew, for the Archfather's migraines," he explained. "Not the ideal time to pick, but beggars can't be choosers, I suppose."

Frederick slipped off a pair of boots, but he wore no cloak or coat. He had not gone far for the herbs. He would not have gone far from his partner. Frederick might look more like a woodland faerie than a warrior, with his mop of light brown hair, pale brown eyes, and gentle demeanor, but anyone who mistook his tall, lean stature as a sign of weakness would be sorely disabused of that notion the moment they attacked him or Rosalind. He had sparred regularly with Frederick back at Whitehall, and he knew that the man could shift from carelessly light to gracefully lethal in a heartbeat. He was also deeply overprotective of Rosalind and would not have left her if there was even a hint of danger here. If Freddie had momentarily wandered off, it meant that they could reasonably expect a night of peaceful sleep.

"Ros, all clear," he said in his usual lumbering tone, and they shared a nod. "Mistress Calendula, it's truly wonderful to see you here, healthy and well."

"Wait a second, your full name is Calendula?" Nox asked, amused. "As in, the flower? The bright orange flower that's pretty much the epitome of sunshine?" He waved his hand at her dark hair and pale face. "No offense intended; it just doesn't really make sense. How did you come to pick that name?"

The two women exchanged a look, Calen's face accusing and Rosalind's guilty.

"It's a long story," she said, just as there was a knock at the door. "And that had better be dinner."

Twenty-One

May 3, 622

Calen

 Calen could not remember the last time she had felt so full, literally, and figuratively. Dinner had been the most deliciously slow-roasted beef she had ever tasted, though her opinion was most likely skewed by the fact that she had been eating only rations for the past nine days, and Stokely-approved meals for the past eight years. She had absolutely devoured the buttery mashed turnips and potatoes and had unabashedly eaten piece after piece of the warm, fresh bread she used to soak up the juice that had escaped the mountain of meat she had piled onto her plate.

 All of them had eaten heartily, and enjoyed a bottle of rare red wine, which Bastian himself had brought to their table. He had been happy to share his supply with them, but had politely declined their offer to join their party for the evening. Everyone else was currently enjoying small ramekins of some kind of pudding that had been brought in for dessert, but she did not think she could eat another bite if she tried.

 As she sat sipping the last of her wine and watching her friends around the table, she could almost allow herself to believe that she was just a woman enjoying a pleasant evening with company she enjoyed. She could almost convince herself that she was safe here, that they were all safe here. She could almost imagine a world in which peace would follow her into tomorrow as she went about her perfectly ordinary life. She could almost.

The nagging weight that lived behind her rib cage reminded her that there was something she was in danger of forgetting. Delicately clearing her throat, she caught the attention of the other three.

"While this has been absolutely amazing, we should talk about what I plan—"

"No," interrupted a suddenly stricken-looking Rosalind.

Calen turned her warm, small hand into her own. "We have to talk about what happens tomorrow, and in the days following."

"No, we don't," Rosalind said, her eyes wide. "Not tonight, anyway. We've only just found each other, Calen. I know that tomorrow brings its own fair share of difficult decisions, but you are safe tonight, and we are together. *He* has had the last eight years, don't let him take tonight."

Both men shifted in their chairs, Nox studying his hands crossed on the table, and Freddie looking away toward the fire.

What had gotten into them?

Rosalind continued. "I just mean, I think I know what you are planning, Cal. I figured it out on the ride down here as well. Looking at the map, and tracking your trajectory..." She looked down at Calen's hand in hers and squeezed it a little tighter. "If you really are planning on leaving, *really* leaving, then...well, I think we deserve a night where we can just be us again. Pretend you never met that awful prick and have a night where you remember that life can be good, and that there are people right here who care about you."

In an instant, she was transported back to that time, so many years ago, when touching Rosie had stopped making sense. It had stopped being casual contact between two friends and had morphed into...more.

"We will talk, I promise. In the morning."

What would Rosalind look like in the morning? And why is it getting so damned hot in here?

Calen sighed but did not move away. "Okay, you're right," she said, nodding. "But it's still pretty early, I don't think I want to head back to my room quite yet."

"No, you shouldn't do that," Rosalind quickly responded. She was so close that Calen could smell the jasmine and vanilla oil she infused her bathwater and moisturized her warm honey skin with. The scent was familiar and pleasant, but somehow, she could not seem to breathe it in enough.

One of them really should tamp down the fire, it was getting stuffy in the suite...Yes, that was the problem.

"So, what do you want to do?" Rosalind asked, and Calen could feel each puff of warm breath that carried Rosalind's words as a caress on her own mouth. She spared a look to the men to see if they had any suggestions, but neither spoke. Freddie actually started to twiddle his thumbs, and Nox's eyes darted back and forth expectantly between her and Rosie. Whatever was wrong with them, it was apparently getting worse.

"I know!" she yelled, pushing her chair back from the table. The sudden movement and obnoxious scraping noise caused the other three to startle. "Cards! We could play cards." She looked at each of them in turn, her eyebrows raised in question, but they just looked back, puzzled, making her feel even more flustered.

"Of course no one brought cards," she said to herself, and realized that she was clenching the loose fabric of her borrowed pants in her fists. "I'll go check at the front desk to see if they have some cards we can borrow." Her legs were wobbly as she made her way to the door.

***

Within a few moments, Calen had procured not only a deck of cards, but a piece of paper and pencil to keep score for whatever game they decided to play. She rounded the corner of the hall, making her way to the end where all their rooms happened to be, but Freddie and Nox were leaving the suite as she approached.

"Where are you two going?" she asked. "I don't know any games for two players."

"You sure about that?" Nox asked, a sly grin forming under his mustache.

"What's that supposed to mean?" she asked. He did not explain.

"Good night, *Mistress Calendula*," he said, before unlocking the door to his room and disappearing inside.

She turned to Freddie. "And what about you?"

"Uh, yeah. No games for me tonight. I actually thought...I thought that perhaps I could check out your room, see what the amenities are like here. We always stay in a double when we're here..." He completely avoided eye contact with her.

"What on Earth are you talking about, Freddie? My room is like yours, just with a smaller bed and less furniture."

He cleared his throat and risked a quick glance at her. She could see that his cheeks were tinged pink. "Still. Perhaps I could just spend some time in your room, and perhaps you could spend some time with Rosalind? Have a... private moment together?"

A private moment. Alone with Rosalind. There was the humming beneath her skin, once more making her feel warm and... Realization hit her like a bolt to the chest.

It was not that she was naïve, just inexperienced. But now that it had been put in front of her, the puzzle pieces all fell together. The men had been acting strangely because they had recognized the tension in the room that was the natural product of her chemistry with Rosie. They had probably noticed how her body had been reacting to it all night. She suddenly felt embarrassed that she had not realized what was happening sooner.

Maybe the fire was too hot? Really?

Not that it was entirely her fault. She was no virgin, but she had never had a romantic experience that was actually pleasurable, so how should she know what it would be like to actually want someone that way? She had never once found herself attracted to Stokely. She had known exactly what kind of man he had been from their first meeting, and he had repulsed her even then.

Rosalind, however...made her want to squirm a bit. It had not been that way for the entirety of their friendship, but at some point, in their last year at Grandview, everyday interactions had developed an added layer of complexity. It was as though their lives had developed a new texture that neither knew how to explain, and both were too afraid to explore. Eight years later, Calen thought she could finally recognize what it was. They *wanted* one another.

That was surely not what Rosalind had meant by saying that they could have this night to be themselves again? Was that really a luxury that they could afford right now?

Freddie seemed to read the conflict on her face. "You okay?"

"Yeah," she mumbled, rubbing her hand down her face. "Just, um. I don't know…"

"Calen, she cares about you a great deal," he said. "Ros misses you, and just wants to spend time with you. In fact, I'm surprised she didn't kick us out the minute we finished with dinner."

"She kicked you out?"

"Didn't have to."

She pinched her lips together, thinking. The playing cards were growing damp in her clammy hand, and she wanted to fidget, but she stilled her body and looked to the suite door, as if it would somehow give her guidance. The emotions warring inside of her quieted, and the confusion and nervousness were pushed to the periphery of her awareness as she was pulled by the overwhelming need to be close to Rosalind. The same thing had happened earlier, in the entryway. Calen had seen her standing there, as breathtaking as always, and any hesitation had fled before the force of Rosalind's tug on her heart. Truly, there was nowhere else she would rather be in that moment.

"Okay," she whispered. She handed him the cards and reached into the pocket of the soft, over-sized pants for the cool metal room key. He wrapped his long fingers around the key and pocketed it, inclining his head.

"Have a lovely evening, Calen," he said, then turned to the door across the hall.

"Freddie?" she said, and he glanced back once more. "I care about her a great deal, as well."

He smiled. "I know."

"I hear the single beds are amazingly comfortable, you should...you should try that one out tonight."

His smile broadened. He unlocked the door and stepped inside. She made her way to the suite door and entered quietly. Rosalind stood by the fire, stirring the logs. She looked up when Calen entered, and her breath caught, the iron poker in her hand all but forgotten.

"I tried to get them to stay," Rosalind said, shrugging.

"It's okay," Calen said. "I think they wanted to give us some privacy to..." To what? Talk? Sleep? *Not* sleep? She could tell by the slack look on Rosalind's flushed face that her mind had run through the same list of options, and her mouth fell open. "Talk!" Calen blurted out. Both women laughed, and the tension in the room eased. It was still there, thick and charged, but more of a comfortable hum than it had been a moment ago. Rosie raised her eyebrows at Calen and held her hand out to the small couch by the fire. She crossed the room and flopped onto the couch, grabbing a pillow to hug, and Rosie joined her a moment later.

"I don't know how they expect either me or Freddie to sleep on this thing," she said, eyeing the couch. "It's too short for either of us, and they're crazy if they think I'm sharing a bed with him. He flails." She flopped her arms around to demonstrate, and Calen laughed again. Rosalind stopped moving and watched her, as if enjoying the sound.

Rosalind tucked her legs up under herself and leaned forward onto her own pillow. She noted absentmindedly that the tailors in the capital must charge extra for thread strong enough to keep all of Rosie's curves contained in a dress that tight, then immediately shut down that train of thought.

Just a private moment to talk, which was all it was.

Rosalind began fidgeting with the trim on the pillow, her eyes darting back and forth. "Calen, I have so many things I want to say to you, and I don't know where to begin." She looked up then, and the anguish in her eyes was unbearable. "I'm so sorry," she said, just above a whisper. "I promised I would always be there for you. And I wasn't. I tried. I really did. I swear it. But life...life just got so busy and hectic in the capital. And I know that's no excuse. I made a vow to protect you, and I didn't. I'm just so, *so* sorry. Please forgive me—"

"There is nothing to forgive," Calen interrupted her. She took Rosalind's hands. "Rosie, there is nothing to forgive! We were just kids back then, and I had no right to think you should spend your life saving me. I was scared, and you were strong, but it was unfair of me to expect that! It's not your fault that he is a fucking monster, and it's not my fault, either. But it is my responsibility to stop him, and I'm going to do that."

"By running away? Do you think that will actually work?"

"Rosalind, I'm not just running away. I'm *disappearing*. I've sent letters to Brother Marcus at Black Rock as well as Revered Jessamin at Grandview, Seeker Pierre, and the Archfather. I've given them everything they need to strip Stokely of his title and pull his mana. There is no way I will be denied justice this time."

"This time?" Rosalind asked.

"Yes. Five years ago...the hearing at Black Rock? Remember? You were summoned but you declined to show up—"

"What?" Rosalind asked, reeling back on the sofa.

"It's okay, I understand you had a lot of responsibility back then."

"No, Calen," she said, shaking her head. "I never received a summons. You think I would have declined? Not for all the coin in the Colonies!"

Calen's shoulders slumped. "Are you...serious?"

"Absolutely! I was never called to Black Rock, Calen. I swear it."

So, Rosalind had not abandoned her in that hour of need? The anger and shock in those green eyes told the truth. She had never been summoned.

"That corrupt bastard. I knew Brother Finneas was dirty, but I had no idea it was that bad," Calen said.

"That's why he's gone, Cal. He lost his position two years back after the Seekers discovered how unworthy he had become."

"Three years too late."

"Yes, three years too late. But maybe that means you don't have to leave? The new Head of the Order could—"

"No," Calen cut her off, shaking her head. "I cannot stay here, for one more moment than necessary. And I cannot put other people in danger. He will come for me, there is no stopping what I've put in motion."

"But you could learn to defend yourself," Rosalind said, rising to her feet. "You were always so strong, before. You could use your mana to protect yourself!"

"I *was* always so strong," Calen clarified. "Not anymore. I barely use my power, and I stay closed most of the time. Working rituals has become really difficult lately. I don't think...I don't think I could do more than that."

"What about when you're fully open?" Rosie asked her. "What does it feel like, how does your mana behave then?"

Calen traced the pattern on the pillow and waited for Rosalind to sit beside her again. "I wouldn't know. I don't do it."

"Why not?"

"I never have, Rosie. It scares me, especially lately. These past few years, my mana has just gone completely wild. I don't know. I guess I'm afraid to try."

Being 'fully open' was a tempting prospect, especially the way she had heard it described in the past. Most ritual workers spent their energy opening their mana just enough to wield it to achieve a goal: a seed blessing, a healing, a marriage union. But there were times that they were called upon to allow their mana to flow freely throughout their body in order to affect a group of people, or a large area of land needing deep recovery. It was said to be a transcendental experience, and one that actually made the Vessel more powerful, instead of less.

"You're afraid of your own mana?" Rosie asked. Calen nodded.

"What if I could help you? I'm not supposed to talk about it, but back at the capital, the work I'm doing with the Archmother has taught me so much. Her mana is unruly, also. It travels and enters her brain." She waved her free hand around the crown of her head. "Makes her see and hear things that aren't there. I've pretty much become an expert in how to use my mana to help control hers. Maybe I could do the same for you? Keep you safe if things go sideways?"

"Wait," Calen said, surprise raising her eyebrows, "you want me to open fully, here and now?"

"Sure, why not?" Rosalind answered.

"Oh, I don't know. Enclosed spaces, lots of breakable objects, a maniac hunting me who can use my mana signature to find me?"

Rosalind studied her, stroking the back of Calen's hand with her thumb. "Calen, what if you are powerful enough to take him on, and you just don't know it because you've never really discovered what you are capable of doing?" Truthfully, she had never even considered that possibility. "More importantly, when are you going to stop letting him *take* from you? I know you are afraid it will draw his attention here, but this power is yours," she said, resting her hand on Calen's lower belly. "You deserve to know just how strong you really are."

Something about the warmth in Rosalind's touch set her head spinning and made her feel a little reckless. "You're right," she said. "This is my power, not his."

Rosalind's eyes lit with joy. "So, you want to try? I promise, I'll keep you safe."

"I know you will," Calen said, smiling.

Rosalind hopped up from the couch and walked to the bed, throwing the blankets back and moving pillows to form a nest in the middle of the mattress.

"What are you doing?" Calen asked.

"Well, the first time you try this, you should be as relaxed and comfortable as possible," Rosalind answered, and waved for Calen to join her. The invitation sent a pulse of heat through her body. She walked to the other side of the bed and crawled to the center, aware of Rosalind's gaze on her.

"Lie down," Rosalind instructed, her voice a husky whisper. Calen obeyed. "Close your eyes and visualize, just like opening for a ritual." Rosalind's mouth was so close to her ear, and all she could think of was getting drunk on the scent of jasmine and vanilla. She pushed the thought away and tried to concentrate, gently running her consciousness along the sides of the power resting at her core, and it awoke, swirling about playfully. The turquoise being shimmered and changed from light to dark but did not expand much. She could almost sense a fearfulness. Even its gentle song was subdued.

"Do you mind if I use my mana?" Rosalind asked.

"Go ahead." Her voice was low and heavy.

She watched as thin tendrils of Rosalind's power joined hers. They were coral pink, strong, and sure.

"Calen, you're pulled in so tightly. Try to relax and let the energy flow through you."

Once again, Calen followed. She took a deep breath and tried to release the tension from her body. Then she invited the swirling ball of power within her to send out tendrils of its own. It grew, and began reaching out from its center, but still seemed hesitant. Rosie's mana moved slowly, but with purpose, brushing up against hers and coaxing it to flow. Eventually, her power built and changed, expanding outward from a hard, tight core to a soft, airy cloud. Just as Rosalind began to pull back, her mana broke free, filling every cell of her body. Every inch of her suffused with power in an instant, the energy moving, ebbing, and flowing and overflowing and ebbing again.

Like watching a performance of dancers, Calen could see the pattern and texture of every cell in her body as they lit up with turquoise and came alive like they had never been before. There was no part of her that had not merged with her mana and as spectacular as the experience was, it was also terrifying. Somewhere in the distance, she could hear Rosie reminding her to stay calm and breathe, but all she could think of was how overwhelming the power was. She was going to break and slip beneath this alien thing, just as she had all those years ago.

"Breathe," Rosalind whispered, sounding suddenly close. "You can do this."

Inhaling as deeply as she could, Calen felt her power press against the confines of her skin. What would happen if she could not get it to stop? As if finally sensing her fear, her mana halted, then slowed, then settled. The gripping terror slowly gave way to something more akin to excitement, and Calen realized that she actually felt good. *Really* good.

There was no anguish, no pain, no screaming; just the rapture of celestial power flowing through her body and the increasing realization of just how close Rosalind was, which was a decadence in and of itself. Her skin was ablaze, like a thousand tiny explosions of pleasure. Gooseflesh rose along her arms and the sensation of her own clothing was almost too much to bear. Her mana's song, *her* song, had reached its crescendo, and it had the most exquisite harmony. Her heart fluttered effortlessly in her chest.

She opened her eyes and through dark lashes saw Rosalind resting on her elbow, looking down at her, a living goddess. A languid grin found her full lips.

"There you are," Rosie said.

"This is incredible," she said, blinking. "How is this even possible? It doesn't hurt. I just feel amazing, and powerful."

"You are amazing and powerful," Rosalind said, leaning in closer, "and so very beautiful."

Rosie lifted the hand resting on Calen's belly and brought it to her face, tracing the pad of her middle finger from Calen's forehead slowly down her nose, to her lips, then around the curve of her chin. As Rosalind's finger trailed deliciously down her throat and found its way to the crest of her clavicle, Calen let out a soft moan that she would swear belonged to someone else.

Her breath grew entirely too shallow and ragged for comfort. It had been such a small gesture, but it was by far the most intimate way anyone had ever touched her.

"Cal," Rosie's voice came, soft but warning. "There is something you need to understand. You really are more powerful like this, but you are also more vulnerable. You have to be careful when you're fully open. Do you know what I mean?"

She nodded that she did understand, but of course, she had no idea what Rosie meant. All she knew, in that moment, was that she could wield this power to far greater ends than she ever had before. It was also obvious that Rosie's voice was a perfectly tuned wind chime dancing in a soft summer breeze, and the gold and green flecks in her eyes were locked in a sensual swirling motion. She desperately wanted Rosie to touch her again. A giggle escaped her lips, and Rosie smiled.

"I forgot how powerful *that* feeling is the first few times you open fully."

"I feel drunk. Is it always like this?"

"No. It always feels wonderful, but you learn more control over time." Rosalind reached to sweep away a lock of errant hair, but Calen caught her hand and pulled it to her chest, interlocking their fingers. The warmth of her palm was both too much and not nearly enough. She needed more.

"Kiss me, Rosie."

"Calen, I've waited to hear those words for ten years, but I can't," she explained, tenderness and regret in her voice. "Not like this. You aren't yourself right now, and I would be taking advantage of you."

"Okay. Well then, how do I close off? I've never had to pull in my power this way."

Rosie smiled again. "Are you sure you don't want to stay there just a little longer?"

"Not if it means I can't have you with me," Calen said. She would have the rest of her life to explore her power this way, once she found her way to safety. She only had tonight to explore this need with Rosalind and even drunk on her own power, she knew that the latter was every bit as important as the former.

"Okay then," Rosie said, "I will help you. Just take your time."

Calen focused, and a moment later, coral-colored power was within her again, circling her own mana, tucking it back into smaller tendrils and coaxing it down into her belly. Just as she had done after every ritual, she clenched down around her power and closed off. Unlike every ritual she had ever done, her mana did not weep, and there was no pain. In fact, she felt completely different now. Her mana calmed as she expected it to, but it somehow seemed more solid, and it still glowed within her. It rested, but peacefully this time.

She felt more level, like she had mostly returned from the trip. Rosie was playing with a lock of her hair, humming.

"Welcome back," Rosalind said playfully. "How do you feel?"

Instead of answering, Calen sat up, close enough to count the pale brown freckles that specked Rosalind's delicate nose and kissed her.

Twenty-Two

May 3, 622

Rosalind

Calen was kissing her. For a heartbeat, Rosalind was locked in place by shock, but it quickly passed as she realized Calen was kissing her. What else was there to do but kiss back? She adjusted her mouth just so, and her lips locked in a perfect fit with Calen's full, beautiful pout. Sliding her fingertips into the soft hair at the nape of her neck, she pulled Calen in closer and parted their lips with the slide of her tongue. The tender skin tasted of the remnants of good wine.

Their mouths remained sealed in a slow, sensual kiss as Calen rolled onto her back, allowing Rosalind to press into her with a wanting body that had waited so long for this moment. But where Calen's hands should have been exploring her curves, they were held out to her sides, as if she did not know what to do next. A wave of surprise and shame flashed cold within her, remembering what Calen had only recently been subjected to. Was Calen trying to move *away*?

Rosalind placed her hands on the pillow and pushed herself from the heat of the kiss.

"Shit!" she blurted. "Calen, I'm so sorry. I just...I just..."

She just, what? Begged forgiveness not thirty minutes ago, then assumed all was perfect between them? Assumed Calen wanted this as much as she did?

"You just stopped kissing me," Calen said, with a voice like liquid velvet, her large, dark eyes hazy and her cheeks flushed. "You should kiss me again."

"No, I shouldn't. I'm sorry."

"You're sorry for what?"

"For assuming that...this was okay. I was ready to devour you whole, without even asking if that's what you wanted."

"I'll be honest, Rosie, I don't exactly know what that means," she said, and her blush deepened. "I don't really know how this works. But I'm willing to let you take the lead. I mean, if you want to."

The vulnerability in Calen's voice was almost too much for her to handle. How had she not done more to protect this woman? Did she even deserve this? How could she ever go back to a life without her in it, every day? She leaned in and kissed Calen, but more tenderly this time.

"Calen, I will show you everything, if that's really what you want. I will give you everything I have," she said. Though that last part was a lie, Rosalind knew. Calen already had everything. "But I also want you to know that we don't have to do this. Not now, not ever. I have always been yours, and I will always be yours."

Calen was shaking her head softly. Her dark, thick hair had dried in loose waves that were spread out across the pillow, tickling her wrists.

"Don't do that," she whispered. "Don't treat me like I'm broken, please."

"Oh, Cal. I know you're not broken," she said, rubbing the tip of their noses together. "But I also know you've been through so much. And he...he hurt you."

"Yes, he did. But you aren't him. Don't you think for even one moment that you are like him." Calen's hands finally found her, gripping her waist with an intensity that matched her words. "Besides, weren't you the one who pointed out earlier this evening that I should stop letting him take from me? I might not understand how this works yet, Rosie. But I know I've wanted this for a long time. I've wanted *you* for a long time. He has stolen this moment from me, *from us*, for eight years, and I won't let him have it for one more night. I won't let him have me." Calen brought her hands to the sides of Rosalind's face, her fingertips grazing the sensitive flesh just behind her ears and pulled her back into a kiss.

Rosalind melted into her, and Calen's tongue rose to meet hers in a kiss that lasted an eternity before they came up for air.

"Calen, look at me," she said, and her breath caught at the sight of those incredible eyes on her once more. "I need you to know that if it's too much, if you want me to stop—"

"I know," Calen interrupted.

"I will stop. I don't want to hurt you."

"I know. I trust you."

Those three words made her chest ache in a way it never had for anyone else. *I trust you.* No matter what tomorrow held, and all the days after, she was going to earn those words from Calen with every opportunity she was given. Tonight, though, she would make the years worth the wait.

Closing the distance, their mouths crashed together once more. Calen's hands found their way down to her hips, and the two shifted until Rosalind was nestled between Calen's thighs. She began trailing kisses down the side of Calen's neck, stopping at sensitive spot that made her gasp. It was taking every ounce of willpower to maintain control, but she needed to take her time and live in every second. She wanted to commit every breath to memory.

Their embrace changed and grew furious, each desperate for more. Dress and blouse and pants and undergarments came off in a flurry of motion and before long, there was nothing between them but heat and need. The feel of herself flush with Calen's soft, warm skin was almost enough for her to come undone. Their bodies pulsed in perfect rhythm, pushing one another deeper into passion, closer to release. Her hands moved of their own accord, exploring every inch of Calen, giving pressure exactly where she knew it was wanted.

Breathing became panting, became moaning, became an incensed song of craving. She pressed into Calen's mouth, swallowing the needy sounds escaping it. Calen went over the edge, crying out as her body surged with years of desire finally fulfilled. Her legs began to shake and close around the sensation, and her chest rose and fell in jagged breaths that filled the space between them as Rosalind broke the kiss and pulled away. One of Calen's hands was fisted in the blankets that they had not even bothered to crawl beneath, and the other was gripping Rosalind's thigh, her fingertips digging for purchase against the intense euphoria racking her body.

"Is that what it's supposed to feel like?" Calen asked.

She laughed against Calen's chest, nodding.

"Is there more?"

"Absolutely." Taking her time, she dragged her swollen lips between Calen's breasts and down her belly, eager to explore with her mouth where her hand had so recently been. Calen let out a cry of elation that calmed into panting whimpers. They moved more intentionally, now, the two of them creating an intimate dance that was accentuated by the slide of one pair of hands tracing the curve of smooth thighs, and the other pair tangling in strands of cinnamon hair.

Rosalind was lost, completely intoxicated by the heady mixture of the scent and taste of *her*. They swam together in the liquid heat of passion, Calen moving steadily closer toward that rush of exhilaration, with Rosalind close behind. She could live in this moment, forever. After tonight, there would be nothing beyond her closeness with Calen. Never again would she allow this woman to be hurt. Never again would she need to seek forgiveness. And never again would Calen forget just how deeply she was loved.

"Yes," Calen moaned into the warm night air, and they both went over the edge, bonded in a way that no one else would ever touch. She would live in this moment forever.

Twenty-Three

May 4, 622

Stokely

Stokely watched Jinn sweep into the dark, quiet room that served as a meeting place for True Eternal members. The cabin was old and run down, but no one had lived there for quite some time, and it was only used sporadically for members to touch base after long periods apart, or to pass off smuggling victims from one kidnapper to another. He was not technically a member, despite numerous attempts on behalf of the leadership to recruit him to their cause. As it stood, they shared a set of ideals and resources that each needed, so a tentative partnership had been formed, but nothing more. He was reluctant to give up his standing with the First Order, which he would ostensibly be forced to do, should he join with Jinn and her merry band of psychopaths. Being First Order simply offered too many juicy little luxuries that he was unwilling to give up until he was required to do so. He may have believed in the teachings of the leader of True Eternal, a figure known only by the name Temple, which in actuality were the same teachings that had been passed down from one generation to the next (zero originality required on the part of their current figurehead). But True Eternal had yet to prove they could give him the kind of power he could *take* as a Brother of the First Order.

Power that would be within his grasp soon, he was certain. He had felt the seismic shift in his chest that always accompanied the successful location of his partner by their shared consecration stone. Calen had been stupid enough to open to her power this evening, and he had ample opportunity to get a lock on her general location. Something had changed, he was sure. The feel of the pull was different than in times past, as if she had somehow pushed against him, but he would figure that out later. For now, he was downright giddy with the realization that she was so close, as the Stone was never that powerful across any distance. He would have her in hand by week's end.

Jinn made her way from the front window, where she had been speaking with a small group of strays who had gathered here for the night hoping to find a safe place to sleep on one of the myriad pieces of disgusting furniture strewn about the place. As she approached his isolated corner, she slowed her steps and took on a more deferential bearing.

He knew that her reverential attitude toward him was due to two separate, but conveniently intertwined reasons. The first was her standing with True Eternal. Women were always expected to defer to men, always. It did not matter that she was a breath's space away from being a member of leadership, the distance would always be a chasm she could not cross. It did not matter that she was often the strongest and smartest among them. She was still a woman, and women did not hold control. In a disorienting contradictory stance, Jinn was such a strong supporter of True Eternal and their ingrained hierarchy, *because* it kept her in place, not *despite* that fact. She relished her subjugation and believed that, as with all women, it was the true order of nature.

The second reason she softened around Stokely was far more banal. She was desperately in love with him.

Blessed Vessel, he missed Calen. In his more honest moments, he knew he was possessed of her. He longed for the feel of his fingers closing on her elegant swan's neck, the way she dug her fingernails into him, no matter how futile the effort. His muscles strained for the fight she would put up, to be required once more to subdue her. He missed the sting of unpredictable words from the woman who refused to cow under his condemnation. Something, well, everything about her, made his body sing in anticipation of their feuding.

But Jinn? Not so much. She was tall and wiry, with a face like a hawk and a body that needed more meat on it. She was not without her merits, however. Never one to push back against mistreatment, Jinn offered a different flavor for him to enjoy.

As it had turned out, she was quite the masochist. She offered no resistance and actually enjoy the hurt and humiliation he leveled at her en masse, and he found that it could be a pleasurable sort of release for him, too, if not exactly what he wanted. Her own blood was her aphrodisiac, and he suspected that she had never met someone as willing to cause her pain as he had been. Hence, the pathetic puppy dog eyes that swiveled his way before casting downward again.

"Master," she bowed. They never used his formal First Order title for fear of wagging tongues that might jeopardize their alliance. He never wore his own clothing or jewelry, and he was referred to simply as "him" or "Master." He had heard some Eternal members refer to him as "Jinn's friend," which was about the most specific modifier he allowed to be used. Odds were good that some of them knew his true identity, but the more they did to keep it under wraps, the less likely he was to incur the wrath of the First Order.

"We have word from one of the local strays that your partner and her companion have been spotted at an inn in Sandria, just southwest of here by half a day or so," she said, refusing to meet his eyes.

Sandria. Well, that was even closer than he had thought. Stokely had been there on several occasions, as it was a large mountain village that held the shop of Minoken, a man known for his craftsmanship with watches. His had been a family heirloom given to him by his grandfather, the last man he had ever respected on this Earth, and Stokely considered the watch to be one of his most important possessions, ranking second behind his Consecration Stone. He personally accompanied the timepiece into the mountain pass and vacationed there while waiting for it to be serviced once every three years or so.

"We can be in Sandria by tomorrow morning," he mused. "We'll set up a perimeter and flush them out."

"Master," she spoke again. "Please forgive my boldness, but do you think it is wise to travel in this weather? The rain has stopped, but the mountains are treacherous at night even without the prospect of slipping on slick rock."

Stokely studied her for a minute and smiled when she shifted uneasily under her gaze.

"That is an excellent point, Jinn." He watched her discomfort grow as she fought back the urge to preen under his praise. "We will need to stay in place for the night, then go hunting at first light."

Stokely would be 'staying in place' in the small village just outside the tree line that disguised this cabin. He would sooner sleep in the half-frozen mud than trapped in this dank little cabin with a group of cagey, homeless adolescents who would stab him for his prized watch regardless of who he was.

"And... Would you enjoy company this evening, Master?" Jinn asked, her voice shaking around the edges.

A smile tugged at his lips. He would enjoy company this evening, but what he needed was rest, if he was to chase down his missing well of mana come morning.

"Perhaps another time," he said, and her disappointment was palpable. "What news do you have about the other matter?"

"We have rerouted her. She will be riding with us within a day or two," she answered.

"Good. That's good. Make sure she is handled properly. A black eye, *maybe* a split lip, but nothing more. I want an insurance policy, not a ruined girl that I have no more use for."

Jinn nodded vehemently and he caught her mid-motion, taking her chin into his hand more roughly than absolutely necessary, forcing her to meet his eye. "I mean it, Jinn. If any of your little pricks actually hurts her..." he trailed off. She had imagination enough to fill in the blanks.

"They won't Master, I promise," she said. "I'll cut off the hands of any who dare."

"Good. She is as valuable as Calen." He released her from his grip, and she sagged forward, jealousy written on her face. "Do you have anything else you need to share with me?"

She shook her head to indicate that she did not.

"We will meet in the morning, here. Do not do anything stupid," he said as he swept past her and out into the cold spring night.

Twenty-Four

May 4, 622

Calen

First light in the mountains had always held a special place for Calen, where she felt that her spirit had transcended into a higher plane of existence. Ever since she had been a girl growing up in a sheltered mountain hollow, she had arisen before dawn to let the first delicate rays of the sun kiss her face and reinvigorate her soul for a new day. This morning, however, the life-affirming force that had filled her heart to the brim currently laid curled around her. Cool milk met warm honey in a dozen points of delicious contact. She desperately wanted to turn around wake her so they could start all over again. But she also knew that making love to Rosalind was a luxury she definitely could not afford this morning.

Still, she wiggled in closer, pushing her round backside into Rosalind's warm, soft body. Rosalind let out a low sound that closely resembled a cat purring, instantly sending Calen back into the small hours of the night and the memories they had made there. A warm flush crept up her neck. Had they really done those things?

Rosalind had been more then generous with her affection for Calen in that sacred space they had created for themselves. She had delivered one kind of pleasure after another, seeming to genuinely delight in pushing Calen over the edge time and time again. It was as though she was trying to make up for ten years of missed opportunities.

Then, it had been Calen's chance to show the same level of devotion to Rosalind as had been shown to her. The inexperience that had made her so insecure mattered little once her desire took hold. Sure, there had been a slight learning curve, but Rosie had been a patient and attentive partner, allowing Calen to explore her body and discover all the ways she could make Rosie moan, or gasp, or even purr. The experience had been far more than just physical gratification, and Calen could not remember ever feeling so close to another person in her life. Melancholy stung the back of her throat.

This morning, when the sun finally crested the horizon, her world would shift again, and she was not yet ready for that. The moment of her departure would arrive all on its own, so there was no need to rush it. She could afford to lay here just a little while longer, soaking in the feel of Rosalind's arms wrapped around her.

* * *

"What are you doing?" Rosalind asked a short time later, sitting up in bed.

Calen finished tying the lace of her boot, avoiding the view. It would be difficult enough to leave without the reminder that Rosalind was wearing nothing underneath the sheets.

"Nox and I will continue on foot, if he still wants to go with me," she said, her voice unsteady. "And you and Freddie will go back to the capital, where you will be safe."

"Back to the capital?" Rosie asked. "What do you mean? You don't want me to go with you?"

Calen could not meet her eye. "Of course, I want you to go with me, Rosie. I'm so grateful to have had this time with you, but my plan must remain unchanged. Trust me, this is for your safety."

"My safety? What about yours?"

"I will be okay, Rosie."

Rosalind fidgeted on the bed, picking at the quilt currently serving her early morning modesty. "Are you sure this isn't just payback? For how I left you?"

Calen looked up then, and her stomach twisted at the guilt she saw in those emerald eyes.

"No, Rosie. How can you think that? I meant what I said, last night. I meant *everything* I said last night."

"Then let me go with you."

"I can't," she said, crossing the small suite to sit on the bed. "He is too dangerous; you don't understand what you are up against."

"Oh bullshit, Calen," she said, barely holding back tears. "Sweetie, please. I know how to protect myself—"

"No, you don't!" Calen interrupted. "Not against him. He...knows things. He has friends who help him, protect him. I have no doubt that they are with him now, and they won't hesitate to hurt you if they find us. He needs me, but not you. I know the ways he would exact his revenge against me, and they would all leave me alive to continue to forcibly serve his needs. But you and Freddie...you wouldn't survive the encounter if he had it his way. It's bad enough that I'm going to ask Nox to continue on with me. I won't put you two at risk as well."

"Calen, if he has people helping him, then you should, too."

"No."

"Please, Cal, he's just a man—"

"He's not just a man, not anymore!" Anxiety mingled with forthcoming heartbreak, and she stood to pace the room. Her power was closed off but swirled in response to her emotions. "He's been stealing my mana, Rosie. I'm not sure why, since it's different from his. I have no clue what he's doing with it, but I know he's up to something."

"He stole your mana? But I felt it last night. You still hold so much. How was he taking it without your consent?"

"The same way he takes everything from me without consent. He waits until I'm too weak or too out of my head to fight back."

"If you can fill with mana, you can empty of it too," Rosalind mumbled, repeating what had been drilled into them as students at Grandview. It was the same line used to threaten any Vessel if they misused their mana or could not learn to wield it properly. It was also considered an extreme violation, outside of those parameters.

Calen lifted the hem of her shirt and pointed to the faded purple pattern on her abdomen. "He used our stone. I don't know how, but that is what this mark is from." Rosalind's eyes grew wide, and she shook her head in disbelief. "This is what I mean. He knows things. He has skills that we've never even been taught about. He's *unbelievably* fast and powerful. And now he has my mana, and I have no idea what he will do with it."

"All the more reason I should be by your side!" Rosalind said.

She sat down on the bed once more, taking Rosalind's hands into her own. A small tear slid off of Rosalind's lower lashes and skimmed her cheek before falling to splash on her thumb.

"No, there has to be a way," she whimpered.

"You said that you know where I'm going, that you figured it out?" she asked. Rosalind nodded once. "So, you know that even if you traveled with me, we couldn't stay together? Not forever. You have to be here; your work is too important to leave. If you were to go with me, to flee The Colonies, you would regret it every day we spent together."

Rosalind let out a small sob before composing herself again. "Then we find a way for you to stay."

"No," Calen said, shaking her head. "He will never stop hunting me, and he will hurt anyone who stands in his way."

Rosie shook her head, her mouth open and silently pleading. "Please," she finally said, "I can't lose you again."

The wall around Calen's emotions crumbled, and tears welled, fat and hot. She blinked quickly and they sped down her cheeks, tracks to mirror those on the beautiful face of her friend, her lover, her everything. Neither spoke for a long time.

***

Rosalind

How on Earth was this actually happening? Rosalind continued to ask the question to the universe, but no answer was forthcoming. Calen was leaving, and there was nothing she could do to stop it. With all the power and influence she held, she had no choice but to stand and watch as Calen walked out of her life. If she tried, if she forced Calen to stay, then she was really no better than Stokely, in the end.

She would never give up on finding a way to be with Calen, but for now, she needed to help her get to safety. Knowing that it needed to happen and *accepting* it were two completely different things, however, and right now she was having a very difficult time accepting.

Somehow, she needed to find a way to be the stronger one and release the embrace first. Calen was already losing too much, she deserved to know that Rosie would be steady for her and would support what she needed, even if it was not what either of them wanted. Calen was already dressed in her traveling clothes, and the thick wool of her jacket muffled what was likely to be their last private moment for a long time.

"Remember everything I told you last night," Rosalind said, opening her puffy eyes to meet Calen's. "You are amazing. You are powerful. Remember how it felt to *own* your power, and whatever you do, don't you ever forget..." The words would not come. The memory was still too fresh, too bittersweet.

They had laid in that incredible space together last night, holding hands and staring into each other's eyes, the haze of passion still thick in the air. Calen had made some silly joke about proving Nox right, and Rosalind had laughed. "I love you, Cal," she had whispered against her lips without even thinking. The words just came out, unbidden and more truthful than anything else she had ever said in her life. At first, she thought Calen would bolt. Surely, that was going too far. But Calen had kissed her and said, "I love you too, Rosie."

Now, she wondered if it had been a mistake to open herself so completely. How could she possibly survive the gaping chasm that had opened in her heart? Surely there was some fatal ailment that accompanied pain this severe.

"I could never forget," Calen whispered, and leaned in for one last, tender kiss. "I could never forget."

Then she pulled away and Rosalind looked down, certain she had accidentally been gutted with the move.

"Travel smart," she said, trying to still her spinning head. "Be safe, you two."

Nox walked around from behind her, carrying his pack in one hand, and a small satchel of food in the other. "I convinced Bastian to let us take his best jerky and cheese, and there are dried berries and a loaf of bread courtesy of the cook who I'm fairly certain was flirting with me."

"You're fairly certain everyone is flirting with you," Rosalind joked, thankful for a moment of levity. She pulled him in for a hug. "You take care of her. I mean it, Nox. You take care of her, or I will hunt you down myself. And please check in every chance you get."

"I'll miss you too, Red," he said, the corners of his eyes crinkling as he smiled at her.

Then Rosalind watched as the love of her life walked out the front door and into the uncertainty of a world where she was being hunted.

"What now, boss?" Freddie asked from over her shoulder.

"Now, we pack up our things and follow them," she said, matter of fact, as she turned to look up at him.

"You sure that's the best idea?"

"Of course not, Freddie. But there is no way we can just go back."

"So, we stalk Calen and Nox, instead?"

"That is the plan. I need to know that she is safe, even if from a distance."

He studied her face, tilting his head to the side. Whatever he saw, he gave a nod to himself and shrugged.

"I'll get our stuff loaded."

Twenty-Five

May 4, 622

Nox

Nox followed Calen at a pace that would allow her privacy as they moved in the opposite direction of Rosalind and Freddie. The sun had risen into a crystalline blue sky and the utter absence of clouds meant that its rays were quickly warming the crisp mountain air. Despite the slow, steady pace that the rain had fallen the day before, the trail was only slightly damp, and the hike was easier than he had expected.

He had yet to ask Calen where she was leading them, instead allowing her to take the reins on that particular conversation when she felt ready. Nox had been working under the supposition, rather naively he now realized, that she simply wanted to be 'away.' Away from Stokely, away from society. He figured that would materialize in the form of a secluded cabin in the woods, or maybe a swamp shack further south, if she wanted to *really* get away from Stokely.

However, they had left Rosalind and Freddie behind, under the guise that they could not go where Calen intended to go. Nox had realized, rather stupidly, that she meant to *leave* the Colonies. If that really was the case, then this jaunty little trip just changed by an order of magnitude. Her 'simple plan to find safety' had just become a 'complex journey they might not survive.'

Well, it had always been that, he just had not known it. Truthfully, he was a little angry at Calen for withholding such important information from him for so long. He chose to hold his tongue on that point, remembering that he had basically shown up out of the blue and refused to leave her side. So really, it was his own fault for getting into this situation in the first place.

Then, there was the question of why she would really refuse the help of her friends, who also just happened to be two of the most talented Vessels on the continent. He had read enough novels in his life to recognize the storyline of the 'self-sacrificing hero,' and he understood it to be an important literary tool. Watching it play out in real life, however, it seemed short-sighted and unnecessarily theatrical. Not to mention, painful.

"I can hear you thinking back there," she called over her shoulder, breaking the silence.

"Apologies, I'll try to keep it down," he said.

"Or, you could just say what you are thinking and get it over with."

"You want to know what I'm thinking?"

"I already know what you're thinking. I just want you to say it aloud so we can move on."

"Oh, all right, if you insist," he said in mock acquiescence. "I was thinking that the sky is the color of cornflowers today."

"Nox," she said, not sounding even vaguely amused.

"Cornflowers are my mom's favorite..."

"Nox."

"...flower. They didn't grow where I lived as a child..."

"Nox!"

"...but they did where she grew up..."

"Nox, please," she plead, "just say it."

He watched the back of her head bob up and down as she took lunging steps over the ancient limestone boulders that blocked their path.

"You made a mistake," he finally said.

"Be more specific."

"You should have let Rosalind and Freddie come with us. They could have helped, and they definitely wanted to be here."

Calen did not respond right away, but she did slow down to allow him to catch up. When his strides matched hers, she shot him a tentative, sidelong glance.

"Nox, I'm not very experienced at having friends. I've never really had many, aside from my siblings growing up, and Rosie once I went to Grandview. But, against my best attempts to thwart you, you seem to have...grown on me a little. And I know we aren't really friends, but this is about as close as it gets for me." She looked up at him sharply. "And don't even think of making fun of me or I will push you down a mountainside the first chance that I get!"

He threw his hands up in a gesture of surrender. She continued.

"Anyway, I'm going to tell you a story. When I was eight, I traveled into Breckridge, the small village closest to the hollow where my family lived. There weren't many shops in town, but there was one that carried small, hand-carved wooden toys. Mr. Turner owned the shop with his wife; he built things, and she painted them. Well, this time, they had created a wooden butterfly that was suspended by delicate twine that moved the butterfly when you tugged on the string. Mr. Turner told me that it had taken him two weeks to chisel out the details, and another two weeks for Mrs. Turner to paint it, and that if I wanted it, he could sell it to me half price on account of the fact that I was always so polite and helpful. I think they mostly felt bad for my family situation. Anyway, it was absolutely gorgeous. I knew right away that I had to have it."

Her voice went soft, and he could tell by the faraway expression on her face that she was remembering exactly how it had looked that first time.

"I became obsessed with having that butterfly. I gathered herbs and berries to dry, I saved one of my uncooked breakfast eggs every morning, I offered to do chores for the neighbors in my free time. I did everything I could to earn coins. When my mom went into town about two weeks later, the butterfly was still there, and so she sold everything I had given her to take to town. I had made enough, and even had a little left over, but I didn't care. All that mattered was that my mom came home with my precious butterfly." Calen stopped for a moment to shift the pack on her shoulders, a small smile playing across her lips.

"I was so happy! It's a little silly to say now, but it felt like life was perfect when I would lay in my bed and watch its wings flap gently in the wind I made with the string. It was the first time something so beautiful had ever been *mine*. It was the most special thing I had ever held. Until...my younger brother, Elian, got mad at me because I wouldn't help him with the extra chores he had earned by angering our pap. He was determined to ruin my day, since his was already awful."

Nox nodded, knowing where the story was headed. "And he broke your butterfly?"

"Yep, ripped the wings clean off, and stomped on them until they broke into chunks of splintered ruin. He felt terrible about it by that evening, but it didn't matter. The damage had been done and it couldn't be undone. I never asked for anything that special again, for fear of how badly it would hurt when it was inevitably taken away from me," she finished, looking down at her feet.

"Calen, Rosalind isn't made of wood," he said.

"No, you're right. She's made of flesh and blood and bone, and is infinitely more breakable than a wooden toy," she pointed out. "Rosalind is...a perfect, cool day walking through the forest, with the sun dappling through the leaves, then a breath whispers through the trees and fills you with unexplainable ease." She looked at him quickly and blushed at the admission. "Aside from the fact that I would sooner die than see harm come to her, she matters to so many other people in this world beyond me. How could I ever be so selfish as to claim her as my own, when I know what kind of monster hunts me? He wouldn't just snap off her wings. Stokely would unmake everything that makes her special. He would break her in ways she would never recover from." A new fury filled her voice. "How could I ever do that to someone that I love? How could I ever misuse her, especially after..."

One suspicion confirmed. Although, there had been no denying the manner and degree of the attraction between them. They were two forces of nature irrevocably drawn to one another. The north and south poles of a magnet, incapable of escaping the eternal pull that brings the two halves crashing back together. He knew how difficult it must have been for Calen to leave that morning, and he had yet to be convinced that they would not succumb to that inevitable pull once more. There was only so much the human heart could take.

"And she can't go with you to Reclamation because she is too important here?" he asked, feigning nonchalance.

Calen pulled up short and looked at him, guilt playing across wide eyes.

"I'm sorry I didn't tell you sooner, I know it's a big deal. You don't have to go all the way there with me, Nox." He looked at her flatly. "I mean it! You have truly been amazing..."

"I know."

"...and I'm actually grateful that you have accompanied me this far..."

"Of course you are."

"...and I will have nothing but fond thoughts of you..."

"As you should."

"...if you decide that this is too far, too much, now that you know I plan to sneak into Reclamation."

Suspicion number two confirmed.

"You do understand that this is going to be an extremely long, difficult, dangerous journey?" he asked.

"Yes." Calen hung her head.

"You know that they might not even let you cross, right?"

She nodded.

"And you still think that this is the best course of action?"

She looked up then. "Yes. It's the only way to find safety and shut down Stokely's access to more power."

"Calen, is there an actual plan here?" he asked, trying to not sound annoyed. "With details explaining how we don't get confiscated or killed at the border?"

"Of course," she answered, sounding very annoyed.

He exhaled loudly and studied her for a moment.

"Well, you better share them with me while we walk," he announced, matching his action to his words. "Perhaps I need to emphasize, once again, just how long this journey is about to be?" He looked over his shoulder just in time to see a quizzical smile cross her face. She started to follow.

"So, you'll go with me, even though you think this trip will be dangerous and possibly futile?"

"I'm going *because* of those reasons," he clarified. "Besides, you just told me that we're friends now. And what are friends for, if not to accompany you on an insanely long, dangerous trip to try to illegally cross into a hostile neighboring country?"

"Exactly," she answered.

Twenty-Six

May 4, 622

Calen

Calen took in the grand scale of the magnificent scenery as they emerged from a mountain pass and the space that had previously been occupied by a wall of limestone yawned open to reveal a smoky, verdant valley in the flush of spring. She could have almost forgotten the storm of the previous day.

Her soul had found some tentative balance within the opposing forces of her emotions. She felt the duality of lightness at having spent the night wrapped up with Rosie, and of weighted agony at the acknowledgment that she probably never would again. With every step, she felt the certainty in protecting Rosie, but also the wrongness of walking away from the most important person in her life.

The feeling of Nox's stare itched at her neck, and when she turned to him, curiosity etched the space between his dark eyebrows.

"What?" she asked the ground in front of her, not wanting to look away from the path that was becoming more tumultuous.

"You are humming?" he asked slowly. Calen realized that she had been, and it made her smile.

"Oh, yeah," she answered.

"I didn't know that you liked music."

"Who doesn't like music?"

"Let me expand upon that thought. I didn't know you liked anything beyond grumpy cats and feisty, green-eyed women."

"Of course I like music. It's actually a really old song," she started, then changed her mind.

"Story time again?" he asked, but his tone was inviting.

"Yeah, this is a good one, though. Well, sort of. I started having nightmares after my Consecration, when I was sent to Grandview." A flash of memory. Water. Power. Rough hands. "Our housemother could not have cared less. I wasn't exactly her favorite, so she was content to let me wake up crying and covered in sweat. But one morning, our Head of Order, Jessamin, asked why I was looking so rough, and I when I explained my lack of sleep, she took an interest. I may have actually been *her* favorite. She was like a mother to me once mine had given up and decided I was no longer hers. Anyway, she would come into the dormitory after I had a nightmare and hum that song to me while stroking my hair. She told me that it had been passed down for generations through her family, and though no one knew the words anymore, they had never forgotten the melody."

"Yeah, I can't imagine my Head of Order coaxing me back to sleep with lullabies," Nox said, smiling.

"One night, I awoke from a particularly vicious nightmare to find someone already sitting at my bedside, humming, and stroking my hair. Rosalind, well, Kiely then, but you know that. But Rosalind, whom I had only had a few random conversations with, had learned the song from her bunk so that I wouldn't have to wake up afraid and alone anymore." Tears flushed her eyes at the sweetness of the memory. "I was thirteen and she was fourteen. We were inseparable from that point on."

His smiled warmed. Sometimes, he was so earnest with his emotions that she could not tell if they were real or if he was actually mocking her.

"She always took care of me," she said, "I could never figure out what I had done to deserve her." He was still watching her.

"While we're sharing, I'm going to tell you what my father used to tell me when I was a kid," he offered.

"Oh, this is going to be good," she said, expecting the type of story that involved tattling, or snot, or other things distinctly childlike. She guessed wrong.

"Love isn't earned, it just *is*. My brothers and I would get into trouble of one form or another, and I was always worried that he would stop loving me for being bad. Obviously, he never did."

"Obviously," she agreed.

"But he would tell me that love is not earned, it just is. You must nurture it, so it can grow, protect it so it can survive. But real love never has to be earned."

The ache in Calen's chest deepened. "That's beautiful," she mumbled.

"Yes, it is. And no, you can't steal it. It's my profound thought, get your own," he said, bumping his shoulder to hers.

"Speaking of last night..." Nox started. Her cheeks flushed.

"Not sharing details, Nox. We aren't that good of friends."

"I wasn't asking about *that*," he said. "But I was going to ask if anything else happened last night that you would like to share with the group?"

Everything that had happened last night was too intimate for Calen to share. "Why are you asking?"

"*Well*," he said, dragging out the word, "quite frankly, Calen, you are leaking."

Leaking? What kind of double entendre was that?

"Wait, what?" she stammered out, hoping that this conversation was not about to take an embarrassing turn. "Leaking what, exactly?"

"Mana. I've cleared my vision several times to check for other mana trails, and you're leaving a pretty steady one today. At first, I thought it was maybe from last night's...antics. But we've been walking for a while and it hasn't let up," he finished, trying to sound unconcerned but failing.

"Shit," she muttered, and instinctively picked up the pace of her steps.

Calen was not concerned so much about her mana as she was the man who would trail them more quickly if she really was leaving a trail.

She had already concluded that something had changed following last nights 'antics,' just not the ones Nox knew about. Her mana seemed to have metamorphosed in the aftermath of her learning how to open fully. She had taken the steps to close off the same way that she had done for years, but her power was not so easy to contain as it had always been. It was calm and still, emanating a sense of peace. But it was also somehow bolder and more confident, turquoise ebbing and flowing gently in her core, not pulled in tight like an atrophied fist as it had been before. Apparently, she would have to add 'leaking' to the list of changes.

"Did something happen?" he asked again.

"Rosalind taught me how to open fully," she shot back.

"You didn't know how to do that before last night?" he asked, his voice more curious than accusatory.

"No. But that doesn't matter, we need to move!" she shouted, then nearly broke into a jog.

"Slow down," he warned. "This trail isn't exactly stable."

"Not helpful, Nox," she threw over her shoulder, but did take his advice.

He did not do her the disservice of asking if she had closed off properly. She would have to be a complete idiot to be walking around open, given their current situation. He did, however, ask how he could help. She shook her head, trying to think of a solution but coming up short.

"Just keep scanning. I'll watch the trail; you watch for movement or mana."

She hated the fearful dread that now knotted her stomach, but at least she was not sad anymore.

Twenty-Seven

May 4, 622

Nox

Nox and Calen kept the punishing pace of two hunted rabbits for another hour before they came to a fast-rushing stream, swollen to the shores from the recent spring thaw forcing its way down the mountain. He guessed that it had to be twenty feet across at that point, the depth unknowable due to a strong current and violent rapids.

"I have an idea," he said, "hear me out." Her head swiveled slowly toward him. "I think I can jump it."

Calen laughed. She actually laughed. "Wait, are you serious? Oh goodness, you are." She stopped laughing. "Nox, even if you could, I most definitely cannot. I don't have magical First Order legs, remember?"

"Well, I could...I could carry you," he responded, giving his most reassuring smile. It did not work.

She stared. "No. Absolutely not. Think about what will happen if we *don't* make it across. That's the end, this whole thing is over. It's an unnecessary risk."

"Okay, what do you think we should do, then?"

"We head upstream to where it narrows enough for us to safely cross. Or jump."

Her big idea was to go around?

Nox thought maybe he needed to remind her of the urgency of

their situation. He considered, briefly, that he could make the jump across, then jump back, to demonstrate his ability. But he realized that he could either fail and die by 'knocking-of-noggin on big rock,' or exhaust his energy and be rendered incapable of any more travel for the day. He looked up and downstream, but there were no downed trees to be seen.

Calen was watching him expectantly, and he realized that she was waiting to hear his opinion on the matter.

"Lead on," he said, holding his arms open upstream.

***

Three hours. They had lost three hours, in his estimation, on their little detour upstream. The sun was quickly making its way toward the western horizon, and they would likely have to camp in the woods tonight.

Great, how fun it would be to sleep on sticky leaves and lumpy rocks again.

They had run into the most massive briar patch he had ever seen, and as it turned out, the only way out was through. Calen had refused to use her *magical Third Order hands* to clear the patch, arguing that they did not need to draw any more attention to themselves. Nox was forced to use his sword like a machete to cut a path. He was certain he would find ripped clothes and scraped skin when they stopped for the night.

After the world's worst game of 'thorny peekaboo,' they had faced a muddy uphill climb due to the riverbank being flooded. He could have handled that just fine on his own, but he would not leave Calen to struggle alone.

At least they were almost back to where they had started. He could see where the two of them had stood, deciding how to get across, before making their detour. On the other shore, he recognized the downhill path they had taken by the small plates and chips of slate that likely marked a rockslide sometime in the past. Nox decided it would be a good time to clear his vision and check for mana trails, and—

"Shit!" he exclaimed. His head swiveled back to their side of the river in time to see a man's head poke around the trunk of a massive red maple just ahead. He smiled at them, then slithered the rest of his body around the tree and into the open, moving unhurriedly. He was not wearing his obnoxious golden robes, but Nox recognized 'Brother' Stokely, nonetheless.

"Out for a stroll?" Stokely mused, holding his hands out wide to indicate the forest around them.

Calen had gone completely still in front of him, with the exception of her labored breathing. He waited for her to speak, but she remained frozen.

Carefully unsheathing the thin dagger from his thigh, he sidled up behind her, already sorry for what he was about to do. He could only hope his plan would allow her a chance to run for safety, and that she would forgive him for not sharing the details beforehand. Nox grabbed her arm roughly and dug the tip of his dagger up under her chin.

"For fuck's sake, Stokely, it took you long enough," he shouted, then began to shove Calen forward.

"What? What's happening?" she shouted, her voice pitching upward toward hysteria. "Nox, what are you doing?"

"Walk, bitch," he said roughly. He shoved her again.

"Nox, please! What are you doing?"

"There is a village downhill, with a call center," he whispered through the fake smile plastered on his face. "Nod if you understand."

Her head tipped forward almost imperceptibly. He continued to use his body to push her toward Stokely.

"Let me go," she growled.

"Oh, this is too good," Stokely crooned. "Did you think he was helping you?" He threw his head back and barked a laugh so loudly that it startled a flock of chimney swifts into flight. Nox could not wait to bury his dagger in the hollow of that throat.

"How could you do this?" Calen shouted. He was fairly certain that she had heard him before, but her angry act convincing.

"Yeah, and like I said, it took you long enough," he said with a sneer toward Stokely. "She's fucking unbearable."

Stokely crossed his arms over his chest, looking amused. "Yes, she really is. Let me guess, you got to that point of the path," he said, pointing across the river, "and couldn't just jump to this side due to the dead weight of a completely useless ritual worker who refused to follow orders?"

"Does she ever just follow orders?" Nox joked, and once again mentally begged Calen's forgiveness.

"Well, if you know the *right* way to command them." The way he crooned out the words made the hairs on Nox's arms rise. He knew in that moment Rosalind had not been exaggerating. This man was a monster, completely undeserving of his title in the First Order. How had he not been thrown out?

"I did not have that problem, for once," Stokely said, looking Calen up and down, "I jumped it with no problem, and I've just been enjoying this lovely afternoon, awaiting your arrival. Now, the gentlemen traveling with me don't have my particular skill set, so they followed your track upstream. You have nowhere to go, you are trapped. You made it entirely too easy, Calen. Really."

Nox stopped their march ten feet from Stokely. Calen was practically panting now, and tears streamed her cheeks. Nox would bet his entire first edition collection that it was hatred and disgust on display, not fear.

"I don't know about you, but I could use a drink," he said to Stokely, pretending to ignore Calen altogether, save the dagger he still held at her throat. He slid the pack off his right shoulder and let it fall into his hand, grasping the strap tightly. Stokely had not answered but was still staring at Calen.

"Run on three," he whispered.

The movement of her hair was the only indication he had of her understanding. "Fuck you First Order bastards, I hope you die the deaths you deserve."

That a girl.

Stokely giggled at her rage. "You're the fucking worst, Calen," he said, opening his arms to her, "but I've still missed you. We have *so* much catching up to do."

His voice was laden with the type of anticipation that said Calen might not survive their 'catching up.' Nox was really going to have to make him bleed.

"One," he whispered, shifting the dagger so that she would not accidentally nick herself on her flight.

"Two." He felt her muscles tense in expectation.

"Three."

She planted her feet and launched herself away from him just as he filled to the brim with mana, his muscles humming and ready.

Then, the world erupted in chaos.

***

Calen

Calen did not have time to plan beyond sending an unequivocal command to her legs to run. Fortunately, she correctly predicted Nox's next move and jumped to the left, taking off at a sprint towards the woods as Nox side-armed his pack to the right and sent it flying at Stokely. The momentary surprise was enough to give her an edge, and she made a wide arc around him as he clumsily caught the bag.

Unfortunately, Stokely had also let loose his mana, and with his superhuman reflexes, he immediately whipped the bag back at Nox's feet, tripping him. Stokely let out a guttural growl and lunged for her, catching her by the ankle. She fell sideways and turned onto her back, her own pack now trapped beneath her, giving her leverage as she kicked him in the face with her free foot. He grunted, blood sprouting from his left nostril, but grabbed the offending foot and pinned it down beside the other. She panicked and began flailing her legs, trying anything to get free.

Just as Nox was coming up behind Stokely, her mana *flared* to life. Of its own accord, it spread and whipped through her core, pushing at the boundaries of her skin before breaking free. For a split second, both men's eyes went wide as bright turquoise energy burst from her, sending weak tendrils grasping for Stokely's face, before whipping back into her abdomen.

The moment passed, and Stokely pivoted on his knees in anticipation of his approaching opponent. He released Calen's ankles, and she scrambled backward just as Nox slammed into Stokely, tackling him to the ground.

"Run!" Nox screamed in a tone Calen had never heard from him before. She shot to her feet and willed her legs to move faster than they ever had.

Go. Downhill. Run.

Calen reached a small crest in her flight down the mountainside and spared one backward glance at the struggle behind her. Both men moved unbelievably fast, and in the blur of Stokely's pale blue mana combined with Nox's deep, royal blue, it was difficult to tell the source of the punches and kicks they exchanged. It looked like a dance, both men knowing the steps and completing them in synchronous beauty. But then Stokely broke from the sequence they had likely been taught at Black Rock and commenced his own brutal pacing. His hands glowed such a bright blue that it was difficult to watch them as they came forward and knocked both weapons from Nox's hands. His foot arced up and kicked out with such force that an afterimage followed Nox as he flew backward and slammed into the ground.

She put her energy back to the path she had charted out in front of herself, but a moment later, Calen was stopped in her tracks as a pained scream ripped through the understory. Nox was pitched forward on his hands and knees, blood and saliva escaping his mouth to paint the fallen leaves before him a sickly crimson. He reached his hand forward, and she watched as his mana drained from his arm, incapable of fighting any longer. Stokely looked down at him, his shoulders heaving with effort, his fists hanging bloody at his sides.

"No!" she yelled, fear and anger surging through her. Her mana once more responded, this time by breaking free of its confines and pushing her fully open.

Both men glanced in her direction and Nox yelled once more for her to go. She stumbled backward a few steps, disoriented by the power moving through her. Fear and guilt warred within her. How could she leave Nox like this? They were friends, were they not?

Stokely turned back to Nox and punched him with such forceful violence that Calen heard the crunch of his face breaking. He crumpled into a pile of boneless flesh on the forest floor, his blood now forging a tiny, grotesque rivulet flowing away from his head. Stokely looked over his shoulder at her once more and smiled.

Fuck.

Calen turned and ran, hard. Still fully open and incapable of stopping to close off, it was all that she could do to keep moving. If Stokely caught her, she was dead.

Go. Downhill. Run.

Twenty-Eight

May ?, 622

Calen

Would the horrors of this day never cease?

It had been hours since she had fled from Stokely. From Nox. Blessed Vessel, Nox. Did he live, still? Did *she* live? A sob escaped her throat at the memory of Nox's blood spraying through the forest understory, the way his body gave out, the smile Stokely had for her.

He had chased her for what she knew must have been hours. It was a complete mystery how she had evaded him well past sundown, possibly even past midnight. Well, maybe she was not entirely clueless. The few times she caught sight of him during their little cat and mouse game, he was grinning, joyful, and complete unhinged. If she was not mistaken, he was enjoying this particular round of torment.

Calen hauled herself off of the boulder she had stopped to rest upon and begged her feet to move. The blisters on her toes had long since burst, and her socks held a disgusting combination of dried, flaked scabs, and wet ooze that could have been blood, sweat, pus, or any combination of the three. It was a bad idea to take off her boots to find out. They would never go back on her feet, if she did.

"Move," she croaked, as if her feet might be more willing to follow a verbal command. They were not. Her body convulsed, a reaction to the mana she still could not close off, and just as she pitched forward, her legs made the executive decision to keep her alive just a while longer. On the march once more, she made her way to the edge of the forest, where she poked her head out, allowing her body a temporary reprieve against a tree that was only just wider than her body.

There was no sign of Stokely, but she could make out a large log building perhaps five hundred feet to the south. Studying the structure, she noticed the mana-enhancing heating and cooling system situated in the back, humming softly beneath the sound of spring peepers putting on a show.

"An Opus Home," she mumbled. It had to be. They were the only structures in this part of the Colonies that were allowed to use that technology. Hope flared in her chest. She could make it another five hundred feet, and Stokely would not dare come that close to the place. He had an unnatural dislike of Opus Homes that Calen guessed stemmed from his deepest fear: being powerless. The unfortunate souls that found their final resting place in an Opus Home were all former Vessels that had burned themselves out and could no longer live safely within society. They retired to mountain valleys and coastal promontories to live out their numbered days. Surely, she would be offered safe haven in such a place.

The sky to the east lit an eerie purple as lightning streaked through the clouds, warning thunder rumbling on its heels. The wind was already picking up, and that storm would be on her soon. She needed to hurry. Looking down at her feet, she sobbed again. Just five hundred feet.

As she emerged from the woods, light droplets met her face, and she realized how hot and sticky she was. And damn if she had ever been this thirsty in her life. She held open her mouth as she walked, letting the tentative drizzle wet her tongue.

Too dizzy to really consider, a loose strand of thought floated in her consciousness. Could she survive being open for so long? Maybe she was already dead, and this was the afterlife the universe had devised for her. If that was the case, she decided, then all of nature was one cruel joke. A coyote bayed in the distance, and she closed her mouth and opened her eyes. She was still walking, by some miracle, and as she scanned her surroundings, the storm lit. Was that a man, standing just beyond the trees? Had he seen her? Was that *really* coyotes, or was it laughter?

"No...no no no..." she whimpered. Another flash, another glimpse. But there was nothing, this time. Her mind was warping. Her body was ready to give out. Was she imagining things? It did not matter. She turned back toward the log building and forced her body into the closest semblance to running she could manage. She cried out as spikes of pain shot through the soles of her feet and straight up her legs. Somehow, she made it to the covered porch and collapsed, crawling the distance to the massive front door. Her weak pounding was all but swallowed up by the gathering rainfall.

"No," she said, her voice a pitiful squeak. "Help me. Please, someone help me."

Her mana, exhausted and slow, but still bright, pulsed in her core.

"Go away," she told it. "You are nothing but trouble."

It pulsed again, then *shifted*. The tufts of mana that suffused her arms grew more solid, as if they were being filled from within. The heat built to an uncomfortable peak, and her hands felt heavy with the substantial increase in power she held. All of her body pulsed, and she felt full to bursting.

Knock, it whispered. If she was not dead, she was hallucinating. Still, she lifted her hands once more and pounded. The coffin lid of a door vibrated, and the small bell hung at the apex of the doorway jingled. Her mana drained back into her belly, and she slumped forward, resting on the door. Within moments, it ground open, prompted by a tall, blonde woman in clean, tidy clothing. Her crystalline blue eyes found Calen instantly.

"Oh, dear," she said. "Can I help you?"

"Sanctuary," Calen whispered, then fell to the woman's feet as black crowded her vision and oblivion claimed her.

***

Her eyes drifted slowly open, vaguely aware of the (ultimately accurate) sensation of being watched. She lifted her head briefly, scanning the room for the source of the niggling at the back of her mind, before letting it fall back to the soft pillow that smelled of fresh air and clean soap. Someone had probably line-dried the pillowcase recently.

That had to be a good sign, right? Deranged lunatics generally did not put clothes out to hang dry in the sun, did they?

The swishing of shifting skirts caught her attention and she attempted once more to find the source of the unseen, watching eyes. She had to sit up fully to make out the shape of a woman sitting in a wooden chair in the corner of the room.

"Hello, Revered Calendula," the woman said. She rose from the chair and crossed the small room to part the plain curtains that hid a small, partially-opened window. The act allowed the entreating cool breeze to brush Calen's exposed arms and she shivered, noticing the thin shift she wore, rather than her travel clothing.

"Your clothes were soaked through with sweat and caked in mud," said the woman. "But do not worry, we were discreet, and your clothes will be clean soon enough, if you wish to change back into them."

Her affable voice was at odds with her tall, athletic stature and strict-looking face. Upon closer inspection, though, Calen found her pale blue eyes to hold a compassion required of a woman in her position, caring for every broken soul that crossed the threshold of this place. She was undoubtedly the woman who had welcomed her inside after her fraught flight from a pursuing Stokely. It had been no small miracle that she had found this place, wandering, fully open, completely helpless, through the unfamiliar, dark expanse of woods that she had begun to fear would be her final resting place.

The sun shone bright, but was dappled through the leaves of the ancient trees that surrounded the large, log and stone building. It had to be early afternoon, but she had no idea *which* afternoon.

"Thanks, I would appreciate that," Calen answered. "I don't plan on staying long. What day is it?" Realizing that would not help her, as she had lost track of the days on her journey, she clarified. "I mean, how long was I out for? How long have I been here?"

"You arrived here the night before last."

She had slept for thirty-six straight hours. Which meant, she had evaded Stokely for thirty-six straight hours, while sleeping. The likelihood of that seemed slim, and she began to grow suspicious of the situation.

"What did you say your name was?" she asked warily.

"I didn't. Forgive my poor manners," she answered, gesturing first to herself, then to the room around them. "My name is Sister Matilda, and I run Opus Mountain Home."

"Sister Matilda, thank you for taking me in. You saved my life. Forgive my briskness, but how is it that you know my name?"

A flash of...something, crossed Sister Matilda's face, and her answer was slow in the coming. "Because I know the man who hunts you," she finally said, as she sat down on the windowsill, tucking her hands into her pockets.

That could mean anything. And if this woman happened to in league with him, Calen was a sitting deer awaiting the crossbow bolt. Her apprehension must have shown on her face.

"It's okay, Revered, he's not here," Matilda said. "You are safe. You begged sanctuary, and you have it, Mistress Calendula."

"Just Calen," she said, huffing as though she had just run a mile in a dead sprint.

"Okay, Calen. I promise, you are safe in my care."

"How do you know...How is he not here?"

"He *was* here yesterday morning. Since you are the only mysterious, unannounced guest that has arrived here in oh, say, fifteen years, I figured it was you that he sought. He asked for you by name."

"Then what, he just politely left?" Calen asked, crossing her arms across her chest.

"Honestly, no. It took quite a lot of convincing. But it did help that this place seems to frighten him."

Calen had hoped for as much, but how would this woman know?

"You gathered that insight in the few moments he spent here?"

"We have a... history," Sister Matilda said, tilting her head to the side. Calen waited for her to say more, but Matilda was holding back for some reason, so she decided not to push this point. If anyone understood a need for privacy on this particular point, it would be Calen.

"You promise you won't hand me over to him?" Calen asked.

The shocked expression on Matilda's face was matched by the furious shaking of her head. "Of course not."

"Do you know where he is now?"

"If I had to guess, I would say somewhere in town. In Acera. It's less than a mile down the hill. I am sure he found somewhere to stay while he thinks of another plan to bully me."

Yep, she knew Stokely, alright. He undoubtedly had another tactic ready to deploy.

"Why did...why would you help me?" Calen asked, incapable of silencing the persistent voice that told her she could not trust anyone, especially a member of the First Order.

You could trust Nox, a different voice whispered. An immediate swell of anguish filled her chest, but she shut it down and shoved it away. There would be time to mourn later, she needed to focus on survival for now.

"Why would I help you? Besides the fact that it is my sworn mission in life to help those who need it?" She leaned toward Calen. "I told you, because I know the man that hunts you." A knowing glint flashed in her eyes. We are allies, it said.

Maybe she would be safe here, for a little while. Calen had so many questions that needed answers, but her mind was every bit as exhausted as her body, and trying to make sense of her thoughts was like gathering leaf litter from a mud pit. She pressed the butts of her palms into her temples and massaged, desperate for relief from the headache that had bloomed in response to the bright sunlight.

"I should let you rest," Sister Matilda said.

"But I have more questions," Calen said half-heartedly.

"As do I. You will have your answers when I have mine, after you have rested. Someone will be here to escort you to dinner at six. I would suggest you try to sleep until then, no one will disturb you."

Sister Matilda stood and closed the curtains, plunging the room into blessed darkness. She shuffled out, closing the door behind her, but there was no tell-tale *snick* of it being locked.

Not a prisoner, at least.

Calen closed her eyes against the swimming motion of exhaustion claiming her and found a heavy sleep soon after.

***

The young woman escorting Calen to dinner was going to have a neck injury by the time they got to where they were going. She had explained that Sister Matilda's office (where they would have dinner together, even though that was never where Sister Matilda took her dinners, but oh well I guess this was a unique occasion) was at the opposite end of the building that was more like a resort than anything else, and that it would take them a few minutes to get there. Anna, Calen thought she had introduced herself as, had snuck a few quick peeks at her as they left the room, but was now staring wide-eyed at her, craning her neck detrimentally to do so.

"Is everything okay?" Calen asked. The question seemed to have broken a trance and the young woman jumped and shook her head. Then she nodded her head.

"Oh, yes, Revered Calendula," she squeaked.

"Please, call me Calen."

"Yes, Mistress Revered Calen," she said in a rush. "Umm, oh. It's just that, well, we don't get too many ritual workers who are still, umm..." She wiggled her hands in front of her. "...who are still *well.*" She beamed at her own word choice. Certainly, the implied 'unwell' that she used to describe the inhabitants of Opus Mountain Home was far kinder than how the general public referred to them. "Brain-rotted nutters" was a popular one back where she lived. Had lived.

"Are you not—" It was Calen's turn to wiggle her hands in their silently-agreed upon pantomime for Vessel.

Anna rose up onto her toes for a few steps, throwing her hands up as she answered. "Oh no! I'm not— that is, I don't have...I mean, umm, some of the girls here are Vessels. Weak ones, else they would have other jobs to do. But Sister Matilda lets them come here to help. I'm — we're— the rest of us...well, some of us are just...wayward girls."

Wayward and anxious, apparently.

"Well, Anna of the Wayward Girls," she said, trying to make it sound like a badge of honor, "I'm glad you are here. These women need someone like you to take good care of them." Calen offered her a reassuring smile and Anna seemed to relax at the compliment.

"Oh, thank you for saying that Mistress Revered Calen," she said less urgently. "Not that I've been much help these last few days. They've all gone kinda—" She flapped her hands around her ears and made an odd sound in her throat. "—kinda wonky."

Calen had not spent enough time around burned out Vessels to know what entailed normal behavior, let alone 'wonky' behavior. Perhaps that was the source of the low din of noise that echoed out into the hall from two large, open doors that they had passed a few moments ago.

"Well, here we are!" Anna announced before unceremoniously entering through the open door at the end of the hall. She swept her hands forward toward the woman seated at the desk. "You know Sister Matilda already."

Matilda rose and Calen noticed just how imposing she was. Where Anna had been too short to meet her eye without looking up, Sister Matilda had to be at least four inches taller than her, with an even more commanding presence in the small space of her office. She had changed into a short-sleeve knit shirt, and her defined arms hinted further at her physical prowess. Calen had no doubt that this woman knew how to handle herself, but she still may not be powerful enough to protect against Stokely, if the need arose.

"Thank you, Anna. You are excused for the evening," she said kindly. Anna bowed and scampered out of the room. Matilda swept her hand to the side, indicating a small table that had already been set with chilled water, wine, fresh bread, and two large bowls of what smelled like a rich vegetable soup. "I'm not in the habit of taking my meals in here, so please forgive the tight confines of our dining area. Given our current circumstances, this was the best place for us to meet in peace."

As soon as she was in front of the bowl of soup, Calen's stomach remembered that it had not been fed in forty-eight hours. Matilda watched her warily, eating her own meal at a much more dignified pace.

"In my experience, it is unwise to eat too much, too quickly, after an ordeal like the one you have faced," Matilda offered. "But if you can keep that down and you are still hungry, I will happily send for more food."

Calen's mouth was too full with the salty, tangy soup to answer, so she nodded her understanding instead.

It took her all of six minutes to finish her meal, and Sister Matilda took her forfeited napkin on the table as her cue to start the question-and-answer portion of the evening. She continued eating her own dinner, but asked between bites.

"I do hope I'm not too far out of line when I say that this is an odd situation?" she started.

"Not at all," Calen said.

"So, then, would you mind terribly, if I asked for you to explain to me how you got here?"

"I was running away from Stokely," Calen said, and Matilda waited for more of an answer. When it did not trot itself out, she raised her eyebrows at Calen, asking for more.

"Why, Mistress Calen, were you running from Stokely? I do not require a general explanation, as I would advise any and all women to run away from him. But specifically, why were you running away this time?"

Calen watched her, unsure of how much she wanted to reveal to this woman. Kind eyes and compassionate behavior did not necessarily facilitate access to all of her wounds.

"I think you could save me a lot of time and stress explaining my history with Stokely if you would tell me more about yours," Calen said, sounding more combative than she had meant to.

Sister Matilda politely dabbed away some errant broth and studied her while chewing.

"You have been with him for, what, eight years, yes?"

Calen nodded.

"But you must know that he had two partners before you?"

Another nod.

"Well, I never met the partner that he bonded directly before you. As I understand it, they hadn't worked together for very long before she suffered and *unfortunate accident*?"

"Two years," Calen supplied. "And it wasn't an accident, but I suspect you already know that."

Sister Matilda gave her a look to confirm that she did, in fact, know.

"Before *her*, he had Zolya. Has he ever mentioned her to you?" Sister Matilda asked, a new tenderness in her voice.

"No. Not on purpose, anyway. He used to wake up with nightmares, yelling her name. But he never openly spoke of her." Those dreams would send him into fits of reclusive bitterness, followed by exaggerated violence.

"I don't suspect he would. And I'm not surprised she haunted his nightmares." She paused, as if recalling a memory of her own. "I'm not sure how much you know about the ceremonial arrival of a Vessel to this place, when they have emptied fully and are ready to live out their lives in the relative peace we can offer them?" Calen shrugged, almost completely, embarrassingly unaware. "If their partner still lives, they accompany them here, along with their closest friends, work companions, and family members. Most accept that this might be the last time they will see their loved one. It's a difficult, but dignified rite of passage. They are often dressed in their finest clothes and are brought here in love and respect, everyone working to keep them as comfortable as possible until they are settled into their room."

A pained look pinched Matilda's eyebrows together, and for the briefest moment, Calen could see the toll this work had taken.

"You want to know my history with Stokely?" she continued. "Aside from the whispers and rumors that have followed him since he was an adolescent? Here it is. I know him by name and appearance, because I am as haunted by him as he is by Zolya. I can still see him, dragging her by the arm, up the front steps of this building. I can see the arrogance and disappointment on his face as he throws her at my feet, broken and alone. I can hear the way he curses at her and me and Opus Mountain Home and all the 'wretched waste' we represent. I can remember him looking me in the eye and telling me that she was my problem, because she was useless to him." Matilda took a deep breath, anger rolling off of her in waves Calen would have thought her incapable of before. "He brought her here, broken in so many ways...face bloodied, missing her front teeth, looking like a scared, half-starved, wild animal. I don't think her eyes stopped moving for the first three days she was here, constantly darting around the room, looking for the next attack. She smelled like—" she lowered her voice in borrowed embarrassment, "—like she had not bathed in at least a week. He just left her here and stormed off, more affronted by his misfortune than by her fate."

Calen realized in brief flash of awareness that *that* had been the most likely fate she would have faced if she had stayed with him. Matilda grew quiet for a moment, but Calen could sense that there was more to the story.

"It took us weeks to get her settled in, but once she felt safe, she started to talk again. The things that she told us were not fully-formed stories, more like...the highlights. The things that she absolutely needed us to know. The things that Stokely did to her. Things that I could never prove. So-called accusations based on the words of an unwell woman."

There was bitter resignation in her voice. Calen knew then that Sister Matilda had also seen the ugly underbelly of the Order to which she had pledged her life, and was every bit as angered about it as Calen was.

"Things he continued to do to his future partner, until she decided to run away and find a better life," Calen said. "I had help from a friend, but he...Stokely followed us and found us two days ago. I escaped, but I don't think he made it." Soundless tears streamed down her face. Nox had deserved better.

The two sat in a heavy silence until Calen finished crying. Sister Matilda pulled her chair around to her side of the table and offered her a clean napkin to blow her nose.

"I'm sorry to hear about your friend. I'll do what I can to find out what became of him, but it might be difficult. We are on lockdown until further notice."

"Because of me? Stokely?" Calen asked, guilt souring the soup in her stomach.

Sister Matilda tipped her head side to side. "Partly. I would not put it past him to grab one of my girls traveling into town as a means of flushing you out. But that's not all."

"Okay? What else is happening? If you don't mind my asking."

"Well, Calen," Matilda said, standing, "that was to be my next line of questioning. I was hoping you could help me figure that out."

"How do you mean?"

"Come with me."

Twenty-Nine

May 6, 622

Stokely

Could his luck have been any better?

He had successfully tracked down Calen and spent a thrilling night haunting her through the woods. The way she had cried and ran, mana open wide, her terror palpable...he would have to make that a routine part of their joined lives. Just thinking about it made him throb with anticipation.

She had fallen apart, before the end, and was forced to beg for safety at that pit of human waste. There was no doubt that she would be so broken by the time he arrived that she would follow him like a beaten puppy.

Not only did he have Calen under control once more, but here he stood, face-to-face with Brother Frederick, the pathetic lapdog of Calen's friend from Grandview. The one who had been a thorn in his side for so many years. The one who he thought had eventually given up. But it was too big a coincidence to believe they were here on other business. He adjusted the collar of his shirt and smiled at the man. Up, he realized begrudgingly.

"You look familiar," he said.

"I should," Frederick answered.

"Franklin, is it?" The man did not respond, but he did narrow his eyes. Stokely wanted nothing more than for him to indulge the fury that was playing behind his light pupils. "Please tell me this means *she* is here too. The whore, Rosalind."

Frederick clenched his fists. A little more goading, and he was definitely going to take a swing. Glee bubbled up in his chest.

"Of course, she is with me," Frederick finally said. "Some of us take our vows seriously. Some of us protect our partners."

"Yes, yes, you deserve some kind of prize," Stokely said, reaching out to adjust Frederick's disheveled tunic. "I have just the thing in mind. How does this sound? You can continue to interfere with what *I'm* doing with *my* partner, and the both of you can suffer the same fate as Calen's other little friend...bleeding out your inconsequential lives somewhere in the woods." The momentary panic on Frederick's face was absolutely delicious.

"Where is she?" Frederick asked.

"So, you *do* want to find out just how powerful I have become?"

"Where...is...she?"

"There are things you cannot even comprehend, Franklin, about this power that we hold. Now, I personally would be absolutely delighted to destroy both you and your whore partner, but I'm going to give you one last chance to turn around and head back. I won't even tell anyone how pathetic it was."

"What have you done with Calen?" Frederick asked, his voice shaking.

Stokely took a step closer, the toes of his boots touching Frederick's. "Follow me and find out, if you are feeling brave enough." He turned his back on the man and stalked away.

Block by block, Stokely made his way back to the safehouse outside of Acera proper, where he was to meet up with his allies. Block by block, he looked, ever so discreetly, to see if the ridiculous oaf of a man was still following him. Of course he was, incapable of resisting the bait Stokely had dangled before him.

Once at the cabin, he walked past the two men stationed at the front door, a sad attempt at security. They spent most of their time arguing and the rest of the time sleeping. It did not matter much. Anyone stupid enough to try to steal from this place would soon find that the real weapons were inside, and they were always ready to be wielded.

"Jinn," he barked out. "Is everything ready?" The woman ambled from the small bedroom at the back, and her shoulders fell inward at the accidental eye contact. There was no time for this deferential bullshit today. He needed her vicious side. Grabbing her by the chin, he lifted her face to his. "Enough of this. Is everything ready?"

"Yes, master," she answered, her eyes wide.

"Good. And bring Jerico, I suspect we'll have company this afternoon."

Thirty

May 6, 622

Calen

"Are they always like this?" Calen asked.

"No, they are not," Matilda conceded. "And to be honest, I was hoping that perhaps you might know why they are behaving this way?"

"Me?" Calen asked, surprised. "Why would I know why they are behaving this way? I don't— I don't even know how burn outs act ordinarily."

"Please, do not call them that," Matilda requested, "it is undignified."

"Sorry," Calen whispered. She had not meant the insult but felt the heat of embarrassment on her cheeks.

"It is alright, I know the term is used loosely. Three days with no sleep to separate them has made me a bit touchy. I had hoped that you might be able to explain things because all of this started a few hours before you arrived."

"And what is 'all of this?' I can't make out what I'm seeing." In truth, her eyes bounced from one side of the room to the other, trying to understand what the woman were doing. Her ears strained to pick out the individual voices and the messages they carried.

"They have been speaking of someone coming, someone they could feel. Several of them tried to escape, the night you showed up on our doorstep. They ran rampant through the home, crying, or laughing, or simply asking to be joined with *her*. It was madness." Matilda lifted her hand unconsciously to her jaw, and Calen noted that the three angry scratch marks marring her tan complexion must have been inflicted during the upheaval that had preceded her unexpected arrival.

"And you thought I would understand why?" Matilda nodded. "I'm sorry to disappoint, but I've never been here, and I don't think I know anyone here. I have no idea why they would have reacted to my presence." Her head had begun to throb, and her feet, still pocked with blister marks, cried to be placed beneath the cool sheets of her room once more. But Matilda had been helpful, so she had to try to respond in kind. "What are they saying?" Calen asked her, tilting her chin to the room. It was unnerving having all those wide, wild eyes on her, the way their mouths moved in a silent prayer she could not understand. Matilda studied her.

"They are all saying some version of the same phrase. It started as 'she is coming,' or 'she is near.' Now, I think you will find, if you are willing to get close enough, that they are saying 'she is here.' 'She has come for us.'"

"And you think that by 'she' they mean...me? No. That doesn't make sense. I wasn't even supposed to come here, how could they have known?"

"So, you can understand my confusion at this situation?" Matilda said, not unkindly.

"Will they be okay?" Calen asked. "Will they go back to...normal?"

"Honestly, I think—" Matilda started to say, but an earsplitting scream rent the air, cutting her off. Both women scanned the crowd for the source, who quickly identified herself by standing on her bed and screaming, this time until her breath was exhausted. The woman's loose gown hung lifelessly from her gaunt frame.

"Zolya," Matilda said.

"Zolya?" Calen asked. "How can that be? It has to have been—"

"Sixteen years," Matilda confirmed, then she took off down the wide aisle that ran between rows of beds, and Calen followed, not wanting to be far from the only one not staring at her in that eerie way. They reached Zolya's bed just as the woman collapsed to the mattress and pulled her legs to her chest, shaking and rocking in an upright fetal position.

"Zolya, sweetie. It's me, Sister Matilda. Are you okay?" Matilda asked her.

"Matilda!" Zolya rasped, sounding terrified. Her hands shot out and she locked Matilda's shoulders in a grip so tight Calen could see her fingers shake. "Maaatttiiiillllddddaaaaa," she dragged out the name, sounding tortured this time. Her eyes opened so wide that Calen could see the full whites around the light brown irises, and she sucked in a ragged breath.

"Zolya?" Matilda asked again, gently working the woman's hands away from her shoulders.

"He's here!" Zolya cried out.

"He's here?" Calen asked, afraid she already knew the answer. "Who is here?"

Zolya's gaze shot straight to her, and Calen flinched at the severity. "You know. He's. Here."

Her heart kicked up its pace, and the sensation pumping through her veins pushed away any thought but those surrounding terror.

"Oh, shit," Matilda muttered under her breath. Whatever assurances she softly issued to Zolya were lost to the sound of frantic thoughts. Could she just stay inside and wait for him to leave? No. He would eventually overcome his hesitation at entering an Opus Home, and she was unwilling to feed these women to the beast of violence he would be by then.

"He has it, he has all of it," Zolya shrieked abruptly. "He wants to take more. His insides are like a maze. Shields and pits." Then her eyes glazed over, and her body seemed to dissolve into the soft, feather down mattress.

Calen stood and began to back away but was stopped by two women standing at the foot of the bed. They stared with a mixture of awe and fondness beaming from their sweaty, sleep-deprived faces. "Heal us," one whispered.

"I...I can't—" Calen stammered out.

"Mari," Matilda called to the caretaker across the room. "Please see Prudence and Josie back to their beds."

"What did they mean?" she asked, but Matilda looked as puzzled as she felt.

A sudden silence descended the room, then was shattered by a loud BOOM that issued from the front door and echoed through the entire building.

"Was that an explosive?" Matilda asked.

The sound had sufficiently frightened the rest of the women on their pilgrimage to Calen, and they scurried back to the relative safety of their beds. Released from the surrealism of the moment, Calen exhaled and clenched her shaking hands together. This was all too much. Time needed to slow down. She had to have a chance to plan an escape that did not involve a building full of dead Vessels.

"You know who that is, don't you?" she asked Matilda, who nodded tightly and gestured toward the hallway. The few caretakers that were not already present streamed into the room, the one named Anna bringing up the rear, all former traces of nervous anxiety gone. Her face was a mask of resolute determination.

"Is that everyone?" Matilda asked Anna.

"Yes, Mistress," Anna answered.

"What will they do if he breaks inside?" Calen asked, not so certain Anna's small frame would last long against the might standing just outside.

"He is not the first to bring hatred to our doors," Matilda answered her. "We have protocols in place to ensure the safety of everyone here."

"Then you should stay here, with them. He's here for me."

"They will be fine. You will need my help more." It would be futile to argue with this woman, especially if she hated Stokely as much as she claimed to. Calen nodded, and Matilda closed the large double doors, releasing her mana into the lock, and three heavy bolts slid into place, entombing the people inside.

Denied time to think and a plan for escape, Calen had no choice. She would have to face Stokely, once and for all.

Thirty-One

May 6, 622

Calen

The front door of Opus Mountain Home had not, in fact, been blown off of its hinges, as it had sounded. As Sister Matilda planted her feet, bent her knees, and heaved, it became obvious that the source of the loud noise had been power, unleashed in a starburst pattern disturbing the previously beautiful wood grain of the door.

The source of that power stood on the covered front porch; his tall frame silhouetted by a sun quickly approaching the western horizon just beyond the ancient hardwoods that enveloped the Home. The door rumbled open just enough for Calen to see him standing there, faced away from her, hands clasped behind his back in a display of ease. Stokely. He surveyed the land around them as if he had built the place himself and was savoring the rewards of a hard day's work, completely unbothered. When he turned his attention toward her, his eyes swept the length of her body, and a smile that some unknowing fool might mistake for friendliness exposed his perfectly straight, white teeth.

"Calen," he said, "glad to see that you've awoken from your nap. I do hope it was restful."

A light breeze picked up, but instead of smelling of the fresh mountain stream flowing nearby, it choked her with the scent of his cloyingly rich, unnatural cologne. It brought back the suffocating sensation of living within his orbit, the constant proximity of his body to hers, and rage spiked within her. She could feel her mana stir, wanting to push out against its own boundaries. Apparently, she was not alone in her desire to break free. Calen could not, however, afford the disorientation of opening fully. Not here and not now. She pulled in a measured inhale, then exhaled slowly, willing her power to calm once more.

Matilda stepped forward, partially obscuring Stokely's access to Calen. "I thought I had made myself perfectly clear that you are not, and never will be, welcome here," she said, sounding more annoyed than afraid.

"And I thought I made it perfectly clear that this doesn't involve you," Stokely shot back without removing his glare from Calen. "Now, run along and take care of your useless hags. Those of us with actual power and purpose need to speak. In private."

Matilda laughed, and the sound was so startlingly inappropriate that both Calen and Stokely looked at her.

"Stokely," she said, "and yes, I refer to you as only that, because as far as I am concerned, you forfeit the right to hold the title of 'Brother' long ago. You may think as highly of yourself as you would like, I am no stranger to spending time with folks who are lost to their own delusions. But make no mistake, everyone else sees you for what you are: a fraud. The only power you hold that is worth any value is what you have stolen from others. You are small and pathetic, and I do not answer to you."

Calen's shock at Matilda's frank words lasted only a moment before she stepped around the taller woman to stand between her and Stokely. She knew by the look on his face that violence would soon follow if she did not find a way to de-escalate the tension.

"Stoke, that's enough," she said, surprised by the steadiness of her own voice. She lifted her chin and squared her shoulders, trying to make herself seem bigger than she was. It did not help that she was barefoot and still dressed in the linen nightgown and robe that made her look like one of the permanent residents of Opus Mountain Home, but she did her best. Again, her power stirred in response to her need, excited to remind her how much strength she truly had. "I am going to ask you to leave." She looked in his eyes, then, and his scowl shifted away from Matilda and back to her.

"Yes, Calen, I couldn't agree more. We need to leave this... place. Immediately."

She narrowed her eyes at him and intertwined her arms across her chest. "Stokely, I am not going with you. I am staying here, and you need to just leave." She could feel the flimsiness of her request, but staying rational was the only hope she had of getting through to him. Brute force would not work, he was simply stronger than she was. Running and hiding were clearly out of the question. So despite the impending impotence of her speech, she continued on. "There is no world in which we can work together again. Not after what you've done to me, after what you've done to Nox." Her voice cracked around his name. She did her best to clamp down on the emotions welling in her chest, but she could feel the heat creeping up her neck, nonetheless.

"Nox?" Stokely laughed. "Consider that a favor to our Order. The strong weeding out the weak. Did you actually think he could protect you? Against me?"

Calen felt Sister Matilda shift, but she held her arm out to bar the other woman from advancing forward.

"Leave, Stokely. Now," she said.

"And let you escape your *responsibilities*?" he asked, but what Calen heard was, "and let you escape your *punishment*?"

She knew that if she offered a rebuttal, an argument would ensue. The sooner she got rid of him the better.

"Let me make it clear, Stokely. I am not leaving here with you. I'm never working with you again." And a day will come when you get what you deserve, she did not say. "There is nothing that you can do or say that will change my mind."

He reached his hands out toward her and began to giggle maniacally. The sound made her skin crawl. If past experience had taught her anything, it had been that the same things that brought him pleasure would bring her pain. Her mind flew through the possibilities of what could be the cause of his sudden outburst of humor.

"I'm so glad you said that, actually! Truly, Calen, your timing is absolute perfection."

Stokely stopped laughing and trained his eyes on her, bringing his immaculate fingers to his mouth to release a short burst of whistles. He smiled wickedly. She realized he was watching for her reaction. Her gut told her that whatever was about to happen was going to be very upsetting, and it was.

From out of the carriage came two figures, one leading the other. Calen had to squint against the orange evening light to make out the taller of the two, but when she did, her face contorted into a snarl at the sight of Stokely's sadistic sidekick. She grabbed the second person, much smaller and younger, by the hair and yanked their head back, exposing a face marked by a swollen lip and eyes that were sad and sunken, but unmistakably recognizable. Her stomach dropped, and despite her best efforts to deprive him of the joy, Stokely read the fear and anguish on her face and sighed, content.

"Avonelle?" she whispered, the air knocked from her lungs. "You bastard, how could you?"

She looked at him then, understanding the elation on his face. He leaned forward, smothering her with his presence in the personal space that she had grown accustomed to owning. How had she lived with this for so long?

"Oh, Callie, how could I *not*?" he asked.

"Who is that?" Sister Matilda asked, correctly assessing the change of stakes in their already high-cost standoff.

"My new toy," he answered acidly. "Calen and I found her some time back in some mountain backwater. And as it turns out, she's just chock full of surprises!" His smile returned.

"So what? You went back for her just so that you could manipulate me?" Calen asked. "Leave her out of this, it has nothing to do with her!"

He clicked his tongue as if correcting a misbehaving child and straightened his posture. "No chance of that happening," he said with a fatalistic tone. "You already know she's unique, Calen, so don't play stupid. Now, whether or not you took the time to figure out *why* she is unique, I don't know. But I did."

Stokely reached out and began stroking up and down the length of her arms. Calen recoiled away with such force that she bumped into the cool stone wall of the building.

"Keep your hands off of her!" Sister Matilda yelled fiercely, stepping into Stokely's reach. Before Matilda could think to defend herself, he swung a backhand attack at her face with such force that his arm *whooshed* as it moved away from Calen. Blood exploded from her nose as she stumbled backward and sprawled out on her back. Calen could see Matilda's eyes, swimming and stunned. He had not even looked away from Calen, who now found herself wrestling a white-hot anger that seemed to stoke the power within her. He placed his hands on the river rock edifice of the Home, pinning her in on both sides.

"Let's wrap this up, shall we?" he said, pleasure radiating from his smooth, mint-scented breath. "The little one is mine, now. There is nothing you can do to change that. She is far more special than you realize, and I will not be without her."

She did not know if that meant he had smuggled and consecrated Nelle the same way he had done with her, but it was clear that he had every intention of bonding her. He had not kidnapped her only as a means of manipulating Calen, he had kidnapped her with the intention of using the both of them.

"She is young, you know. Very impressionable. Innocent," he cooed. "I know that you remember how difficult things were for you when we started working together. Don't you, Calen?" She did not need to answer. They both knew that the first few years they had worked together had left an indelible mark on her soul. They both knew she would never let that happen to Nelle. "So perhaps if you come back into the fold, things won't be so...difficult...for her?" He had not even bothered to veil the threat.

"Calen, no!" Matilda groaned, her voice muffled by a quickly swelling face. Calen held up a hand to stop her protest.

"Besides," he said in a low, conspiratorial tone, "aren't you curious to learn how our sweet little friend feels so connected to us already? It's quite the juicy little secret."

Calen met his eye, searching for any sign of humanity, any chance that she was not throwing her life away. All that stared back at her was a seething mix of desire and animosity. It was taking every ounce of inner strength he had to not simply grab her and haul her away. He wanted her to go willingly. He wanted her to submit.

In the moment that stretched out, Stokely glanced briefly over his shoulder, and the woman holding Nelle spun her around and punched her once in the stomach. The girl doubled over, a loud grunt leaving her petite body, and she fell to her knees.

"I'll go!" Calen shouted at the same time Matilda yelled, "No!"

Both women had involuntarily lunged forward, far too much space still dividing them from Nelle for it to make any difference. When Matilda realized what Calen had said, she swiveled her head, still trying to recover herself.

"Don't do this, Calen," she pleaded. "We'll find a way."

Calen knew that those were desperate words that held no weight in the real world. The only way for them to stop a man like Stokely was to remove the power he hid behind, both the personal and the systemic. He had proven too many times over the years that he was not above using his superior physical strength to steal that which was no offered. He reveled in the privilege his violent tendencies afforded him. And she had seen firsthand that the only person who had the right to strip him of that, his Head of Order, was unwilling to do so. Calen knew that if there was another way, she would have to work to find it while also protecting Nelle, if she lived long enough.

"I'll go," she said more resolutely.

Stokely straightened, looking down his nose at her with such satisfied superiority that she had to clench her fists to keep from slapping it off of his face.

"Good, let's go. And don't even think of stepping back inside that place. I still have your old clothes; you won't need anything else." He turned and sauntered down the front steps, reminding her of every time he had bullied her, gotten his way, and walked off as if it had been nothing.

"What are you doing, Calen?" Sister Matilda said, finally climbing to her feet. "He'll burn you out, or worse, kill you." She was pinching her busted nose to keep it from bleeding, but at least she was on her feet again.

"Yes, he probably will," Calen said quietly. She found Matilda's worried gaze.

Matilda was shaking her head. "No, no, no. You cannot expect me to stand here and watch him carry you off! I swore an oath, Calen, and I have never abandoned it. I won't abandon it now."

Calen was surprised by the tranquility of her own voice. "Sister Matilda, sometimes our oaths take different forms. You are *not* abandoning yours; you are allowing small sacrifice to save many others. Please, I have to go."

"Revered Calendula, your death will not be a 'small sacrifice!'"

"Perhaps not. Perhaps it *will* be more than 'just the words of an unwell woman.' Perhaps it will be enough to end this," Calen finished. If death awaited her, perhaps it would not be so bad. Her life had certainly been a difficult one, but she had also experienced love and beauty and meaning. Unbidden, Rosalind's face swam to the front of her mind, relaxed and joyful, whispering the three most exquisite words she had ever heard. Calen would hold onto that vision, that feeling, as she met her end.

Matilda's shoulders fell, realization dawning. There was nothing she could do to stop Calen from sacrificing herself.

She needed to move now, before they both lost their nerve. "Thank you," she whispered as she clasped Matilda's broad hand in her own. Then Calen walked into the warm light of a sun that would soon set.

***

"How did you get her away from her family?" she asked the back of Stokely's head.

"Are you kidding? They were overjoyed at the prospect of their little girl going off to train as a Vessel."

"But you aren't a Seeker, you can't just take her that way! So, what? You take her to The Well and beg for her to be consecrated?" She almost reminded him he was not allowed more than one partner at a time, but the thought of her own impending death stilled her tongue.

"I won't have to; she already holds mana. Up," he said to Nelle. The girl stood without taking his hand. "A bit too much Jinn."

"I'm so sorry, Master," the bald woman said, genuinely seeming disappointed with herself.

"Master?" Calen asked, unable to hide the disgust in her voice.

He smiled. "Work on the inflection, Cal. It should have a sound of reverence."

"Fuck you, how does that sound?" His smile broadened.

Distant hoof beats echoed up the mountain pass leading to the Home, and they all turned toward the sound as a second, more distinct call caught Jinn's attention.

"That will be company, Master," the woman said to Stokely's feet.

"Handle it," he commanded, and she bowed quickly before breaking into a sprint in the direction from which the loud, sharp whistle had come.

Company? Who could possibly be joining them, and why would it concern Stokely?

"Now, where were we?" he said, turning to face Calen, his hands firmly on Nelle's shoulders. "Ah, yes. The girl with the secret mana, whose parents always knew she was special. The girl who was conceived on a lover's trip deep in the mountains, fourteen years ago. Whose parents thought themselves blessed when they were surrounded by a beautiful turquoise blue mana as they swam in the midnight stream…you remember that night, too, don't you Calen? You lost consciousness, but you were overflowing with power. Seems it found a second host."

Her breath caught at the implication. "That's not possible."

"The proof stands before you."

Nelle looked up at her, then, with eyes no longer innocent and curious. "I tried, Mistress Calen. I did what you said, but he found me." She began crying then.

"This is not your fault, Nelle," she said, reaching to comfort the girl, but Stokely yanked her backward, Nelle nearing losing her footing.

"No, it is not her fault, it is yours, Callie," Stokely said. "If you had just stayed, all this pain could have been avoided. We could have welcomed her into the fold, together."

"Like some demented version of a family? You cannot be serious, Stokely."

"She holds our mana, Calen. We are a family, now."

The sound of steel against steel rose from over the hill, and Stokely's face took on a look of impatience. "That'll be your whore friend and her fairy partner, Cal. If you want them to leave here alive, you will get in that carriage right now."

He shoved Nelle toward the open door, and the girl scampered up the steps, pressing herself to the far side of the bench. Stokely grabbed her arm and began dragging her, but before he could pull her inside, she wrenched her arm away.

"Wait," she said, the furious bits of a plan coming to mind. "You have me, Stokely. Let Nelle go. I know you can sense her mana, and she's not very strong. You don't need her." He narrowed his eyes. "I will go with you, I swear it. I will stay with you, just let her leave. Sister Matilda can see her safely back to her family. Please."

He moved back out of the carriage and his scowl changed, impeded upon by a victorious smirk. "Oh, that's the best part of her little secret. It doesn't matter how weak she is; she has a Seeker's distribution. She's not worthy of training as a full Vessel, but she will still be capable of finding strays. And no one will notice, or care, when they go missing."

Blessed Vessel, he was going to use Nelle to find other victims. He would drain them all, just as he had planned to do with her.

"She's just a girl, Stokely. Don't do this to her," she pleaded.

"You were just a girl, too. And look what I did for you. Once you know all the ways to *properly* use mana, you will be incredible."

"You are a maniac."

"Maybe," he said with a chuckle, "but this is good news for you Calen. It means my plans have changed and I've decided to keep you around. Think of how powerful we can be together." He moved with superhuman speed and took her by the arms before she knew what had happened. His breath was hot on her face. "You will be by my side, forever."

"What?"

"Did you think this was all some useless attempt to take mana? There is a plan, Calen. One that you are a part of. I will teach you everything, we can become invincible, take what this world owes us."

"No." She ground the word out, her body quaking against the sensation of his hands on her. "I will not go with you, not until you release Nelle."

He spun them both, pinning her against the side of the carriage. Sister Matilda was advancing across the clearing, but before Calen could call her back, Stokely pulled a small dart from the holster at his thigh and threw it blindly in her direction. She spun, but it still lodged itself in her shoulder, the force of impact driving her backward.

Stokely's full attention came to her once more, and he growled as he pressed their consecration stone between her breasts. "I will break you as many times as it takes for you to learn, Calen. You are mine. You always have been and always will be." He had not even finished speaking before she was overcome by the searing pain of her mana be ripped from her body, then everything went white.

Thirty-Two

May 6, 622

Rosalind

Rosalind was going to have to kill this bitch.

Halfway up the drive to the Home, she and Freddie had encountered a bald mound of meat watching over two horses. He had instantly advanced on them, swinging a cudgel in each hand, surprisingly nimble for a man of his proportions. They had handled him within a few minutes, her lucky strike on the back of his head sending him toppling, unconscious. Now they were set to face off against the vulture that had descended from where Calen was being held.

She was far more wily than her partner had been, and her greasy gray mana moved in ways Rosalind had never seen before. Somehow, it left her body, but then she pulled it *back in*, barely registering the effort. It was not like when she healed someone, and it moved from one body to the next. This woman's mana formed a whip that cracked the air beside Freddie's ear before being reeled back.

"You are the unnatural one, aren't you?" the vulture asked, as the three of them circled, jockeying for position. "Master says you're in love with her. It will be an honor for me to kill you."

"Well, good luck with that," Rosalind said, panting. She really should have taken up Freddie's offers to spar with more frequency.

"You're too late, you know. He already has her."

Freddie moved then, swinging his thin sword toward the woman's wielding arm. She turned, lashing out with her mana to sheathe it around the blade. He twisted at the elbow and her mana snapped, the tendril wrapped around his sword dripping to the ground. She bellowed and fell to her knees, scrabbling at the earth where it had already been swallowed. Freddie swung again, but she rolled away, the tip of his sword catching her cloak to pin her in place. Rosalind advanced on her, taking the brunt of the woman's foot as she kicked out from her position on her back. It knocked the breath from her and she stumbled back, seeing stars.

"Go!" Frederick shouted, going to his knees to wrap the woman in a headlock. "She needs you!"

"Freddie—"

"I said go!" he yelled in a tone she had never heard before. "I've got this."

The woman beneath him was struggling but losing. Her attempts to wield her mana were feeble, the gray power oozing from her hands but finding no purchase.

Rosalind ran, the strangled sound of Calen crying out reaching her as she topped the small hill that brought Opus Mountain Home into view, Stokely's carriage parked in the wide, open expanse out front. She had to continuously blink to keep blood from seeping into her left eye from the split skin just above her eyebrow. It had been pure luck that the thug's cudgel had only glanced her and not made full contact. He would have cracked her skull.

She immediately locked in on Calen's location, hidden behind Stokely's solid form. Forcing her legs to pump faster, she pulled her cloak pin, releasing the oppressive fabric from her shoulders as she ran. The only weapon she actually had was a small, needle-point blade that Freddie had made for her two years ago. It would be necessary to sneak up on him if she had any chance at hand-to-hand combat with this man.

Unfortunately, he had already clocked her approach, and half-turned toward her. He had Calen pinned by the throat. Her vision swam with fury, and she charged straight for him. He moved to meet her onslaught, bringing Calen with him, clawing at his arm for release. He held tight.

"Rosalind, so nice of you to join us," he said conversationally as she closed the distance and smashed into him ungracefully. Her knife found flesh along his rib cage just before he swept his arm around her neck and spun her body, locking her chin in the crook of his elbow. She flicked the knife in her hand so that the blade faced backward and rose her arm to strike, but his teeth sinking into her earlobe stopped her, and she cried out in pain.

"Drop that fucking knife or I snap her neck," he growled into the shell of her ear. His mana encircled Calen's throat, creating an ever-tightening noose.

She willed her shaking fist to release the weapon, and it did so, one agonized finger at a time. The knife dropped to the hard-packed earth and Stokely instantly kicked it backward and out of reach.

"I'm so glad you're here," he said, his words and tone a discordant pair. "I'm curious to see just how spectacularly you will break. Now, this might hurt a bit."

Rosalind did not have time to respond as Stokely immediately lifted his foot and brought it down on the back of her calf. She could just barely make out the blue glow of his mana, but the results were undeniable. The force of his foot was enough to snap her leg, and she watched as the jagged white thing that used to be an intact bone ripped through her flesh with a sickeningly wet sound. She howled in agony and fell to the ground when he released her, now as useless as the knife that lay ten feet away.

Thirty-Three

May 6, 622

Calen

"Rosalind, no!" Calen choked out around Stokely's grip.

Calen had already made peace with her own fate, as it was only her chance to protect Nelle, but she had no idea how to save Rosalind. Stokely would finish his business with her and move on to Rosie. Her only fleeting hope was that Freddie was close by and would arrive in time to get her out of here. There was no way she was leaving on her own, sprawled out and screaming in pain that echoed through the forest.

"This stupid bitch was helping you the entire time, wasn't she?" Stokely asked, turning his attention back to Calen where she half-knelt in the dirt. "You know I'll have to make her pay for that, right? I wonder if she likes it rough?"

Calen met his glare with her own furious one. "Go ahead and try. I hope she rips off your cock and shoves it down your throat."

He smiled slowly. "Believe it or not, I have actually missed that filthy little mouth of yours. Now, where were we?"

He wrapped his arm around her, pressing their bodies together, her thin, linen gown the only barrier. She tried to move away, and in the shift, she saw a glimpse of someone standing behind him.

Nelle. What was she doing?

The tip of Rosalind's discarded blade peaked between Stokely's ribs and bicep, and he lurched upright, screaming. Blood blossomed across his side. Nelle had stabbed him. The blade *whicked* as she pulled it back out, and he cried out even louder. His grip grew tight, and Calen feared he may actually snap her neck soon. The girl made to stab him again, but he turned, releasing Calen in a burst of force. She flew backward, away from Stokely's mana-enhanced arm, slamming forcefully into the ground, her head bouncing at the edge of the grassy edge of the lot. Shuffling onto her hands and knees, she watched as Stokely fell upon the girl, raising his hand to strike. Rosie had seen it too and was attempting to push-crawl her way to Nelle with her destroyed leg dragging behind her. She was never going to make it in time, and neither was Calen. It did not matter if Stokely needed Nelle. If he was too deep in his rage, he would kill her anyway, and deal with the regret later.

Calen was powerless. Once again, she knelt before this man and watched as he violated everything decent in this world. She had tried, *really* tried, to escape. To save herself. To prevent other victims from suffering her fate. And yet, there he stood, monumentous in the setting sun. Inevitable. She was powerless.

Not powerless, it whispered, and pushed against her belly.

No…no, she was not that weak, small person anymore. Even without her mana, she had the strength to stand up to Stokely, spurred on by the coals of rage and regret she held banked in her chest.

But she did have her mana, and it was ready.

There was no time.

No time to wait. No time to open. No time to coax, to ask, to plan, to hope, to hesitate. There was only a desperate need and a bone-deep fury. She could not let this happen. *They* could not let this happen.

The world around Calen slowed and warped as she released her tenuous hold on her power and allowed it to explode through her. In an instant, she was glowing turquoise, radiant and terrible. Her power screamed from the base of her throat in an other-worldy language that rent the air with vibrations compelling the universe to respond. It poured from her hands with enough force to send tremors breaking up the hard, dusty soil in a rippling wave of disruption. Her skin burned with the power longing for a target, now that it had room to breathe. It needed a purpose.

She gave it a target.

Her dark, angry eyes shot open and locked on Stokely, who had risen to his knees at the outpouring of her mana. Digging her hands into the now-loose earth, she did not have to ask, she did not have to direct. She barely had to form the thought and her power obeyed, lancing out from her palms, and crossing the distance in an instant. Her mana shot from the ground in the same intricate pattern it had at her last seed blessing and slammed into Stokely's chest, knocking him to the dirt beside Nelle's still body.

Calen caught sight of her small, unmoving frame and her anger redoubled as she screamed her fury once more. Even from this distance, she saw the wave of fear that swept over Stokely's face.

He had good reason to be afraid.

Sister Matilda ran to Nelle, scooping her up in capable arms and moving her back to the porch. She hovered her face above the girl's broken mouth, waiting for confirmation that she still breathed. Relief swept across her features, and she nodded once toward Calen.

"She lives," Calen heard over the rhythmic pounding of her heart in her ears.

She could feel the power humming through her, energizing the air around her, suffusing the Earth beneath her, and it was like nothing she had ever experienced before. Tendrils of her power coiled outward awaiting the next need to be fulfilled. It had not poured from her, had not left her body, had not severed their connection. She and it had remained intact, her mana tethering her to the universe around her. Through that connection, she could feel…something. It was as though her power had struck a tuning fork at the perfect frequency and it vibrated through her. On some elemental level, she knew that whatever it was, it recognized her. It could feel her anguish, and it waited to see what she would do.

"Calen, that was—"

She cut off whatever Stokely was about to say by spurring her power to action with a heart-rending wail. The coils flared out and reached for the roots of the countless plants and trees growing around them. She needed, and they obeyed, bursting out from the ground and ensnaring Stokely's arms and legs. She flexed with her power, and they pulled him prostrate. Rising to her feet, her connection to her mana never wavered as she stood tall and walked to where Stokely lay spread-eagle, utterly helpless.

Her power rolled from her in wisps of turquoise that curled and danced before pulling back into her skin, and his gaze held a mixture of fear and awe that she had never seen before. Lifting her palm, she watched her mana swirl and move. Had it always been like this?

"Cal," he said, his voice quavering. She flexed anew and filled his mouth with another fleshy root.

"No," she said, sounding altered. It was no longer her voice alone that spoke. Now it carried two wills, sharing one throat. "No more. Never again."

Rosalind's knife lay a few feet away, and she plucked it up gingerly before straddling Stokely's abdomen. She pressed it into the soft spot under his chin and wondered if she could actually kill him. The thought had taunted her for so long, but with the possibility of it literally resting in her hand, Calen hesitated. She knew that killing him would mean more to her than it would to him. It would be another piece of her soul forfeit to his monstrosity. She tipped his head back with the weapon, and his eyes gave away the truth. He did not think her capable.

"Calen," Rosalind called, her voice heavy with the exhaustion of holding injury-induced unconsciousness at bay.

"I have to do this, Rosie," she said.

"No, you don't. Think. If *he* can fill, he can empty. Take back what is yours."

Calen scrutinized Stokely's face. If he had been afraid before, he was absolutely terrified now. He tried to shake his head, but her vines held fast. She tenderly took their consecration stone into her open palm. Such a magnificent thing, abused in such ugly ways. Had it a consciousness, as her mana did? She was now convinced of that fact. The small knife thudded as it fell back to the dirt, and she concentrated fully on the smooth, teardrop-shaped object in her hand.

How to begin? Perhaps, if she made her need known, it would respond in the same way it had just moments ago. Her mana would do what she commanded, and the consecration stone would follow suit. A single tear slipped along Stokely's hairline as she pressed the Stone into his chest, closed her eyes, and asked. Her mana flowed from her hand, into the stone, and crossed the barrier of his flesh with an odd popping sensation. It instantly connected with its own kind, a well of her mana that he was holding in a strange grid-like pattern around his internal organs. The two halves of her power within Stokely began to intertwine and rejoin. Then, she simply pulled.

It resisted at first, held tight where it had been tucked away for years, but her need was insistent, and so the mana began to flow. At first, it was slow and sluggish, but as it broke free from him, it began to move more easily, sluicing through the liquid interior of the stone and back into her body. The experience was one of absolute ecstasy. For her, anyway. Stokely was squirming and moaning and trying, in vain, to speak. If she could make this moment last forever, she would. If she could exact this revenge over and over again, she would do it for herself, and Zolya, and Jamilla, and all the countless other people he had hurt in his pursuit of absolute power. She would be his reckoning.

The wave of exuberant mana returning to her crested, and as the last swirls of turquoise left his body, she expected the flow to stop on its own. But it did not.

Where her power ended, it was intertwined with his, embedded in his muscles, joints, and nerve fibers. She was no longer intentionally pulling, but it continued to move into her. Stokely started to scream in earnest, bucking his hips against the roots in response to what was likely the most pain he had ever experienced in his life. She could tell he was begging, pleading for her to stop, but it was too late now. Her mana kept pulling on his, moving it from his cells in an ever-growing torrent of power. After an eternity of his muffled screams, something changed and his mana stopped its disentanglement and was left floating aimlessly, like Spanish moss from a tree, no longer properly attached to its host. Stokely's body went slack beneath her as he lost consciousness.

Calen let out a ragged exhale. Done. It was done.

Suddenly, she felt a lurching, something attaching, something moving beneath her palm once more. Instead of the light blue mana she had associated with Stokely for so long, she was flooded with a muddy blend of creamy, turquoise-tinged pink mana.

Not his, she realized in a panic. It fled from him, pouring into her in a wave that blotted out her thoughts. Actively trying to visualize cutting off the source of mana did not work, and she lost all control. She even tried to rip her hand away from the stone, hoping to sever the connection, but it was held fast. Whatever was leaving him had no intention of stopping halfway. She was caught in the deluge of power flooding into her body. This was not like the night she had learned to open fully. This power was too much, and if it did not stop soon, it might actually destroy her. Human bodies were not meant to hold this much of the universe within them. Her muscles began to flex and cramp, her skin going hot and her vision swirling. She could only just make out the shape of her hand glowing atop the Stone, mana pouring through it but also *outside* of it, directly from his body to hers. If only she could pull it away...

Weak and dizzy, power flared within and around her in an exquisite, lethal aurora. She was not strong enough to take it all, and she was powerless to cut it off, held fast in the fatal dance.

Small, cool hands tried to take the sides of her face, flinching away from the searing heat before finally gaining purchase.

"Calen, close off!" Rosalind shouted over the hissing of power ripping through the air around them. "Calen, please, you have to close off!"

She tried, ineffectually, to wrest the power under control. There was nothing she could do but fade out...

...flow ebbing... slowing... so dizzy... burning... igniting... bursting... collapsing... cool arms... green eyes... the cries of her best friend as she tumbled away from life...

Thirty-Four

May 6, 622

Rosalind

"Calen, please stay with me!"

In one moment, Calen's body was held rigid by the immense power that rolled through, out, and back into it as it looped tighter and tighter, trying to fill an overflowing vessel. The heat around her had rippled the air and forged a boundary that Rosalind had to push through to reach her. In the next moment, Calen had collapsed in an exhausted heap, her face smashing into the soft flesh of Rosalind's shoulder. Only the delicate clinking of their stone shattering marked the passage from one dramatic state to the next.

Rosalind gently rolled Calen onto her back in the cool dirt and swept her hair from her face. Her dark eyes were bleary half-moons, the top lashes brushing the bottom ones before sliding open again. Her breaths were shallow and thready, her chest barely moving with each brief inhale exhale.

"Calen, can you hear me?" Rosalind almost did not recognize her own frantic words.

Calen moaned as her head lolled to the side. Tears slid from Rosalind's eyes and sizzled as they met the scorching skin of Calen's cheek. Power still engulfed her, seething, coiling, flowing.

"Calen, if you can hear me, I think you need to close off," she said, trying to calm herself enough to think straight. "Cal, you can do this. Control it. Close it off before it kills you!"

Rosalind became distantly aware of voices now trying to convey instructions to her. But those voices did not matter, not when she was watching Calen's life force burn up, threatening to carry her away on wisps of swirling mana.

"Don't leave me, Cal! Please, don't leave—"

Frederick's hands swept under her arms and tried to haul her away from Calen's calamitous form.

"No!" she let out in a feral scream. There was nowhere else that she could exist away from this time and this place. A queasy feeling of hopelessness crept up from her stomach and into her throat. Calen was slipping away from her and in the instinctive rush of despair that accompanied that realization, she wrapped herself around the inferno consuming her and threw her own powers open wide. With all the force she could muster, she entangled every strand of her power around the maelstrom of Calen's and pushed, trying to wrestle it into submission.

"Calen, you have to close off," she tried once more, weakly. Her mana continued to work, coaxing, and moving the amalgamation of all of Stokely's past horrors into the only place it had left to go: Calen's core. She wielded like she never had before, sweat popping out on her forehead from exertion as much as from the heat of the feverish body she held. Slumping to the ground with Calen, she studied the exquisite features of her face, realizing that in saving her, she was likely forfeiting herself. Frederick must have realized the same thing, judging by the crazed look on his face as he gripped fistfuls of hair and knelt beside them, just outside the storm.

"It will be worth it, for you," she whispered as her own tired eyes fluttered shut. "I love you, Calen." Stroking her dark, wild hair, she breathed in the scent and hummed. Calen had always loved that song; it made her feel safe.

She continued to push herself to the brink, never letting up on the force with which she worked to convince Calen's power to settle in and spare her life. Her coral mana glowed brighter and worked harder than it ever had, and she watched as it was consumed by the fury raging within Calen. Eight years she had done this work, losing hardly any power in all that time. But here, in this mountain hollow, holding the love of her life, she watched it burn up, losing tendrils of mana at a time. There was nothing to be done about it. Losing Calen would be far more devastating to bear than burning out.

It was almost like a dance, now. The thought was a comfort to her. One last intimate act for them to share, one last special moment. Rosalind felt a shift in the tide as the energy engulfing them began to slow and settle within Calen's body, still cradled lifelessly within her arms.

Minutes or hours or lifetimes later, Rosalind's mana released. In a sensation like being cut from a tether tied to her rib cage, she knew she had done it.

Frederick was there, delicately disentangling the two of them. He had not left her side while she had worked, while she had taken herself apart to hold Calen together. He deftly lifted her with arms strong enough to make her feather-light. She was fading out, watching the dusky orange sky roll by above his head as he carried her...somewhere. Her eyes would close soon, she knew. But for how long, she did not.

"I'm sorry, Freddie, I had to..." she mumbled.

"I know, Ros. Apologize to me when you wake up from this," he answered as he slid her into the carriage, "because you will."

"Get them to the healer on Fourth Street." A woman's voice. "I've got the girl."

"Keep a look out, I lost sight of the woman." Freddie's voice. "She's dangerous."

Doors shutting. Silence. Muffled hooves. Faster now. Faster. Air moving against the sides of the carriage. Silence. Darkness. Nothing.

Thirty-Five

May 8, 622

Rosalind

Rosalind was drowning, spinning in the churning ether between dreaming and awakening, incapable of discerning up from down. With a jolt, she broke through the surface of sleep, but did not shoot up in bed. Her depleted body was incapable of such an unreasonable task as sitting up. Every inch of her ached, feeling as though her bones had been hollowed out and filled with lead. Her heart, however, seemed to have been spared that fate as it vigorously galloped in her chest with the unattainable goal of keeping up with her body's need for injury-healing blood. The pained groan that left her throat drew Freddie's attention from the bedside chair. He sat on the edge of the mattress and reached for a bowl of water balanced on a tray by her feet.

"You're awake," he observed.

"I survived. Hooray," she muttered.

"The healer said that you need to re-hydrate before he can do anything else." He wrung most of the water from a clean, white cloth and brought it to her lips. Rosalind drank the scant water it offered, but it was like the first drops of rain on hard-packed clay. She needed more.

"Help me sit up," she requested weakly, and he clasped the back of her neck to prop her up, fluffing pillows behind her back. She motioned for the cup on the tray, and he obliged. After she had drunk roughly her own body weight of the cool spring water, she sat the cup down and looked at her partner. Really looked at him. He had a few minor cuts on his face and bruises on his neck, but it was his eyes that suffered the most injury. They were puffy and red-streaked. He had been crying, and recently. She placed her hands on his.

"Freddie, I'm sorry," she said, the dampness in his eyes renewed.

She was not sorry for what she had done. They both knew that she would do it again in a heartbeat, if that was what it took to keep Calen alive. Just like they both knew he would not interfere, if that was what she required. No, she was not sorry for that part. She was sorry, however, for hurting him in the doing. She was the closest he had to a family for hundreds of miles, and he had almost lost her. He was a quiet and gentle man, and the only person in the world who truly understood him had almost died while he sat idly by and watched because she had commanded him to do so. He had undoubtedly sensed the closeness with which she brushed against death in that struggle, and for delivering him that anguish, she was sorry.

Freddie nodded and looked away. "I'll get the healer," he said, and stood to leave.

"Wait," she stopped him with a plea. "I don't need the healer right now, Fred. I need my friend, my loyal partner." The look on his face said that he had no desire for her groveling. "I mean it. Even if that was a bit melodramatic." He exhaled through his nose and looked toward the door, then back to Rosalind before settling himself back in his chair by the bed.

She studied his eyes once more, not sure if she had the strength to ask the question that was threatening her sanity with its lack of an answer.

"Is—" she started. "Did... did Calen—" She could not finish the question.

"She's alive," he answered, not needing her to.

Rosalind felt the stone of worry crack inside her chest. "So, she's okay?"

"She's...well, you'll see," he said, his brow furrowing.

Her heavy head fell back onto the pillow holding her upright. "What does that mean?" she asked, her throat already needing more water.

"That means," he studied the ceiling as if it might have right words, "she has changed." He turned his palms upward, as if he did not know what more to say. "But she did survive." He suddenly smiled and leaned forward. "And actually, I can do you one better."

"I cannot imagine many things that would be better than that news."

"But if you could?"

Her mind swam for an answer. "Nox?" she asked tentatively.

Freddie nodded.

"Nox is alive?" she shouted, then immediately wished she had not.

"He is alive. He's here, just two doors down," Freddie answered, looking much lighter than he had just moments ago. "Apparently, some trappers were up on the mountainside checking their snares and heard the commotion of Nox and Stokely fighting. By the time they found him, Stokely had fled, and Nox was in pretty bad shape. They recognized him as a Vessel by his earring and brought him here. He's fairly beat up, but he'll be okay."

Nox, Freddie, and Calen, alive and under one roof. It was more than she could have hoped for with everything they had faced in the past few weeks, but an unnamed sense of doom still lurked in the back of her mind.

"Stokely?"

Freddie shook his head slowly. "I went up to visit at Opus this morning. Apparently, by the time Sister Matilda had taken the girl inside and had her injuries tended, he had escaped. She went out to check on him, and he was gone."

"How?" she asked, her broken leg now throbbing at the memory of how it had been shattered.

"The woman, whoever she was. We heard screaming coming from up the path you had taken and felt whatever Calen had done. The woman took off, into the trees. My best guess is that she waited for us to clear out and then helped him escape." He ran a frustrated hand through his fluff of brown hair.

"Or she dragged his corpse into the woods, where it is currently being devoured by birds," she said, narrowing her eyes at the ceiling.

"We can only hope," he said, standing. They both knew that they had not been that lucky. "You need to rest. I'll be back with the healer soon, and I'll bring you some more water." He gave her a relieved smile as he slipped out of the room and silently closed the door behind him.

Rosalind sunk back down, releasing all of her weight into the bed. A deep weariness claimed her. She felt smaller and weaker than she ever had in her life, but at least she was still here living it. Her friends had all survived this nightmare. While she knew that Stokely was probably still out there, somewhere, she did allow herself the hope of believing he and his companions had not fared so well. Rosalind had personally witnessed the ruinous effect of Stokely losing his mana. If he *had* survived, it had been just barely. If he did still live, it would be as a fractured piece of what he had been before.

That was a problem for future Rosalind to solve, after she slept for the next year.

Thirty-Six

May 9, 622

Calen

Calen sat curled up in the overstuffed chair that looked directly at Rosalind's room. The thin wool blanket draped over her raised knees was more than enough to keep her comfortable in the rising spring warmth that drifted through the open windows of the healer's clinic. Boredom set in as she clocked the second hour sitting in the same spot.

She began shifting wisps of turquoise from her left palm to her right, and back again, the sensation not unlike passing one's hand through a cloud of fog. Only, it was the fog that passed into her flesh. The amazement at it was only surpassed by the overwhelming sense that she should not be amazed. This should be commonplace.

In the three days since her showdown with Stokely, she had spent approximately half of her time sleeping off the after effects of wielding too much mana. The other half of the time, once she had arisen from the sleep of the dead, she had spent making sense of the phenomena living within her. She had been able to figure out how to sequester the different mana into small pockets of energy that were distinct from one another. That part had not been too difficult, as the mana had no interest in sharing space, it had seemed. But figuring out what to do with Stokely's stolen power had been a task. After multiple failed attempts to settle it in the same way she was able to with the creamy yellow, then the vibrant pink, she realized that it was not likely to follow the same pattern. It seemed common sense, now, that Stokely's mana would want to settle in her muscles and nerves, as it had with him.

The ramifications of holding more than one type of mana were yet to be seen, and she was not in any rush to discuss her situation with anyone. Except, maybe, for Rosalind.

The bizarre sensation of having mana live within her arms and legs (and spine, maybe?) was nothing compared to the disconcerting twin flows of energy that rested behind her ribs. They had brought with them the sensation of trauma, and the impressions of memories from their former Vessels. If Calen had needed any further confirmation of Stokely's pattern of abuse and penchant for brutality, she had it now. The twice-stolen mana had once belonged to Zolya and Jamilla, she was certain.

The more she thought about it, Calen thought she understood his reasoning. *There is a plan, Calen. One that you are a part of. I will teach you everything, we can become invincible, take what this world owes us.* He truly sought to make himself invincible. The way he had woven the stolen mana into his organs, safeguarding them against injury. All those years he spent, hoarding his own power. For the longest time, she had thought he was simply a selfish prick who enjoyed hurting others. Now, she understood that it was all part of a grander scheme to make himself something more than human. The idea made her shudder.

The turquoise faltered as she lost focus, remembering what she had felt as she pulled the power him. Hatred. Rage. Destruction. But now, as she felt for the twin pulses of power that she protected with her literal heart, she realized that his depravity had imprinted upon her. She had taken what was not hers to have. She held something deeply precious that she held no claim to. True, she had not done it willfully, and she had no desire to misuse the power, but still…Calen felt a flush of shame at the unintentional violation she had committed. She would need to find a way to make things right.

Calen took a deep breath, focusing on her own hands. Her mana spiraled slowly around each finger on her right hand, stopping to explore the ridges of her obsidian ring, before moving on to coil around the next finger. Like a playful toddler, she thought. It had changed as well. There was no longer the option for her to close off, it simply could not be contained. Her power was *everywhere*. One more mystery to investigate, if they ever left this healer's clinic.

Calen shifted in the soft chair and reached for her mug of linden tea with her free hand. Her power was trying to figure out how knuckles worked on the other, and she was genuinely curious to see how it would react if it pushed up against Stokely's power (now her power, she realized) in her hand.

For the twentieth time this hour, she looked at Rosalind's door. The healer had given her strict instructions to stay away until Rosalind had rested enough to be able to handle company. Calen had remembered most of what had happened on the mountain side, and Freddie had filled in any timeline gaps for her. Well aware of what Rosalind had done for her, she was more than happy to oblige the healer's edict. That had not stopped her from sneaking in to watch a sleeping Rosie, with Frederick's help, of course. And it did not mean that she would not spend all day and night watching her door, waiting for him to lift it.

As if on cue, the door slid open slowly and Revered Jacob, the resident healer, stepped out, immediately meeting Calen's hopeful eyes. His shoulders dropped and he let out an exasperated sigh. There was no doubt that her party had forced him to push the boundaries of what he thought he could heal. While he was specialized in caring for Vessels, he had probably never been faced with the volume and severity of wounds, power-related and mundane, that they had brought to the doorstep of his clinic. Revered Jacob would not be sad to see them leave, when the time came.

"Alright, you can see her," he conceded. "But only for a short time, and if she seems taxed, you must let her rest."

Calen rose, dropping the blanket to the chair and practically running across the waiting area. The mana in her right hand shifted to her elbow and danced in the breeze. As she crossed the threshold, the air left her lungs. Rosalind sat up in bed, her broken leg forming a small hillock under the sage green blankets that covered the lower half of her body. Her posture was relaxed, but it belied a weakness that Calen had never seen in her before. Her face was sleepy, but happy, and her warm cinnamon hair fell in long, loose sheets over her shoulders. Rosalind was as beautiful as she had ever been, but there was no denying that she had sacrificed something of herself in saving Calen.

"I'll get Nox," Freddie rumbled as he moved around Calen, who was frozen just inside the room, staring.

She shuffled to the side of Rosalind's bed, both women locked in an enchantment and incapable of looking away. She could not find words. There simply were none that seemed sufficient. Sorry? Thank you? I love you? How about this weather? There was nothing she could say to convey the depth of gratitude or the abundance of love she held for this woman. So, she did not speak. She leaned forward and kissed Rosalind gently, taking her round face between steady hands. They kissed and cried and laughed and kissed some more until the charged space between them shrank to nothing and they sat wrapped in a tight embrace, hearts pressed together, breathing the same sweet air.

A discreet throat-clearing pulled their attention to the hallway, where Nox and Freddie stood, ending the private moment far too prematurely for Calen's liking. If it had been anyone else, she would have closed the door on their noses.

"Does anyone else think we should have just stayed at Bastian's that night and drank ourselves silly?" Nox asked, a playful grin on his face.

Before she had time to think about it, Calen rose and crossed the small room, standing on tip toes to throw her arms around his neck, narrowly avoiding the sling that held his right arm in place. He let out a slight grunt at the force of her hug, but then wrapped his uninjured arm around her waist. This was the first time the healer had let her see him, as well, but she had no problem finding words for him.

"Thank you, thank you, thank you, Nox," she said into his chest, her voice muffled by his shirt. "You are a good man, and you saved my life."

"What are friends for?" he answered.

"Hey, I told you I was still new at this."

***

The clinic did not offer much in the way of food, relying mostly on the healer's ability to treat patients quickly enough to return to their homes by their next meal, and the services of neighboring restaurants when he could not. That evening, the four of them sat in Rosalind's room, eating an eclectic mix of everything Jacob's apprentice could carry back from the three restaurants on the same block. As it turned out, healing a Vessel required a vast amount of food and enough water to drain a well. The four of them were likely to clean out the larders of the city if they stayed there much longer. Calen barely tasted any of it, eating with haste to fill a stomach that had held for too few meals in the past three weeks. She would have to remember to thank Sister Matilda for her hospitality and ask forgiveness for her poor table manners when she visited next.

"Ya know," Nox started conversationally, "this reminds me of one time when I was traveling with a woman, and we met up with a few of our friends for dinner..." He shot a smirk at Calen, who blushed lightly at the jab, and washed down a mouthful of mutton before speaking.

"All jokes aside, I do want to thank you all for everything you have done. I know it's not nearly enough, but..." She looked to each of them in turn, feeling a different sort of emotion creep up her throat than what she was used to. Gratitude. And belonging.

"Calen, if you are about to tell us that you are taking off again, please know that I will personally tie my broken leg to yours and force you to take me with you," Rosalind said, when Calen looked her way.

Calen chuckled. "No, that's not what I was going to say. I was going to say that I know it's not nearly enough, but I want you to know that if you ever need anything from me, I will be there for you in any capacity that I am able to be."

"Kind of difficult to do that from across the border," Nox commented, raising his dark eyebrows.

"I'm not leaving," she said. "Not anymore. I'm done running."

It was the first time she had voiced her plans out loud, and as soon as the sentiment left her lips, she knew it was the right decision. Freddie nodded his agreement, Nox smiled crookedly, and Rosalind looked like she might weep with joy. She smiled warmly and intertwined her fingers with Rosalind's.

"So, what will you do?" Rosalind asked.

"Well, I've been thinking." She chewed on the inside of her lip, choosing her words carefully. "So much has happened in the past few days that defies any ready explanation." For emphasis, she held her hands apart and pushed mana from both palms, forming an intricate pattern between them, before sending it forward to flick Nox in the nose, then returning to her hands. She smiled smugly; his previous jab returned. All three looked at her with surprise.

"So that's what you meant?" Rosalind asked Freddie. He nodded. Calen looked at her questioningly, but she only smiled back.

"Anyhow. I can't quite explain it, but I have this unshakable feeling that we are missing something. That our understanding of this celestial power is incorrect, or at least, incomplete. I've seen half a dozen unbelievable things since I left Old Roan, and I have no way of understanding any of them." She rested her hands beneath her breasts, feeling the energy humming beneath them. "There are answers here, somewhere, and I need to find them. We deserve to know, after what we've been through."

"Does that mean you will return to the capital with us?" Rosalind asked, her eyebrows rising hopefully. "We've had word from Augustus that he is bringing a small squad from the Capital Guard to escort us back." Calen had forgotten how satisfying it was when Rosalind was eager to spend time with her.

"Yes," she answered. "For a little while, anyhow. But you know that if I really want to find buried information, I need to go to—"

"Black Rock," they all answered in relative unison.

If she were lucky, she would be granted access to the library on the eastern side of the promontory. As the undisputed center of information in the Colonies, it should have tomes dating back far enough to hold answers to her questions. Calen had only been there on two occasions, neither pleasant, and she was not particularly excited to return.

"Perhaps I'll join you," Nox said.

She smiled. "That's incredibly generous, but I cannot ask that of you, Nox. Perhaps while we are in the capital, I will find another unfortunate soul to join me on this leg of my journey."

Nox looked sheepishly at his hands. "I'd love to pretend that my offer was purely altruistic, but alas I must confess that I am in desperate need of training. It was...less than stellar having my ass kicked that way. A few months running the Promontory should do me some good."

"Don't lie, you plan on raiding the library, too," Freddie said, ripping a bite from a chewy dinner roll. Nox chuckled, then winced. Calen suspected that his injuries ran deeper than what he was letting on.

"When do we leave?" Rosalind asked.

All three looked to Calen, silently appointing her as the leader of the group. She returned the look, and they seemed to reach the understanding that whatever happened next, they would face it together.

"When we are all well enough to do so," Calen said, reaching out for Rosalind again. She had refused to allow Jacob to mend her leg completely, knowing how gravely it would drain the man. Healing unassisted would slow their progress, but Calen also knew the price that mending a bone would exact, so she was content to wait patiently. Freddie had been scouting the city since their arrival, and there had been no sign of Stokely or his bald partner, Jinn.

Jinn. Such a small name to hold so much contempt. Calen pushed away the dark thoughts that surfaced with that name, refusing to allow them to taint this moment.

"How was everyone when you visited Opus Mountain Home?" she asked Frederick.

"Sister Matilda said that things had settled down by the morning following," he answered.

"Did you see Nelle when you were there?" she asked.

"I did. She is healing, physically anyhow," he said, sadness in his soft face. "But she has been through a great deal of stress, and her mind will take longer to knit itself back together."

She had hoped to rob Stokely of the opportunity to destroy the life of another innocent person, but now she feared that plan may have failed. Whatever parts of herself that Nelle could recover, Calen would be by her side to help. They had been forged together, somehow, and she recognized her duty to the delicate girl and her fierce heart.

"She comes with us," Calen said quietly. "I will protect her. I have to."

Thirty-Seven

May 10, 622

Zolya

Zolya (formerly of the Third Order), had spent nearly every day for the past sixteen years locked inside the maze of her mind. She, like every Vessel, had been taught during her training that it was a possibility to expend her mana and reach a point of burn out during her career. It was not always guaranteed to happen, but it was more likely to happen to members from her Order, due to the nature of their abilities. Scholar warriors only ever expended power in a fight, Seekers almost never pushed their power outside of their bodies, for any reason. Ritual workers, however, almost always their mana to achieve the goal for which their services had been acquired.

What Zolya had never been taught, most likely because the possibility was so remote and treacherous it was beyond the boundaries of educational necessity, was that this particular fate could be expedited by another Vessel. Say, a power-hungry partner, who could steal her mana from her.

Her teachers had also been quite stingy on their details regarding life after burning out. As it was from her perspective, being stripped of her mana had somehow un-tethered her from the reality of the world around her. She was still connected to life by that tether, but it she had to follow it back through the maze to make her way to the 'here and now' that others were experiencing. Once there, she could only stay for short periods of time before the anguish of knowing what she had lost sent her spiraling back into the labyrinth. And although everyone in this Home was kind and gentle, she could see in their eyes and hear in the tone of their voice what they never could say. This place was a hospice, and she was dying. More slowly than the rest of her companions, it had seemed, but withering away, nonetheless.

Some things helped her find her way back more readily. The smell of roasted fish, which reminded her of her childhood home along the coast. The sound of Harper playing her favorite song on the small piano in the common room. The way Sister Matilda wound her hair into a tight braid, how she had worn it in a previous life. Sister Matilda, herself, was a safe passage back. Her voice, her presence always made Zolya feel confident in ascending to the surface of herself. She still could not stay long, and the 'visits' were usually for check-ins, to make sure she was comfortable, at peace.

Zolya was quickly learning that Sister Matilda was not the only one who could do that, however.

When *he*...Stokely, she remembered with some effort, was close, something about his presence had pulled Zolya back into her body, resting in the large infirmary. It had not been a feeling of safety that accompanied her flash back to reality that time, it had been sheer panic. Zolya had no idea why, but locked in a box in the corner that had his name was also the distinct sensation that he was dangerous. Sister Matilda had been in the room with her, so Zolya had drifted away secure in the knowledge that she would handle it and all would be well again.

It was quite the surprise to her that after sixteen years, something (or, rather, someone) new would arrive that would pull her from the depths in a way that was *hopeful*. But that was exactly what was happening now. She felt herself resurfacing once more, seated with her legs hanging over the edge of her bed. At least she was back in her own room this time. She looked at her hands, held them out in front of her as she always did when she came to. When had they grown so thin?

Was she brave enough to ask for a mirror this time? No. She would take this moment to live in her body for a few fleeting moments. Just long enough to learn about the new visitor and why they made her want to stick around.

"Hello, Revered Zolya," the woman said. Her voice was low and smooth, and Zolya instantly wanted to hear her speak more. "Do you know who I am?" she asked.

Zolya did not, but there was something familiar about her. She continued to watch the woman's lips move, her voice soothing and warm. Zolya rarely spoke, even when she was lucid. The timbre of her own voice after spending so much time locked in silence was often too much stimulation, and all it ever did was make her upset. This woman, though, spoke slowly and gently, her voice comforting. Sister Matilda stood behind her, watching with interest. Zolya managed a small smile for her, the muscles in her cheeks trembling at the effort of pulling up her lips. Matilda smiled back, so Zolya decided to stay a few minutes longer.

"My name is Revered Calendula," the woman said.

Zolya thought about repeating her name but nodded her understanding instead.

"You can call me Calen, if you would like. The reason I came to see you today is because I have something that I believe belongs to you. I would like to try to give it back to you, if I can."

The woman, Calen, sounded nervous underneath the warmth of her voice. Zolya could not imagine why, or what she might have. She had not owned any possessions for quite a long time, and the trinkets she had brought with her were all but useless to her now. If Calen really did have something of hers, it might be better used by her.

She looked at Sister Matilda, confused. Her caretaker nodded back encouragingly, so she looked back to Calen's hands, trying to see what she might be holding.

"May I place my hands on you, Revered Zolya?" Calen asked respectfully. Another smile from Matilda, another nod from her.

Calen slowly stretched her hands forward and placed them lightly on her belly, bowing her head and closing her eyes. Before Zolya had time to question what was happening, she began to feel a presence pushing against her skin, then continuing beyond it. She began to panic, but Matilda suddenly sat beside her and held her still beneath careful hands.

"It's alright, Zolya," she whispered.

Suddenly, there was a swirl of light and color behind her eyes that made her feel dizzy and warm. The swirling expanded, then contracted into itself before exploding outward. She was struck with the feeling that she had done this once before, and instantly the hope she had felt made sense. The force was moving through her, settling behind her navel in an undulating ball of energy and *meaning*. Calen pulled back her hands just as slowly and released a held breath.

"Oh," Zolya muttered, sucking in a deep breath. She wrapped her arms around herself and cried unabashedly, her sobbing hiccups the only sound in the room for some moments. Relief and wonder washed over her. It was hers, and she *did* want it back. She did not know if her grasp on lucidity would be more permanent, now that her mana had been returned to her, but she would try.

She looked into Calen's eyes and was surprised to see sadness and anger there.

"I'm so sorry," Calen said to her. "I know what he did to you, and I'm so sorry."

Oh. Calen was sad and angry because of what *he* had done. She shook her head emphatically.

"No," she said, her voice hoarse from lack of use. "Let's—" She cleared her throat. "Let's not talk about him. How? How did you do this?"

Calen smiled, then, and her chin lifted.

"I don't know," she answered, "but I'm going to find out."

Samantha Jo is a Youth Services Librarian with aspirations of becoming a distinguished voice in the world of fantasy. Inspired by her love of nature and storytelling, she graduated from Youngstown State University with a degree in biology and many creative writing courses under her belt. Her passion for the natural world shines through in her debut novel, Vessel: Bonded Earth Book One. She finds that her day job at a public library provides a wealth of motivation and creative influence for her own writing. Samantha lives in Ohio with her co-nerd and husband, their four semi-feral children, and a barnyard menagerie. You can learn more about Samantha at www.authorsamanthajo.com.

Printed in the USA
CPSIA information can be obtained
at www.ICGtesting.com
JSHW080213250824
68562JS00002B/10